AND THEN ONE DAY

SAMANTHA CHASE

And Then One Day

PRAISE FOR SAMANTHA CHASE

"If you can't get enough of stories that get inside your heart and soul and stay there long after you've read the last page, then Samantha Chase is for you!"

-*NY Times & USA Today Bestselling Author* **Melanie Shawn**

"A fun, flirty, sweet romance filled with romance and character growth and a perfect happily ever after."

-*NY Times & USA Today Bestselling Author* **Carly Phillips**

"Samantha Chase writes my kind of happily ever after!"

-*NY Times & USA Today Bestselling Author* **Erin Nicholas**

"The openness between the lovers is refreshing, and their interactions are a balanced blend of sweet and spice. The planets may not have aligned, but the elements of this winning romance are definitely in sync."

- ***Publishers Weekly, STARRED review***

"A true romantic delight, *A Sky Full of Stars* is one of the top gems of romance this year."

- ***Night Owl Reviews, TOP PICK***

"Great writing, a winsome ensemble, and the perfect blend of heart and sass."

"You know it's not going to be so bad."

"Yes, it is and you're the worst best friend ever."

Rolling her eyes, Courtney Baker leaned over and rested her head on her best friend Scarlett's shoulder. "I think the pregnancy hormones are making you more and more ridiculous every day. When is this baby coming?"

Sighing, Scarlett replied, "Not soon enough. We've got another ten weeks."

"Ugh, poor Mason."

Shoving her away, Scarlett cried, "Poor Mason?! How about poor me? I'm the one whose emotions are all over the damn place! I swear, I cry at the drop of a hat!"

"You've been doing that practically since this baby was conceived. We're all used it by now."

"Well I'm not, and the fact that you're moving so far away isn't helping."

Yeah, she knew this was going to be an issue—particularly the timing—but Courtney knew if she didn't do this now, she never would.

"Scar, we've been talking about this for months now. You know it's something I have to do."

"Oh, please. You've been threatening to move for years! Why did you wait until I was about to have a baby to do it? And you know you don't have to move right now. You don't have a job waiting for you, so what's the rush? Can't you wait until after my little peanut is born?"

"I thought we were calling him a bean?"

"And I thought I told you that no one knows the sex of the baby yet so ixnay-on-the-imhay."

"We've got to get this baby out of you," Courtney said blandly. "It's like I don't even know who you are anymore. No one says ixnay at our age so...stop that."

And then the worst thing happened.

Scarlett started to cry.

Like...ugly cry.

"Oh, God...oh, no...just...I'm sorry! I didn't mean to upset you!" She muttered a curse and reached across the table for a napkin and quickly began wiping her friend's face. "Dammit, you have *got* to stop being so sensitive!"

No sooner were the words out of her mouth than Mason, Scarlett's fiancé, was right there beside them, his attention fully on Scarlett. "Hey," he said softly, "What's going on? There's no crying tonight. It's our wedding rehearsal party and only smiling is allowed." He kissed the tip of her nose before looking over at Courtney. "Everything okay here?"

"She's upset about the move again."

"Ah. Well, you have to admit, the timing's not the greatest," he replied.

"I know, but...for me, this is the way it has to be and she's going to have to understand. It's not my fault that Dr.

Curtis had to retire abruptly and no other local dental practices are hiring. I need to work, Mason."

He gave her a patient smile. "I know, but you have to understand how hard this is on Scarlett. The wedding's tomorrow, the house we're building is behind schedule, and the pregnancy's really kicking her butt..."

"I am right here," Scarlett interrupted, looking first at Mason and then to Courtney. "You know you don't have to move so far away to find a job, Court, and it's not like you have to find something right this second. Why not take a couple of weeks and look some more?"

With a weary sigh, she looked at Mason and said, "Can you...give us a minute?"

Nodding, he kissed Scarlett before standing and walking away.

"What's so secretive that you can't say it in front of Mason? You know I'm just going to tell him whatever it is later, right?"

"And that's fine, but..." She groaned. "Okay, here it is. You know how my folks have always been into paranormal hunting?"

"Yeah..."

Another sigh. "Well...they've both taken some extended vacation time to go on some sort of cross-country trip with a group they belong to."

"O-kay. I still don't see what this has to do with you moving away though."

"When I lost my job and realized the best thing for me to do was move, they decided to list the house as an Airbnb for the time they're away as a source of income."

"What? But..."

"That means I don't have a place to live for the next

three months. They leave on Monday, which is when I need to be out as well."

"Is that all?" Scarlett said, suddenly all smiles.

"Uh, yeah. It's kind of a big deal. I'm going to be homeless on top of already being jobless, sooo..."

"So stay at my place! You know we haven't decided what to do with it yet and it's just been sitting vacant for months! This is perfect! Now you can stay and..."

Courtney held up a hand to stop her. "Scar, I appreciate the offer, but I can't do it. I really..." She looked around the room and spotted one of the main reasons she was opting to move away. Forcing her attention back to Scarlett, she continued. "It's just time for me to have a fresh start someplace that isn't Magnolia Sound. I can't do small-town life anymore. I just can't."

Tears began to well up again in Scarlett's eyes, but Courtney wasn't having it.

"And you can*not* keep crying to get your way," she said with a small laugh. Jumping to her feet, she looked down at her friend and grinned. "This is going to be a good thing for me and you should be happy! Now if you'll excuse me, I'm going to grab a glass of wine."

Walking across the room, Courtney smiled and waved to people she knew but did her best to get to the bar as quickly as possible. Once there, she smiled at the bartender. "Moscato, please." Once she had her glass in hand, she thanked him and walked out onto the back deck of the Magnolia on the Sound–the new B&B that Mason's aunt owned. The house was over a hundred years old, recently renovated, and it was quite possibly the most magnificent house she'd ever been in.

The weather was a little cool and she wished she had

grabbed a sweater, but...it was peaceful outside and the perfect spot for a little quiet reflection.

Leaning on the railing, she looked out at the Sound as she sipped her wine. She'd never admit it to anyone, but she really loved it here. Not the B&B–although it was beautiful–but the small coastal town where she'd lived her whole life. She loved the beach and her friends and family, but...nothing was happening for her here. Not only was her job gone, but she hadn't had a date in months and the men she did want to date–or rather, the *man* she wanted to date–was off-limits.

And it sucked.

If it weren't for the fact that the dentist she was working for had to retire immediately therefore leaving her unemployed, she probably wouldn't have opted to move away. But considering the downward spiral her life was currently in, it seemed only logical to pick up and move someplace new and start over.

But yeah, the timing did suck.

While Courtney was glad that she would get to see Scarlett marry Mason, the thought of not being here when her best friend had her baby was a little harder to deal with. They had always talked about having their kids close together so they would grow up to be best friends too.

Hard to happen when no man has even attempted to touch me in almost six months...

That depressing thought had her taking a long drink of her wine and she was thankful no one was there to witness her guzzling the whole thing down.

"Hey, Court."

Or so she thought.

Turning, she saw Scarlett's brother Kyle walking her way. He was super sweet, a total flirt, and completely harmless. There was zero attraction between the two of them and she considered him to be a good friend.

"Hey, yourself. Having fun?"

Standing beside her, he leaned against the railing as well and stared out at the beach. "I know this is just supposed to be a casual dinner after the whole wedding rehearsal, but I swear Mason's mother has me feeling like I'm a kid trying to sneak a spot at the grown-ups' table." Chuckling, he shook his head. "You know my family's not fancy like the Bishops. This all feels a little weird. Why couldn't we just have a cookout in the backyard at home or something?"

Turning her head, she looked at him and laughed. "Kyle, can you imagine the sophisticated Bishop family hanging out in your dad's backyard? Come on!" Then she motioned toward the inside of the massive house. "And are you telling me you're not enjoying the food here? The menu is spectacular! I'm already planning on putting about a dozen crab cakes in my purse for later."

"Classy," he said, still laughing. They stood in companionable silence for several moments. "So I hear you're moving to Raleigh."

She nodded. "Yup."

"Why so far?"

"It's only three hours away."

"You know my sister is freaking out over it though, right?"

"Yeah, I know," she said sadly, her eyes never leaving the Sound. The sun was going down and it was her favorite time of day. "Once the baby's born, she won't even notice I'm gone."

"Somehow, I doubt that."

It wasn't Kyle who spoke, but his older brother Dean.

As in...the man she wanted most in the world and couldn't have.

Why did he have to come out here? I specifically came out here to escape!

Both Courtney and Kyle turned and looked at him and she did her best to appear calm and cool–and not at all like her heart was ready to beat right out of her chest at the sight of him.

Tall, shaggy dark hair, blue eyes, and dimples. Honestly, every time she was near him, her ovaries sighed. Why did he have to be related to her best friend? If he were anybody else she wouldn't even be giving this a second thought, but because Scarlett meant the world to her, there was no way she wanted to jeopardize their friendship over a guy.

Even if said guy was her ideal man.

Smiling at her, Dean raised his beer as he commented, "It doesn't matter how much time my sister spends with the baby. Nothing can replace a best friend."

And he was sweet too, damn him.

When he continued to stare at her expectantly, she realized she probably should respond. "Nah. I think between the baby, Mason, and everyone coming to see the baby, Scarlett's going to be just fine. And it's not like I'm moving to another country or anything. I'll only be a few hours away."

"Still not the same," he said mildly before looking at his younger brother. "Can you believe our baby sister is getting married tomorrow?"

Kyle shrugged. "Considering she's just about ready to give birth, I'm kind of happy she's getting married tomorrow." He winked at Courtney. "Am I right?"

"Look, I firmly believe in the institution of marriage,"

she said evenly, "but it's not like they *had* to get married. No one has to do that anymore."

"Still," Kyle replied, "I just think it's the right thing to do."

"What is this, 1950?" Dean asked with a small laugh.

"On that note, I'm going to get a refill," she said, stepping away from the railing and raising her glass. "I'll see you two later." She sashayed away and got a brief whiff of Dean's cologne–all fresh, clean, and masculine–and she just wanted to rub up against him and inhale deeply.

Yeah, it was definitely time for another drink.

Or two.

As she made her way back toward the bar, she caught a server walking by with those mini crab cakes she loved so much and grabbed a few. At the bar, she had her glass refilled while she noshed and then caught another server who had a tray of chicken satay. She grabbed some of them as well. She figured if she was going to slam back some cocktails, it would be smart to keep eating.

Out of the corner of her eye she spotted Dean walking back into the room with Kyle and sighed.

It wasn't fair. She'd been crushing on him since she was fifteen and because he was six years older, it was completely inappropriate. Now? Not so much. But he was her best friend's brother and, as such, that meant Dean was completely off-limits. There had never been a conversation between her and Scarlett about this–mainly because she was too embarrassed to admit how she felt. For some reason, Courtney felt her friend wouldn't have a big problem if she had crushed on Kyle or even Hunter because they were closer in age. Dean was...well...not only there a bigger age gap, but he was way more serious and levelheaded than his brothers. He didn't do casual relationships, and for a long time, Courtney wasn't looking for anything long-term.

A fact Scarlett would have brought up as a way of discouraging this crush.

Too bad it didn't work.

No matter how many times she tried to tell herself.

Dean Jones was Courtney's ultimate man and she knew the main reason she never wanted a serious relationship was because he was always right there–small-town living meant they ran into each other a lot. And every time she saw him, it just reinforced why no other man measured up and how it was never going to happen for them.

And now she had to move on with her life.

He caught her eye from across the room and smiled. The weak smile she gave him was forced and rather than think about it, she turned her attention back to the bar and ordered a second glass of wine.

———

Everything felt...off.

Glancing around the room, Dean Jones saw how everyone was laughing and smiling and having a great time and yet...he felt like he didn't belong.

No, that wasn't it; he felt envious.

And how pathetic was that?

His baby sister was getting married in the morning and also getting ready to have a baby of her own. She was six years younger than Dean. He glanced over at his brother Hunter, who already had a kid, and who happened to be two years younger than Dean. Granted, Hunter and his on-again-off-again girlfriend never married, but they started a family. Kyle was next and wasn't in any kind of relationship so there wasn't anything there, but...dammit, Dean felt like his family was passing him by.

Frowning, he took a pull of his beer and continued to scan the room. He knew everyone here–literally everyone. True, this was an intimate dinner for thirty, but he knew each and every face here. That came with living in a small town. As he continued to look around, he realized they were all doing things with their lives like getting married and having kids, or for the older couples, they were traveling and enjoying their grandkids. And where was he? Nowhere, with no one and no prospects of there being a someone.

Yeah, pathetic.

He caught a glimpse of Courtney from across the room and realized they were the only two people in the room who didn't look like they were having any fun. Dean knew why he wasn't, but was curious about why she wasn't. If there was one thing he knew about Courtney, it was that she liked having a good time. She was usually the life of the party– always loud and boisterous and full of laughter.

She's certainly not any of those things right now...

Maybe the fact that she was days away from moving was distracting her, but damn, he wished she didn't look so sad and alone. He was about to go over and talk to her but quickly decided against it. She never seemed to have a problem laughing and joking with Kyle or even Hunter, but whenever he was around, she usually clammed up.

Or walked away like she did when they were on the deck.

It was probably because while they were all growing up, he had to be like one of the parents–always watching his younger siblings while his father was at work and making sure no one got into trouble. It was a lot of responsibility on him and he took it seriously.

Especially when his mother died.

After that happened, he was even more protective of his family and tried to fill the void of losing their mom.

So he was the serious brother, the rule enforcer, and...it sucked.

Before he could think any more about it, the announcement that dinner was being served was called out. He took his place at a table along with his brothers, father, grandfather, and...Courtney.

Smiling, he held out a chair for her and she softly thanked him. Taking the seat beside her, he thought maybe it was prophetic that she was sitting with them. They could talk and he could try to figure out why she was being so quiet.

And maybe he'd finally be brave enough to...

"There you are," Scarlett said as she came walking over. She grabbed Courtney's hand and pulled her to her feet. "I want you sitting with me up at the head table. Sam and Shelby are sitting with us too, so..." Then she looked at her brothers and smiled. "Sorry for making this the lone guy table, but..."

"Or maybe we should call it the lonely guy table," Kyle joked, and Hunter punched him in the arm. "Ow!"

"No worries, little miss," their grandfather said, ignoring the spectacles beside him. "Although, I was looking forward to having such a beautiful girl sitting with us."

"Oh, stop, Tommy. You rascal," Courtney said before walking over and planting a loud, smacking kiss on Dean's grandfather's cheek. "You better save a dance for me tomorrow!"

"You know it!" he called out and Dean swore the old guy was blushing.

Before he could even process where Courtney was

going, their meals were being served. Conversation around the table flowed and once everyone was done eating, speeches were made by both Scarlett and Mason–thanking everyone for coming and talking about how excited they both were for the wedding tomorrow. Honestly, Dean was happy for them. Never in a million years did he imagine his sister marrying into one of the wealthiest families in town, but he knew that had little to do with their relationship. Still, he was happy that Scarlett would hopefully never have to struggle again.

They'd done that enough while growing up.

He raised his glass with everyone to toast the happy couple, enjoyed a celebratory cupcake when they were passed around, and was more than a little thankful that the night was coming to an end. Tomorrow would be even longer and undoubtedly more draining, and right now the only thing Dean was looking forward to was going home and enjoying a little peace and quiet before going to sleep.

Yeah, just call me Mr. Excitement...

Walking across the room, he wanted a chance to say goodnight to Scarlett and Mason. As he got closer, however, he could see his sister looked upset.

Again.

Damn pregnancy hormones. He swore his sister had cried more in the last seven months than she had in her entire life.

When he was beside her, he carefully asked, "Hey, what's going on? What are you upset about now?"

Mason was the one to answer. "Scarlett feels like Courtney had a little too much to drink and is worried about her driving home and...let's just say things got a little tense."

"Dean," Scarlett began pitifully, "you have to make sure

she doesn't drive! She won't listen to me and I realize she doesn't have far to go, but...you have to go after her! She's probably still in the driveway. It's a little chaotic even with the hired valet and..."

"Isn't she sleeping by you tonight?" he quickly interrupted before she got herself even more worked up. "I thought that was the plan–Courtney was staying with you at your place."

"She is, but she's mad at me and said she's not staying over!" she sobbed. "How could she do that? She's my maid of honor and...and..."

Dean looked at her and then Mason before he nodded. "Okay, okay, don't worry. I'll make sure she gets to your place safely." Then he paused. "Wait, when we say your place, do we mean your old place or your place on the beach–Mason's place?"

"The place on the beach is *our* place," Scarlett corrected. "But yeah, I mean my old place. We wanted one last night to hang out there like old times, and now she said she changed her mind!"

And she was crying again.

"I've got this," he said firmly. Shaking Mason's hand, he added, "Take care of her and I'll...I'll deal with Court."

"Thanks, man."

With a quick kiss on Scarlett's cheek, Dean made his way across the room and out to the large entryway while trying to find Courtney. He hadn't seen her leave, but she could've stopped to talk to someone on her way out.

"You leaving too?" Hunter asked when he spotted him in the foyer.

"Uh, yeah. Have you seen Courtney?"

"I think I saw her go out the back door. How come?"

Dean quickly relayed the situation before excusing

himself and walking back through the house. With no other choice, he stepped outside and headed down to the yard. Several people were still milling about and he scanned the property to try to figure out where she went.

A lone figure on the pier caught his eye.

Courtney.

Her shoulders were hunched and shaking and he knew she was crying. With a muttered curse, he started walking across the yard and down the pier. When he got to her side, he stood there and looked out at the Sound like she was.

"You want to talk about it?" he quietly asked.

"Not particularly."

Her words were spoken so softly he could barely hear her. Turning his head to look at her, he wasn't sure what to say.

"I don't need a babysitter, Dean," she said after a minute. "You don't have to stand here and watch over me. I'm not a kid anymore."

Like I haven't noticed...

He laughed softly. "Yeah, I got that, Court, but you know you're not in any condition to drive, so..." And he braced himself for the fight that was sure to come. "Scarlett's just worried about you. You know that. So why don't you let me drive you home and we'll get Kyle or Hunter to bring your car to you, okay?"

She looked up at him and his mouth went dry. It wasn't the first time he noticed how beautiful Courtney was–it was something that hit him years ago–but it was the first time he was seeing the vulnerability in her. For once, she wasn't the sassy, confident girl she presented to the world.

And he had no idea how to react.

"I wasn't going to drive. I know better than that." She gently swiped her hand over her cheek to wipe away the tears and he wished he had a handkerchief or something to offer her. "I'm more upset because she didn't need to humiliate me like that in front of everyone. Hell, she could have just offered to let me drive home with her, but instead, she practically shouts it out for everyone that I've had four glasses of wine!"

A small laugh escaped and she shot him an angry glare.

"Okay, yeah, that was wrong of her, but you know Scarlett's all over the place right now. We've talked about this. So maybe she could have handled it better, but...let's be honest, Court, you're possibly making a bigger deal out of it than it was too."

And then he held his breath and waited for her to argue with him.

But she didn't.

"Everything's changing," she said, her gaze turning back to the water. "There's a part of me that knows it's all for the better–Scarlett's happy, the baby will be here before we all know it, and she's found this amazing love with Mason." She paused. "Then there's me. I'm unemployed, my parents are off chasing ghosts and turning our home into an Airbnb which leaves me homeless come Monday morning, and I'm moving to a city where I literally know no one." She shook her head. "I didn't mean to ruin her night."

Unable to help himself, Dean put his arm around her and hugged her.

And she instantly stiffened beside him.

Trying not to focus on that, he did his best to encourage her. "I know things all seem bleak right now, but you have to believe it's going to get better. I've been hearing you tell everyone how much you hate living in a small town so... here's your big chance to find someplace that's a better fit for you. And...you know you'll always have a place here.

Even if it's not with your folks, Scarlett would always welcome you home whenever you want."

"I know that…"

"But…?"

"But…it's not the same. Everyone's moving forward and I'm just…I'm not. This whole job thing is making me crazy. I mean why did I have to lose my job now?"

"To be fair, Dr. Curtis was like a hundred years old. He didn't exactly instill confidence when you went in for a cleaning."

She chuckled. "First of all, he's only seventy-five, but yeah, he did look a lot older." She sighed. "I just wish he would have sold the practice rather than close his doors. He's been my family dentist since I was a kid–and everyone else's dentist here in town! How could he just leave like that? It's like he didn't even care about all the patients who now have to scramble to find a new dentist or his employees who need to search for new jobs!"

"I'm sure you're not going to have any problem finding a new job," he said, hoping he sounded optimistic. "I thought dental hygienists were always in big demand."

"Not in small towns," she murmured, stepping out of his embrace. Turning around, she faced him, and Dean noticed she didn't look quite as sad as she had a moment ago. "It's just another sucky aspect of my life! I was the youngest hygienist in the office–everyone else had been with him since forever! Most of them are retiring! And so here I am with no job and no prospects and I have to move across the state and hope I find something!"

"So…wait," he said, holding up a hand to her. "Why are you moving if you don't have a job yet? Shouldn't you find the job first and then move?"

"There are a lot of jobs in the Raleigh area so I figured it would be a safe place to start. I'm going to stay at one of those extended-stay hotels while I job hunt and then I'll find an apartment. It's not ideal, but with my parents renting out the house to strangers, I had to get creative with what I'm doing."

"Wow, Court, I had no idea. I'm really sorry."

She shrugged. "Yeah, well...this is my life. Nothing goes my way and no one wants me, so..." She gasped before covering her mouth and turning her back on him.

No one wants her? What the...? Wait, did she mean her folks or did she mean...?

For some stupid reason, he needed clarification–knew he'd go crazy if he didn't know specifically what she was talking about.

Stepping around her so he was facing her, he asked, "What do you mean no one wants you? That's crazy! Your parents are just doing their own thing right now. They probably thought it wouldn't be a big deal to you."

Groaning loudly, Courtney spun around and started to walk away. "I'm going to call an Uber. I...I'll see you tomorrow."

He didn't let her go even three steps before he was in front of her again. "Hey, what's going on? What did I say?"

Her big green eyes stared up at him and he swore she was going to start crying again, but then...something changed. Her expression went from sad to neutral to something he couldn't quite define.

He saw her swallow hard before she seemed to pull herself together. "I wasn't talking about my parents, Dean. I'm talking about guys. Men! I haven't had a date in forever and no one in this town has any interest in me!"

"You're crazy. That's just not possible. I mean...look at you!" he said emphatically, motioning to her body–which right now was encased in a clingy sapphire blue cocktail dress. Her long, dark hair was blowing a bit wildly in the wind but she was still a beautiful woman.

Which is what he told her.

A snort of disbelief was her only response.

"Courtney, I'm serious! You are a beautiful woman and if the guys around here don't see it and don't appreciate it, then they're idiots!"

"Oh, really?" she asked, her voice dripping with sarcasm.

"Yeah, really."

"Then I guess that makes *you* one of the idiots," she grumbled before trying to walk away, but he stopped her.

"Excuse me?"

"You heard me. Then you're an idiot too. Probably the biggest idiot."

"Hey!" he snapped. "What the hell? What did I do?"

Her eyes were blazing with fire when she looked up at him and for the life of him, Dean had no idea why she was so pissed off at him.

"Because you're too blind to see this!" she said right before she snaked a hand around his nape and pulled his head down and kissed him.

Shock held Dean immobile for all of three seconds before he realized what was happening and then...holy crap.

He had no idea what he was expecting, but Courtney's kiss wasn't angry–like her words were getting–but it was soft and sensual.

He was the one to kick it up a notch.

Reaching up, his hands cupped her face as he dove in for more of her. She pressed closer and the feeling of her curvy body pressed up against him from head to toe was enough to turn him on more than he'd been in years.

Maybe more than he'd ever been.

And just as he shifted and let his hands skim over her cheeks, her throat, her shoulders, and before his arms could wrap around her waist, she broke the kiss and looked at him in absolute horror.

"*Ohmygod*," she whispered right before she turned and ran.

For the second time in as many minutes, he was frozen in place. By the time his head was clear enough to think, she was out of sight–and out of the yard. Running across the yard, he spotted her in the driveway. As much as he didn't want to make a scene, he knew he had to call out to her to stop her. Just as he was about to, Dean spotted his brother Kyle standing with her and ushering her toward his car.

"Son of a bitch," he hissed and immediately realized this was probably for the best. She'd had too much to drink, was upset, and would more than likely have no memory of ever kissing him come tomorrow morning.

Which was a damn shame.

Because there wasn't a doubt in his mind–he'd never forget that kiss.

2

"You may kiss the bride."

Courtney held on to Scarlett's bouquet as her friend kissed her new husband. Tears stung her eyes as she watched them, but when Scarlett turned to her to get her flowers, she made sure she was smiling.

As the happy couple made their way up the aisle, Courtney smoothed a hand down her purple strapless gown, stepped forward and linked arms with Mason's cousin Sam, who was the couple's best man. As they began to walk, she trained her eyes forward otherwise she'd be tempted to glance toward where Scarlett's family was sitting. There was no way she was going to be able to look at Dean after the way she behaved last night.

Hell, it had been bad enough facing Scarlett after Kyle dropped her off.

Although, she had no idea how she could avoid him all day. This was a fairly small and intimate wedding – much like the rehearsal dinner was the night before. At some point she was bound to run into him and for the life of her, she had no idea what she was going to do or say when it happened. True, she could simply pretend she didn't remember kissing him and go with the whole I-drank-too-much thing, but that didn't sit right with her.

For starters, she didn't drink that much.

At least, not as much as everyone thought.

And secondly, she wasn't a liar.

So for now, she smiled and looked like the happy maid of honor on the outside, but inside, she was a mess. There were pictures to pose for, first dances to get through, and there were enough friends here that she could make sure she was never alone.

In theory, it was a good plan.

Putting it all into practice, however, was much harder than she imagined. Mainly because she had forgotten that as the bride's brother, Dean – who looked incredibly sexy in a tux – would be part of all the activities Courtney thought she was going to use to distract herself.

Well...damn. Now what?

The wedding was being held at the Magnolia Sound Country Club which sat right on the beach. There wasn't any place to hide – especially once they stepped outside for pictures – and she found herself holding her breath more than once while the photographer started arranging them all for pictures. If all went well, they wouldn't have to be in any of them together.

"Court!" Scarlett cried out, interrupting her thoughts. "Come pose in the family pics. You know you're practically my sister!"

It was like her best friend was purposely messing with her, except...she never told Scarlett that she'd kissed Dean.

Hell, she'd never even told Scarlett she had a crush on Dean!

There was no way to decline posing with the entire

Jones family without it looking suspicious, so she slowly made her way over and kept her eyes on the bride and not on the bride's ridiculously hot brother.

Who kissed like a dream.

Yeah, she wasn't so drunk that she didn't remember how incredible that kiss was or how warm and hot and hard Dean felt all over.

"You okay?" Scarlett whispered when she was standing beside her. "It's not hot out but you're looking a little pale." Then she laughed quietly. "I thought you said you weren't hungover."

"I'm not," she hissed, frantically looking around to make sure no one was listening. "I just..., I'm fine."

Before she knew it, she was posing next to Scarlett with Kyle and Hunter beside her. Glancing at Kyle, she said, "Thanks for getting my car to me last night. I really appreciate it. And the ride." Shaking her head, she added, "And for not passing judgment."

Chuckling, Kyle said, "No worries. I've been in similar situations a time or two."

Somehow she doubted they were *that* similar, but Courtney opted to simply smile and nod.

Pictures seemed to take forever and then they were all ushered back inside. Dean made no attempt to talk to her and she wasn't sure if she was pissed off or relieved. He could at least inquire if she was okay without bringing up the kiss, right? He was always the responsible one – making sure everyone was all right and he wasn't even trying to find out?

Okay, drama queen, make up your mind. Do you want to talk to him or not?

Damn, she hated when her conscience reminded her of how crazy she was most of the time.

Back inside the country club, the bridal party–which only consisted of the bride and groom, Courtney, and Mason's cousin Sam–was taken to a private suite for the remainder of the cocktail hour. There were trays of hors d'oeuvres for them to nosh on along with champagne and anything else they wanted to drink.

"Please stick with water," Scarlett murmured as they were helping themselves to the food.

"Don't worry. Lesson learned."

It kind of bothered her that Scarlett was almost reprimanding her, but considering it was her wedding day, Courtney let it pass. Within thirty minutes, the group was being ushered out of the suite and down to the event hall for them to be announced into the reception.

Things were kind of a blur after that – walking into the room, the announcements, the first dance...there were a hundred people in attendance and they all joined them on the dance floor.

"I hope you don't mind," Sam said at the end of the first song, "but I'm going to go find Shelby."

"Go for it," she said easily. No reason for the man not to dance with his fiancée. Although, now it left her alone in the middle of the floor. She went to follow him when someone tapped her on her shoulder. With a smile, she turned and saw Kyle holding his hand out to her.

"Care to dance?"

Placing her hand in his, she said, "I'd love to." They danced through the next two songs and were going for a third when Dean approached. Her heart sank and she knew there was nowhere for her to go if he asked her to dance.

Which he did.

Once Kyle was gone and she realized the song playing was a ballad, she really felt nervous. Dean wrapped one arm around her and took her hand in his as they began to sway to the music.

And he felt just as good as she remembered.

And smelled even better.

Part of her hoped she had imagined it all–or had exaggerated it thanks to the wine–but no such luck. Neither spoke for so long it was starting to get awkward.

"Your sister looks beautiful," she finally said to break the silence.

He nodded. "She's always been beautiful. But this pregnancy has really made her look radiant." Smiling at her, he said, "I know this wasn't the wedding she wanted. Scarlett's more low-key and I know she was a little self-conscious about being so far along in...well, you know."

Unable to help herself, she laughed softly. "Dress shopping was a challenge; that's for sure. But even with all of Mrs. Bishop's demands, I still think they managed to have it be a little more intimate than the circus his mom was pushing for."

"It's not every day that Magnolia Sound royalty gets married."

Pulling back slightly, Courtney grinned as she studied him. "Oh, my God, did you just make a joke?"

"I've been known to have a sense of humor," he said with a careless shrug. Then he leaned in close. "And you know exactly what I'm talking about."

Yeah, Mason Bishop came from a very prominent family and people tended to hold them in reverence. It was a huge stumbling block for Mason and Scarlett, but they ultimately got over it.

Well, Scarlett did and the baby she was carrying certainly helped.

They were back to being silent before Dean asked, "So how are you doing today? Feeling any better?"

It wasn't like she could pretend she didn't hear him, so with a bit of a frown–and a ton of embarrassment–she said, "Much, thanks. I guess everything's just hitting me hard, but...once I see Scarlett off for her honeymoon and my parents leave for their big ghost hunting trip and I get on the road..." She shrugged. "It will be like I'm starting a new adventure, right?"

He eyed her warily. "You sound...much better than you did last night about the whole thing."

If he was fishing for her to rehash what she said, it wasn't going to happen.

"Do I?" Another shrug. "I guess I was just in a funk last night."

There was a flash of annoyance on Dean's face. "A funk? Seriously?"

"What? What would you call it?" Before he could answer, she went on. "I mean, I guess you could say it was a pity party for one, but...I'm good now. No amount of worrying is going to change anything, and I'm sure once I get settled in Raleigh, I'll feel better. Sure it's hard meeting people and making friends at my age, but I'll go join a gym and download a dating app and go from there."

"A dating...?" He muttered a curse. "Do you have any idea how unreliable those things are? And without a friend to go with you, it's not safe to meet some strange guy alone! You need to be responsible, Courtney!"

"Geez, relax, *Dad*," she said sarcastically. "I know that. I never said I was going to arrive in Raleigh and go out with the first guy who swipes right. Trust me, I know better than that."

"Swipe...?" And yeah, he looked ready to punch someone. Releasing her, Dean took a step back and she was certain he was going to walk away, but instead, he grabbed her hand and pulled her off the dance floor with him.

"Hey! Where are we going?" she asked, stumbling behind him in her stilettos to keep up. They walked by the tables and the guests and the bar and were out of the room before she knew it. Figuring he wanted to talk to her without the loud music, Courtney was certain they'd stop.

Nope.

He kept walking with his grip tightly on her hand until they were outside. The sun had almost set and no one else was around and now she imagined he wanted a place where he could yell and lecture her without an audience.

Like something a big brother or parent would do.

They were out on the club's boardwalk when she finally pulled her hand free.

"I'm not walking on the boardwalk in these heels," she said defiantly. "So say whatever it is you have to say so I can go back inside. They're going to be serving dinner soon and I need to be at the head table with everyone."

Rather than respond right away, Dean raked a hand through his dark hair as he paced in front of her. When he finally stopped, he was a little bit breathless and a whole lot annoyed. "Do you remember *anything* you said to me last night?"

"Um..."

"Less than twenty-four hours ago you were all *'here I am with no job and no prospects and I have to move across the state and hope I find something!'* and *'Nothing goes my way and no one wants me,'* and now you're just okay with it? Just like that and you're over it? How is that possible?" he demanded.

She'd never been on the receiving end of Dean's anger

and she didn't know what to make of it. "I didn't say I was okay with it. I'm just saying..."

"You were crying, Courtney! And now you're all smiles and ready to go on an adventure? Do you even care about anyone? Don't you have anything more than superficial feelings for your friends and family?"

Okay, that was hitting a little below the belt...

"What are you even talking about? Of course I have feelings for all of them! I'm devastated to be leaving them all behind, but this is how it has to be!" she yelled, hating how worked up she was. "Maybe you're okay with staying here and doing the same thing day in and day out, but I'm not! I can't sit here and keep watching all my friends move on with their lives while I'm standing still! There! Is that what you want? Are you happy now that I'm not smiling or being optimistic? Geez, Dean!" She turned away but he grasped her arm and spun her back around.

"What is it that you want, Court, huh? Because I've got to tell you, it's not like there's a lot of people here in town doing anything so spectacular that you should be jealous of! You hit a rough patch. So what? It happens to everyone and there's no mass exodus of people leaving Magnolia because they're not getting their way!"

Her eyes went wide as she stared at him in shock. Was he for real? "So...what...you think I'm doing this because I'm pouting? Because I'm jealous?" she all but screamed.

"Seems that way to me..."

He was just a little too smug. A little too arrogant and it rubbed her completely the wrong way.

"You know what I want, Dean? Huh?" she mimicked. "I want...passion and excitement! I want to have more than living in my parents' house and dating the same guys! I want a great love like Scarlett and Mason have, and someone who actually gives a damn about me as more than a friend!" She was breathless by the time she finished and this time she pulled her arm free and took a step back. "Don't you dare judge me. You have no right."

"That's where you're wrong," he said, advancing on her. "I think after last night, I have at least a little bit of a right."

He couldn't possibly mean...

She took another step back but the heel of her shoe snagged on the wood of the boardwalk and she began to fall backwards. Dean's arm banded around her, hauling her close. His expression was fierce, possessive, and it was the most exciting thing she'd ever seen.

"This time, I want you to remember," he all but growled as his lips claimed hers.

He had no idea what possessed him to do what he was doing, but now that he was kissing Courtney, Dean was pretty sure he didn't want to stop.

And from the way she was suddenly wrapped around him, it didn't feel like she wanted him to stop either.

Thank God.

His hand reached up and anchored into her hair and he knew he was messing it up but he didn't care. Right now his only concern was making sure she didn't forget how they'd kissed. She tilted her head and grabbed onto the lapels of his suit and groaned–or maybe it was him. It was hard to tell because they were both a little frantic. Last night, her kiss had been about seduction, while his was...

Dammit.

Instantly, he broke the kiss and took one step back and then another.

What the hell am I doing?

His kiss was about proving a point and punishing her for not remembering the one last night and he was suddenly ashamed of his behavior.

"Courtney, listen, I..."

"You know what? Let's just...forget it. I really need to get back," she said, and yeah, he heard the slight tremor in her voice.

"Yeah," he said quietly. "Come on. I'll walk with you."

She shook her head as she put more space between them. "I'd really rather you didn't." And without another word, he watched her walk away.

There was no way for him not to go after her–after all, this was his sister's wedding and he needed to get back inside too–but the least he could do was give her a head start. His eyes never looked away until she walked through the large french doors. Once she was out of sight, Dean called himself every name in the book.

Last night, she'd been slightly drunk and more than a little emotional and the smart thing to do was to forget how she had kissed him.

But he couldn't.

Something about the things she said and the way she looked at him told him it wasn't quite an impulsive move on her part–that maybe it was something she'd been thinking about.

And how weird was that? Courtney had never shown any interest in him before. She'd been in his life since she and Scarlett were in kindergarten together. He couldn't remember a time when she wasn't around. Still, it always seemed like she was way more comfortable around Kyle and Hunter than she ever was around him. He figured it was because of the age difference, but...

What if he was wrong?

What if he was just that freaking clueless that he never noticed?

Wasn't part of her tirade last night about him being too blind to see and how he must be one of the idiots who didn't want her?

And had he seriously just blown it again?

Cursing, he stalked back to the hotel and nearly ripped the glass doors off their hinges when he went in. He was determined to get to the bottom of this no matter what. If he had misread things and hurt her feelings, he didn't know if he could forgive himself.

Right. That's the only reason you're chasing after her right now. It has nothing to do with how much you enjoyed kissing her or how attractive she is. Something you know you've noticed even if you don't want to admit it out loud.

Ignoring the snarky voice of reason in his head, Dean walked back into the reception and was nearly tackled by his brother Hunter.

"Dude, where the hell have you been? They're serving dinner and everyone's been looking for you!"

"Oh, uh...just went out to get some air," he mumbled. "Sorry." Following his brother to their table, Dean looked around for any signs of Courtney. He hoped she came back in here and wasn't hiding on account of him.

"Why are you standing?" his father asked. "Sit down."

So he did.

"You feeling okay, Son? You don't look so good."

Where the hell was she? He looked toward the head table and saw Scarlett, Mason, and Sam, but no sign of Courtney.

"Well, shit."

"What's the matter?" his father asked.

Forcing himself to look away from the front of the room, he faked a smile. "Sorry. It's nothing. Just...distracted, that's all."

"What's on your mind? Anything I can help with?"

Great. Way to not draw attention to myself.

Shaking his head, Dean said, "It's nothing, Dad. Really. Thanks." Just then, their salads were served and he was thankful for the distraction.

Out of the corner of his eye, he caught a flash of deep purple–the color of Courtney's dress–and turned to see her whispering something in Scarlett's ear as she sat down. She looked a little flustered, but other than that she looked...

Beautiful.

Sexy.

Tempting.

Yeah, that last one was messing with him the most.

"She certainly looks happy, doesn't she?" his father asked.

It took Dean a minute to realize why his father made that statement and then he realized how he was still staring in that direction. "Uh...yeah. She does."

"Hard to believe my baby girl is married and having a baby. It seems like only yesterday your mother and I were bringing her home." He paused. "I wish she could have been here to see how beautiful our girl grew up to be."

Turning, he saw his father's eyes well with tears. Domenic Jones wasn't an emotional man and the sight of him crying now was a little unnerving. Reaching over, he squeezed his shoulder. "I know, Dad. Me too. You know she would have loved seeing Scarlett today."

His mother had been gone for over twenty years, but times like these–special occasions, holidays–made them really feel her absence.

Beside him, Domenic chuckled. "And she would have been over the moon at another grandbaby."

Dean nodded.

"If you don't get started soon, all your siblings will pass you by."

It was an innocent enough comment–besides Scarlett, his brother Hunter already had a kid. He and his ex were co-parenting or whatever the hell it was called, but they were making it work for their son Eli. Still, that was two siblings with kids and Dean with…not even the possibility of one.

You have to actually have sex with someone for that to happen.

And when was the last time that happened, Stud?

He seriously wished his inner voice would shut the hell up.

"It's not a contest, Dad," he said lowly, stabbing his fork into his salad.

After that, luckily, the conversation turned to how happy Scarlett was and then all the fancy food they were being served for dinner and how they all couldn't wait to go home and take off their tuxes. Dean mentally shook his head because here they were at a very fancy wedding, but it was essentially a guys' table again and none of them enjoyed dressing up.

Could we be any more stereotypical?

By the time dinner was over and everyone was up and dancing again, he was beyond ready to get up and try to talk to Courtney again. So he stood up and scanned the room and watched as his father went to dance with Scarlett and his grandfather made a beeline for Courtney. He rolled his eyes but couldn't help but be amused. His grandfather was smiling from ear to ear and so was she.

"Go figure," Kyle said from beside him. "Gramps gets all the pretty girls."

Dean turned his head so fast that he thought he pulled a muscle in his neck. "What?"

Kyle nodded toward the dance floor. "Gramps," he said. "He's dancing with Courtney and she looks all kinds of gorgeous in that gown. I mean, damn. She's got the body of one of those classic pin-up chicks–all soft curves and..."

Dean smacked him in the back of the head. "What's the matter with you?"

Rubbing his head, Kyle glared at him. "What the hell did you do that for?"

"Since when are you into Courtney? She's practically like a sister to us!"

Ugh...pot? Meet kettle.

"I never said I was into her," Kyle protested. "I was simply stating the obvious. I've always thought Court was pretty, but...yeah. She's like a sister to me." Then he paused. "And why are you suddenly so protective of her? It's not like she's ever been on your radar either."

"No one's being protective," he lied. "I just happen to know that you have a very short attention span with girls and I don't think you should be messing around with her."

They stood watching people dancing and when the song ended, Kyle excused himself.

And cut in on their grandfather and Courtney.

Son of a bitch!

Kyle caught Dean's eye and winked and it was all he could do to stop from storming over and slugging him.

But he didn't.

Instead, he picked up his champagne glass and drank the rest of it down while he waited for the current song to end.

And that's when he cut in on Kyle. With a sincere smile he asked, "May I?"

Courtney's eyes went wide while his brother glared, but once she nodded, he shot Kyle a smug smile and shooed him away. Lucky for him, it was a slow song–he was the worst dancer, but could handle swaying to a ballad.

"So, uh...having a good time?" he asked nervously.

Bowing her head, she laughed softly before looking up at him. "As a matter of fact, I am. I love seeing your sister so happy."

He nodded. "Yeah. Me too." They moved together slowly and all he could think about was how good she felt in her arms. "Um...listen, about before...you know...outside..."

"Let's just forget about it, okay?" she said quietly, her gaze not quite meeting his. "Let's just chalk it up to temporary insanity."

He stiffened. "Is that what it was? Really?"

This time she did look directly at him, her expression a little sad. "Wasn't it?"

Wait...was she disappointed? Had he seriously misinterpreted the whole situation?

She was leaving the day after tomorrow and he knew he would only make himself crazy if they didn't settle this–if they didn't get to the bottom of what she was thinking.

Boldly, he pulled her a little closer. "What if it wasn't?" he asked carefully. "What if it wasn't random or temporary insanity? What if...what if I just wanted to kiss you?"

"You...you wanted to kiss me?" There was wonder in her voice–like she didn't quite believe him but really wanted to.

Hell, he'd be a liar if he said he'd never thought about kissing her–no matter what he said to his goofy brother earlier. Still, it was a line he never wanted to cross.

Until now.

Without breaking eye contact, he nodded. "I still do," he said gruffly. "Hell, Court, just say the word and I will."

Her beautiful green eyes went wide. "But...I don't know...I mean...when..."

She was all flustered and it was completely adorable. The arm he had around her waist tightened, pulling her close until they were touching almost from head to toe. "I'm not sure I can give you an exact date," he teased.

Her breathy "wow" almost made him groan.

This was insanity. He knew that. Right now, he was playing with fire holding her and talking to her like this in the middle of his sister's wedding. And before he could stop himself, he said, "Come outside with me again. Just for a little bit. Please."

He was not opposed to begging at this point.

The song ended and everyone clapped as the DJ announced it was time for the bride and groom to cut the cake. Dean had no idea what they were going to do–there was no way they could leave right now but he knew if he gave her too much time to think, she'd avoid him for the rest of the night.

Unfortunately, he had no choice but to let her go and it became a fun little game of cat and mouse until the reception came to an end. Dean hung back with his family until his sister and her new husband came and kissed them all goodnight. They were going back to their place for the night and leaving for their honeymoon first thing in the morning. Then, he watched as Scarlett gave Courtney a fierce hug. This would be the last time they were going to see each other for a while–with Scarlett's honeymoon and Court's move, it could possibly be the longest they had ever been apart.

Mason gently urged Scarlett to leave and after that, the room emptied rather quickly. In the midst of all the good-byes, Dean lost sight of Courtney and his heart sank. Not that anything else was going to happen, but...he had hoped to kiss her one more time. Once she moved, he'd only get to see her when she came back to visit his sister and even that was iffy.

With a sigh, he walked with his family out to the parking lot. After watching his father and brothers leave along with his grandfather, he knew he was hanging around for nothing.

She had left without saying goodbye.

And it stung.

Opening his car door, he took one last look back at the country club entrance when he saw her. Looking a little lost, she came walking out the front doors while glancing around for...something.

Him?

Slamming the truck door shut, he strode toward her. When she caught sight of him, she halted in her tracks. "I...I thought you left."

He couldn't tell if she was relieved that she was wrong or not.

"I was just getting ready to go," he admitted. "Actually, I thought you had..."

"I've always had a crush on you," she blurted out, and even in the dim lighting he could see her blush.

"Um...what?"

She nodded. "Ever since like the ninth grade, I've had a crush on you." Her voice was a little steadier this time. "After you said what you said while we were dancing, I...I thought you should know that it wasn't all one-sided."

And now he really didn't know what to do.

Actually, he knew exactly what he wanted to do, but he wasn't sure he should.

"Are you going home right now?" he asked.

Courtney shook her head. "I'm going to Scarlett's place. Her old place," she quickly amended. "My car's there and I left some things there so I planned on crashing there tonight. My folks were here earlier but left before the cake because they're getting ready for their trip. The house is a mess and they're bickering over what to pack and...I really just wanted a little peace and quiet after all the craziness of yesterday and today."

"That makes sense."

"Actually, they were supposed to be my ride home because I came here in the limo with Scarlett. But once they started arguing about some other aspect of the trip, I told them I'd find a ride. Then I forgot to ask anyone. I was just about to call for an Uber..."

"I'll drive you home," he quickly replied. "It's not a big deal."

Her smile was a little shy as she thanked him and he motioned toward the direction of his truck. His mind raced with things he wanted to say–things he wanted to ask–and yet he couldn't make himself utter a single word. He knew if he opened his mouth, he'd ask her to come home with him and that was just courting trouble no matter how he looked at it. She was his sister's best friend and he didn't ever want to make things awkward between them.

No matter how badly he wanted her.

As they approached his truck, she stopped and faced him. "I'm leaving on Monday," she said, and all he could do was nod. "And...after the things that happened between us, I was thinking..."

"Come home with me," he said, his tone as fast and shaky as her admission of a crush had been.

"What?"

He nodded, moving in close and cupping her cheek in his large hand. "Come home with me," he said, slower this time. "We don't have to do anything, I just..."

"Okay."

Leaning in, he gave her a searing kiss before stepping back. "I wasn't sure I should ask."

She grinned impishly. "I'm really glad you did."

He nodded.

"How far away is your place?" She sounded a little breathless and he was tempted to simply haul her up into the truck and have his way with her right here, right now.

No. If this was going to happen, he wanted her in his home. In his bed.

"Dean?" This time her voice sounded a little uncertain. "If you're having second thoughts..."

Leaning in, he kissed her again. "Never." Taking her by the hand, he helped her up into his truck before jogging around to the driver's side and joining her.

And he got them to his place faster than he thought possible.

3

WHAT THE HELL am I doing?

The question was on a constant loop in her head as she sat beside Dean on the short drive back to his place. The ten-minute drive wasn't enough for her to come up with an answer. And if anything, it was just enough time for her to obsess about all the scenarios that could happen and all the ways this could go horribly wrong. They had just turned onto his block and she seriously considered telling him she'd changed her mind.

This was crazy! She had no idea what possessed her to blurt out that she had a crush on him, and this time she couldn't blame it on the wine!

You're moving away in less than forty-eight hours. Do this and get him out of your system...

It was hard to argue with that logic and as they pulled into the driveway in front of his small bungalow, she let out a long breath and decided to go for it.

Whatever *it* happened to be.

They made small talk during the ride and it was primarily about the wedding. What was going to happen once they were in his house? Were they just going to talk? Was he going to kiss her and then wish her well? Or was he going to take her in his arms and seduce her?

She was really hoping for option number three.

Either that or she was just going to grab him by the lapels and do her own seducing.

Looking up, she realized Dean was already out of the truck. He was standing at the hood of the truck watching her and she couldn't quite read him. What was he thinking? Either way, she knew she had to get out of the truck too, otherwise she was going to not only look crazy but make herself crazy in her own head!

Slowly, she gathered her purse and carefully climbed down. Dean had walked over to help her and the heated look on his face took her breath away. In his tux he looked sexier than any Bond actor and she couldn't believe she was here with him like this. He walked over and took one of her hands in his and led her to the front door. She'd never been in his home and this was becoming more and more overwhelming.

For so many years, she'd been crushing on him and hoping he'd see her–really see her–and now that it was happening, she felt nervous and shy even as she was beyond excited and turned on at all the possibilities.

Ugh...I am crazy.

Once inside, he led her to his living room and offered her something to drink. "No thank you," she said quietly, taking in her surroundings. The place was small but had a very homey feel to it. Looking around, she noticed an over-sized sofa, large flat-screen TV over a stone fireplace, and sliding glass doors that led out to a deck. Turning, she saw the kitchen and it looked like it was newly renovated. Actually, the whole place looked like it was recently done. It was an older house and she wondered if he did it all himself—which she asked him.

"I did," he said before taking a drink from the bottle of water he was holding. "My plan had always been to renovate the whole thing. It just took a lot longer than I expected."

"I watch a lot of HGTV and always wanted to try flipping a house." She laughed. "Of course, I have no idea if I could handle all the work and aggravation that goes with it, but I think I'd really enjoy the demolition phase."

He laughed softly. "It certainly can be satisfying."

She swallowed hard because that phrase sounded incredibly sexy even if it wasn't meant to be. "So, is this the only house you're going to do or are you thinking of making this a hobby?"

With a shrug, he replied, "I'm going to help Scarlett get her place fixed up so she can sell it. But I'm also thinking of selling this one and doing it again with another house—maybe one a little closer to the water. After seeing Scarlett and Mason's place—both the current one and the one they're building—I'm a little envious."

She laughed softly. "Yeah, I have to admit, I feel the same way." Then her expression fell. "I'm not even going to be near any water after Monday. The only bodies of water are lakes and I doubt I'll find a place near any of them."

"I couldn't imagine living that far away from the coast. I think I'd miss it too much." He walked over and sat down on the sofa and motioned for her to join him.

"I think I'm going to too," she said as she sat and they both went quiet for a moment.

"You sure this is what you want to do? Moving?" he asked, his voice low and deep and...concerned.

Looking at him, she sighed. "I was."

"And now?"

"Now that it's really happening, I'm...I mean...I wish..." Damn. This was all too depressing to talk about and totally *not* what she wanted to be doing either. Shaking her head, she said, "Can we change the subject? Please?"

"Sure," he said with a nod, reaching up to caress her cheek and man-oh-man did it feel good.

Swallowing hard, she studied his face. God, he was so handsome. Why was he still single? Why weren't there women banging down his door?

Although, that would make things pretty awkward if that were to happen right now.

So many thoughts raced through her head and she finally asked, "What are we doing, Dean?"

For just a second, he seemed as if he was going to move away–like he was doubting what was happening–but luckily it didn't take long for him to get over it.

"Whatever it is that you want, Court," he said and she swore she could have orgasmed right there on the spot.

Whatever she wanted? For real? Like...anything? She wondered.

If I only have tonight, then I'm going to go for it all...

Before she could lose her nerve, she moved away from him and instantly missed the feel of his hand on her skin. Standing, she moved in front of him and did her best to hold his gaze as she reached behind herself and unzipped her gown. The sound of the zipper going down seemed overly loud in the room, but Courtney didn't stay focused on that. It was the look on Dean's face that mesmerized her.

She swore she saw his hand twitch–as if he couldn't wait to touch her–but she needed to finish what she was doing. This was her first attempt at a striptease, and dammit, she was going to do it without turning into a trembling mess!

Once the zipper was down, she wrapped an arm around her waist to hold the strapless gown in place–all the while not breaking eye contact. Licking her bottom lip, she dropped her arm, and thankfully, the gown floated down over her breasts, over her hips, and to the floor–leaving her standing in a deep purple thong that matched the gown and her stilettos.

Dean's hand reached out and landed on her hip as he looked up at her to make sure it was okay. Nodding, she silently willed him to stand and touch her everywhere he could at once, but he was a man who clearly enjoyed taking his time.

And hopefully he would.

Later.

Right now, she wanted the wild and frantic man who kissed her near the boardwalk earlier.

"Dean..."

He stood, his hand still on her hip as he took in the sight of her. She'd been naked with men before, but for some reason, standing here in front of Dean in a thong and heels left her feeling way more exposed than ever before.

"Damn, Court," he finally said, slowly licking his bottom lip. He met her gaze and his expression was heated and intense and she braced herself for what was to come.

"Don't hold back. Please."

As soon as the words were out of her mouth, it was madness. His arms banded around her as his lips claimed hers in a kiss she could only describe as carnal. With his hands on her ass, he lifted her out of the puddle of her dress and she wrapped her legs around his waist. They were a tangle of lips and limbs and it wasn't elegant or pretty, but it felt so damn good that she was ready to go up in flames.

She figured he was going to lay her down on the sofa and was surprised when he started walking. His lips left hers to kiss along her jaw and neck and her head fell back to give him better access. Her eyes closed and didn't open until he stopped moving.

His bedroom was dark. That was the only thing she noticed. As Dean slowly lowered her to the bed, she only had eyes for him. Standing back, he stripped off his tuxedo jacket and then the tie.

Looks like I'm not the only one doing a striptease tonight...

Part of her wanted to sit up and help him, but it was hypnotic watching his hands work–slowly unbuttoning his shirt, taking off his cuff links, his belt...

Oh, my...

Clothes hit the floor and when he was finally down to black boxer briefs, her eyes went a little wide.

He was perfection.

She knew Dean had tattoos, but she'd never seen how many. The ones on his arms were visible whenever he wore a t-shirt, but the ones on his chest were completely new to her. Reaching out her hand to him, he joined her on the bed, lying beside her.

Without a word, she rolled toward him and placed her hand on his chest with a whispered, "Wow."

He smiled but she could feel the rapid beat of his heart under her palm. "You like?"

"Um...yeah," she said, laughing softly. "I had no idea you had these." His right arm had a cluster of red roses and a cross with his mother's name on it, and his left had a very intricate tribal design. On his chest, however, he had a massive lion's head and the artwork–even in the dim lighting–was spectacular. She was tempted to ask him to turn on a light but figured there was time for that later. Right now, she was simply enjoying having the freedom to touch him.

After several moments, she looked up at him and gave him what she hoped was a sexy smile right before she pulled him in for another kiss. This one was slower, sweeter, but as soon as Dean rolled her onto her back and covered her body with his, it changed–grew more urgent–and pretty soon all Courtney could think of was how much she wanted him.

All of him.

She began to move beneath him, rubbing against him, and just as she had thought earlier, she was all for him taking things slow later. Right now, however, she couldn't wait. Hell, she'd been waiting for more than ten years to be like this with him and she was beyond impatient.

Her hands began to score down his back until she reached the waistband of his briefs and began pushing them away. His deep chuckle against her lips told her he got the message. But when he still made no move to help her, she broke the kiss.

"Dean?"

"Hmm?"

"Lose the boxers," she said breathlessly.

"Yes, ma'am." And as soon as he was done, he surprised her by ridding her of her thong and of her breath when his mouth trailed a hot path from her breasts and downward. As soon as he settled in to please her, Courtney forgot about everything else and enjoyed the ride.

She was gone.

Dean rolled over and squinted at how bright his bedroom was and realized he was alone. He lay there and listened for any indication that she was still here but he was only met with silence. Cursing, he kicked off the blankets and got dressed. Stepping out of his bedroom, he looked around and confirmed Courtney had left.

Why? Why would she leave without saying goodbye? The night was amazing–beyond amazing–damn near perfect, so why would she sneak out on him like this?

"Coffee," he murmured. Maybe he could think clearer if he had a jolt of caffeine in him.

Five minutes later and things still didn't make sense.

Sitting on the sofa with his mug cradled in his hands, he thought about what could have happened. He wasn't a prude, but even he blushed thinking of the things they did last night–from her striptease right here in his living room to the way she rode him like some sort of rodeo porn star. Yeah, it was quite possibly the hottest night of his life and it pissed him off how he was here alone now.

He'd questioned what he was doing on the entire drive home from the wedding. This was Courtney, his sister's best friend. He had no right pursuing her in any capacity, and yet by the time they arrived at his house, he wasn't looking at her like that. Gone were the images of her hanging out with his family because all he could see was a sexy and beautiful woman who he wanted more than anything.

And look where it got him.

Was that why she left? Was she unable to compartmentalize their history? Maybe she couldn't see beyond him being Scarlett's brother and regretted what they did. That thought depressed the shit out of him. He sipped his coffee and shook his head. How was it possible that they could share such an incredible night after knowing each other for years but she wouldn't feel comfortable just talking to him about it? What kind of men did she date that she didn't feel like she could talk to him about her concerns? Didn't she know him by now? He was the one *everyone* confided in—the guy who was always ready to listen and help! So then why...

And then it hit him.

Everyone came and talked to him about their problems, but not when the problem was him.

Another curse flew out of his mouth and he wanted to throw something or punch something. He seriously contemplated throwing his mug across the room, but everything was newly finished and he was too damn practical to ruin the new paint job.

No matter how mad he was.

So he drank his coffee and stewed until he couldn't take it any longer. Standing, he walked to the kitchen and put his mug in the sink and decided he needed to get out of the house. He wasn't going to chase after Courtney; the fact that she left spoke volumes and he wasn't going to make things worse by showing up at her house and demanding that she talk to him. Instead, he was going to head over to Scarlett's old place. She wanted to put it on the market but it needed some work and he had volunteered to do it in his spare time.

This was how he'd get out his frustration—he'd go replace some rotten wood and tear down a wall or two—demolition would be great therapy right now. Feeling invigorated, he threw on a pair of work boots before going out to his shed and grabbing the necessary tools. Within minutes, he was in his truck and making the short drive to his sister's house.

Scarlett's house was only a half a mile away and yet he felt like he couldn't get there fast enough. He had just turned onto her block when his phone rang. Glancing down, he saw it was his brother Kyle and opted to let it go to voicemail. He was a man on a mission right now and he didn't want to stop and talk to anyone. Maybe after he'd torn down a wall or used a sledgehammer on the kitchen cabinets, he'd feel a little more civilized, but not yet.

He turned onto the long dirt driveway that wove through the heavily wooded lot where Scarlett's little house was. He always hated that she lived in such an isolated spot, but for whatever reason, she loved it. It had always needed a ton of work, but it never bothered her. And now that she was married, she didn't need this place. Hell, she didn't need it for the last four or five months–not since she moved in with Mason–but she was procrastinating. Dean had been the one to convince her it was time to let it go and then volunteered to do the renovations.

And right now, he was glad he did. A day of hard, physical labor was the perfect distraction for him and in his mind, he began a list of what he wanted to accomplish today and what would need to be done first. He was sure that he'd have to hit one of the big home improvement stores for supplies, but he wanted to smash some things first. Then he'd make a list and go buy materials.

As he got closer to the house, he saw a car in the driveway that wasn't Scarlett's.

It was Courtney's.

Shit.

What the hell was she doing here? He knew she mentioned that her car was still here along with some of her things, but...why was she *still* here? There was no way he could have a conversation with her right now; he'd just told himself that he wasn't feeling particularly civilized, so now what was he supposed to do? His phone rang again and without looking at it, he rejected the call. Parking the truck, he sat there and stared at the house for a full five minutes before he said, "Screw it" and climbed out. At the front door, he didn't bother knocking. He simply used his key and let himself in.

And froze.

Courtney was curled up asleep on the sofa.

Letting out a long breath, he shut the door and stepped into the room. The sound must have woken her up because the next thing he knew, she was blinking and stretching and then gasping in shock.

"Dean! What are you doing here?"

"I could ask you the same thing." And yeah, his tone was a little harsher than he intended.

Sitting up, she shoved the blanket aside. "What time is it?" She got up and walked into the kitchen and he noted she had on a pair of black yoga pants and a gray t-shirt. He was tempted to follow her and push her for an answer, but the kitchen was literally a few feet away and he could see her. Clearly she was trying to kill some time because he watched as she got herself a bottle of water and drank half of it down.

She looked at him and must have seen how annoyed he was getting because she finally came back out to the living room. "So, um...yeah," she mumbled, sitting back down.

He figured he was going to have to be the one to speak since she went quiet again. "Look, if last night freaked you out that much, then just tell me," he said, unable to hide his frustration. "We've known each other long enough that you should know me, Court. You know I appreciate honesty."

She nodded but still wouldn't look at him or respond.

"You at least owe me an explanation," he snapped. "I had no idea you'd even left! And now you're just going to sit here and ignore me? Seriously?"

Then she did look at him and her green eyes were incredibly sad. "Last night did freak me out," she finally said and he felt his heart sink. "I'm leaving town tomorrow and... and you're my best friend's brother and I don't want things to be awkward and now they are!"

"Court..."

"I'm serious, Dean! Do you honestly think it will be easy when I come to visit your sister and see you? Do you think I'm not going to immediately think of how I had one of the greatest nights of my life and it was a one-night stand? Like I'm not going to see you and remember how you made me feel or how you saw me naked?" Her cheeks flushed and she looked away to study the bottle of water in her hands. "These are things I should have thought of before I went home with you. I don't want to have to avoid coming to see Scarlett because I'm embarrassed to be around you."

Well, damn. He said he wanted honesty...

Sitting beside her, he sighed. "Okay, I get it. This has the potential to be awkward, but...you don't think I'm worried too?" He waited until she looked at him and then nodded. "Last night, I wasn't thinking of you as Scarlett's friend. All I was thinking was how you look like a damn fantasy and kiss like a dream." He paused. "You have to know that."

She gave him a small smile. "Thanks. I really wasn't thinking of you as...you know, either. You were this guy who I've been crushing on for so long and..." She paused and sighed. "And I knew I was only going to have one chance– one night–and I wanted to know what it was like to be with you."

He had no idea what to say. No woman had ever said such a thing to him and he was a little humbled to know Courtney felt this way.

And it sucked even more that this was all they were going to have.

Not that he thought they would've started dating if she wasn't moving. That would be awkward. He would definitely catch a lot of flack from his family. His brothers would mock him for being a hypocrite, his sister would be pissed that he was messing around with her best friend, and his father would...well, he had no idea what his father would do or say, but he was sure it wouldn't be positive.

So where did it leave them?

His phone rang again and he wanted to throw it and smash it, but clearly someone was desperate to get in touch with him. Pulling it from his pocket, he saw Kyle's name and groaned. Swiping the screen, he snapped, "What?"

"Dude, maybe answer your phone once in a while," Kyle snapped back. "Where the hell are you?"

"I'm at Scarlett's. I'm supposed to start doing the reno on the place. Why? What's up?"

"Scarlett's in the hospital."

"*What?!*" he cried, jumping to his feet. "Why? I mean, when did this happen?"

"They were at the airport this morning for their flight and Mason said she wasn't feeling well. She went to the ladies' room and got sick. Real sick."

"Yeah, but...she's been getting sick ever since she got pregnant. They're hospitalizing her for that?"

Courtney instantly stood up, concern written all over her face.

"It wasn't like the normal stuff. There was blood and she passed out. Some woman came running out of the ladies' room to get Mason and they called for an ambulance. We're all on our way there now."

"Holy shit," he murmured. "Okay, I'm leaving now. I'll see you soon." He hung up and looked at Courtney.

"Give me five minutes to get dressed!" she said as she ran from the room and all Dean could do was focus on breathing and praying his sister and the baby were going to be okay.

4

It was getting dark when they finally left the hospital.

Scarlett had developed an ovarian cyst that burst and that's what caused the health scare. She was put on bed rest for a week which meant her honeymoon was on hold. They were keeping her overnight at the hospital for observation.

The whole day was a bit of a whirlwind–and that wasn't including her confrontation with Dean before they had gotten the call.

After that, things got a little crazy.

First, they argued over driving to the hospital together. Courtney was more than happy to take her own car, but Dean had gone into his bossy mode and told her to just get in his truck.

So she did.

The drive to the hospital wasn't long, but they sort of switched gears and went from two people arguing over their wild, sexy night, to two friends concerned about the same person. And she had to admit, they slid back into friend mode easily.

Throughout the entire day, she sat with Scarlett's

family and was able to forget about last night and this morning. She did her best to keep them all distracted and talking while they waited for word from the doctors. And while everyone was relieved that the baby was fine and Scarlett was going to be okay, it made Courtney re-think her plan to leave in the morning.

She knew Mason was going to be home to take care of Scarlett during her bed rest, but...what if something else happened? What if this trauma caused the baby to come early and she wasn't there for it? Either way, she had to be out of her parents' house and already had a small trailer filled with her stuff. So where did that leave her?

Climbing into Dean's truck, she sighed.

"What's up?" he asked as he buckled his seatbelt.

"Nothing. Just thinking of all the things I still have to do when I get home." It wasn't a total lie, but she didn't want to discuss her dilemma with him because...well...she just didn't.

"Ah," he said. He pulled out of the hospital parking lot and they drove in silence for several minutes. "So, uh... you're all packed?"

She nodded. "Yup. Probably packed way more than I need, but...I'm hoping to find a place to live sooner rather than later and don't want to make a trip back here so I've got a small trailer that I'm going to hitch to the back of my car."

He glanced at her. "You sure that's a good idea?"

"Yeah, why?"

He shrugged. "I just never really think of sedans as towing vehicles, that's all."

Frowning, she replied, "You work on cars for a living and you didn't realize this?"

Another shrug. "Like I said, I just don't think about

sedans doing that. And I don't remember seeing a trailer hitch on your car the last time you brought it in for service."

"Oh, um...my dad put one on for me."

He stared at her for so long she was afraid they were going to crash.

"What? What's the matter with that?"

"Court, you know I think your father's a great guy, but he probably wasn't the best person to install that. I'll look at it when we get back to the house."

And the thing was, this was just Dean being Dean. He was always looking out for everyone and willing to lend a hand whenever needed, but right now Courtney really just wanted to get going. "It's fine, Dean. Really. I towed the trailer home without any problems. I appreciate your willingness to help, but it's late and I just need to run into the house and grab my stuff and go."

Luckily he didn't argue.

Even though he looked like he wanted to.

And he kept looking that way after they got back to Scarlett's.

Standing next to his truck, he waited for her to go in and collect her things. She wasn't stupid; she knew he was looking at the trailer hitch without her seeing him. But when she walked back out with a duffel bag full of clothes, he was standing in the same spot she'd left him in. Walking to her car, she tossed the bag onto the back seat and turned to smile at him, not really knowing what to do or say.

Did she hug him? Kiss him? Climb him like a tree and beg him for a quickie before she hit the road?

He made the decision for her by walking over and wrapping her in his arms and hugging her tight. "Take care of yourself, Court," he said, his voice unusually gruff.

Unable to help herself, she held on tight and simply

relished the warmth of him. "I will."

They stood like that for several minutes before Dean placed a soft kiss on the top of her head and stepped back. He smiled before opening her car door for her. Part of her was a little disappointed that he wasn't asking her to stay or even mentioning keeping in touch.

So it was just a night. You said you'd be okay with it...

That was before she had that night.

And now she was ruined for all other men.

Damn him.

Swallowing hard, she forced herself to smile at him. "Take care of yourself, Dean."

"You too, Court."

And with no other choice, she got into her car with her smile in place and drove away. As soon as she was off Scarlett's block, she let the first tears fall–and they kept falling all the way home. In her own driveway, she took a minute to compose herself because she didn't want to upset her parents. And really, what would she say–that she finally made love with the man of her dreams and he didn't care enough about her to ask her to stay?

Um...no. That would not go over well.

When she finally felt ready, she went inside.

"Hey, sweetie! We were expecting you home much earlier today. How was the rest of the wedding?" her mother asked.

Smiling, she said, "It was good. Really good. You missed some excellent cake."

Her father walked into the room. "Who has excellent cake?"

"Mom was just asking about the rest of the wedding," Courtney explained.

"We took a ton of pictures," her mom explained. "You

both looked beautiful."

"Thanks, Mom." Looking around, she saw several pieces of luggage by the door. "So? Are you all packed and ready to go?"

Donna and James Baker had taken up ghost hunting. For as long as Courtney could remember, they had been interested in all-things paranormal, but it wasn't until a few years ago that they began to actively get involved with a group who researched, documented, and made it their mission to prove the paranormal. Personally, she found it fascinating and always loved to hear about their adventures but had yet to go on a trip with them.

And now wasn't the time to do it either.

While her father walked around talking about all the places they were going to visit, her mother walked around cleaning. Courtney felt bad about not being around much in the last several days to help out, but all the wedding activities had kept her busy.

"Mom, can I help with anything?"

But she waved her off. "You have your own packing to do and I'm sure you'll remember to clean your room and bathroom before you leave tomorrow. I have a cleaning company coming in tomorrow afternoon and then the property management people will handle our guests."

"Is that what we're calling them?" she muttered.

Pausing, her mother stared at her. "Is this still bothering you? I thought with you leaving in the morning, it wouldn't be a big deal."

"It just feels weird, that's all."

"Are you sure? Because you look like something's bothering you."

That's when she told her about Scarlett's health scare.

"Oh, my goodness! And just as they were leaving for

their honeymoon! That is too bad."

"And now I feel guilty about not being here," she admitted, flopping down on the couch. "I know Mason's going to be with her, but after everything we've been through together, it just feels wrong to leave."

Sitting beside her, her mother sighed. "And now you can't even stay here."

"Exactly."

"You could stay with Grandma," her father suggested. "You know she'd love to have you."

While that was true, her grandmother was a bit of a handful at times and Courtney wasn't sure how long she'd last staying there.

"Did you talk to Scarlett? I'm sure she'd understand if you weren't here. After all, no one could have predicted this turn of events," her mother offered.

"I guess." But it still didn't feel right. Of course, she could still leave and maybe come back for the weekend. It wasn't ideal but she knew she and Scarlett would talk every day so it wasn't like she was completely abandoning her. It seemed like the most logical choice.

Or was it?

"So what do you think you'll do?"

"I think I need to sleep on it," she said. "It was a busy weekend and a hectic day and I still have so much to do, so..." She stood and stretched. "I might as well get to it."

The wrench slipped from his hands for the fourth time and Dean let out a string of curses. His focus was total crap today and he hadn't accomplished one damn thing.

"I think you need to call it a day," his father said. "I

know we're all worried about your sister but you're going to hurt yourself at this rate."

Straightening, he looked at his father oddly. "Um...what?"

"It's obvious that you're distracted today. I know I am. But Mason said she's doing fine and is resting. Maybe tomorrow we can go see her after work."

That's when it hit him that his dad thought his mood had to do with Scarlett.

And he was going to keep on letting him think that.

"Yeah. That sounds good. Maybe we'll bring some Chinese food or something," he suggested, wiping his hands on the rag he kept in his back pocket.

"Go on. It's almost quitting time anyway. We'll start fresh tomorrow."

"Thanks, Dad."

"Why don't you call Scarlett when you get home so you can hear for yourself that she's doing okay?"

Smiling, he said, "I will." After he washed up, he asked, "What about you? What are you doing tonight?"

"Tommy asked Kyle and me to go look at some pieces he wants to use in the restaurant. Something about an auction," Domenic said with a shrug. "He needs help moving them if he buys them."

"Oh." He wondered why his grandfather didn't think to include him. "Well, have fun."

Within minutes he was in his truck and heading home. He was tired, filthy, and starving. A hot shower would make a world of difference and then he'd go pick up something for dinner because he was in no mood to cook tonight.

Once he was home, he stripped as he made his way to the bedroom and once he was under the hot spray of the shower, he felt himself begin to relax. Visions of Courtney came to mind—just like they had all day. This particular time he could attribute to his own wild and wishful imagination. Over the course of their night together, he had fantasized about waking up with her in the morning and taking a shower together. Why it had been something he wanted so badly, he couldn't say. But now the image was lodged there and wouldn't leave.

Groaning, he shook his head. It had to get better, right? Eventually he'd stop thinking about her and just...get back to his regularly scheduled life. He had to. It was just on his mind so much because it had all just happened. By tomorrow, hopefully, he'd be able to think about it less and less. What they had was a one-time thing, that's all. It was a combination of years of curiosity and just...

Hell, who was he kidding, and really, what was the point in lying to himself? He'd had a thing for Courtney since she was about eighteen. He could still remember the night of Scarlett's graduation party. She had shown up wearing a white strapless dress that hit about mid-thigh and he just about swallowed his own tongue. He'd always thought she was pretty, but that was the night he realized she wasn't a kid anymore.

And then he felt ashamed for even thinking of her at all. She was six years younger and yet he always felt way older— like ancient, comparatively.

When she kissed him Friday night after the rehearsal dinner, he was shocked, turned on, and ultimately relieved that she felt the same way he did.

Until she took off.

He let out a mirthless laugh as he thought about it. Maybe he should be examining why she felt the need to run off on him not once but twice.

Talk about crushing a guy's ego...

Still, he wished he had forced himself to say something more to her yesterday. He knew she was leaving but he could have said something about how he felt about her or how he wished they'd had more time. Something. Anything.

But he hadn't and he knew he was going to regret that for a long time.

Rinsing his hair, he cursed himself. Thinking about her was not what he was supposed to be doing. He needed to think about something else. For the rest of the shower–which wasn't long–he started thinking about the work he wanted to start on Scarlett's place. After he dropped Courtney off there yesterday, he didn't stay and try to get any work done. His head wasn't in it. But sometime this week, he really needed to get himself organized so he could be prepared to hit it hard next weekend.

Stepping out of the shower, he dried off and dressed in a pair of faded jeans and a black t-shirt–his standard attire. Looking at himself in the mirror, he finger-combed his hair and sighed. He had meant to get it cut before the wedding but hadn't made the time.

And speaking of the wedding, he grabbed his phone and called his sister. Her new husband answered the phone.

"Hey, Dean, what's up?"

"Hey, Mason. I'm sure you've had like a hundred calls today, but I just wanted to make sure Scarlett was doing okay."

He laughed a little. "She is the worst patient. I swear, I think the nurse ran with the wheelchair this morning to get her out of the hospital as fast as she could."

The image had Dean laughing too. "Sounds about right. She's always been like that. Doesn't like taking orders and hates to be confined." He laughed again. "Good luck with that."

"Yeah, thanks."

"Is there anything you need? Want me to pick up some dinner for you guys?"

"I appreciate the offer, but my mother dropped off about a month's worth of food here this afternoon–a combination of groceries and ready-made stuff. We barely had enough room for it."

"Yikes."

"Exactly. Listen, I'd ask if you want to talk to Scarlett but she's sleeping. Although I do need to wake her up to eat..."

"No, don't wake her up on my account. I'll try to call her tomorrow or maybe swing by after work if that's okay."

"Absolutely. We'll just be hanging out and trying not to think about the tropical vacation we're not on," he said lightly.

"I know that must suck, but I have to say that I'm glad you hadn't left when this happened. I'd hate to think of her in a foreign hospital or having to travel in her condition."

"Yeah, we talked about that and we know this is all for the best. Plus, her doctor was already a little against her flying in the third trimester. So now we definitely won't be going anywhere until after the baby comes."

"Damn. Sorry."

"It's all good. The only thing that matters is that Scarlett and the baby are okay."

It was just another reason Dean liked Mason. He knew he genuinely loved Scarlett.

"I'll let you go," Dean said. "I'm going to go get myself something to eat and come back and just chill." He paused. "Oh, I'm going to start working on Scarlett's place this week. I was there yesterday when we got the call, so I didn't get anything started yet."

"No worries and no rush, Dean. Seriously. Don't go killing yourself. We know you put in long hours at the garage as it is so...we're really okay with you doing it at your own pace."

"Thanks. I appreciate you saying that, but I'll keep you up to date so you'll know when you can possibly get it on the market."

"Sounds good," Mason said. "And we'll see you tomorrow."

Hanging up, he slid his phone into his pocket as he walked back across the house. Grabbing a pair of sneakers, he slid them on before picking up his keys and sunglasses and heading out. It was still relatively early–barely six o'clock–and he had no idea what he wanted to eat. There were all the usual suspects like pizza or Chinese food, but neither seemed overly appealing. He didn't mind driving through town until something piqued his interest. Traffic was mild and maybe something would come to mind while he drove. The sky was getting darker–and not because of the time of day. There were some storms predicted, and with any luck, he'd be home before the rain started.

There was the Mystic Magnolia–his grandfather's place–but he was already heading in the opposite direction and it wasn't fully open yet. Still, he was all for helping test the new menu.

"Another time," he murmured.

He drove by the country club and shook his head and Café Magnolia wasn't open for dinner. A little farther up the road was Michael's Italian Restaurant, but the more he thought about it, he wasn't in the mood for pasta. Panda Garden was right next to it and while he always enjoyed some shrimp with lobster sauce, that didn't appeal to him either.

"God, when did I get this picky?"

Driving past the supermarket, he considered going in and just getting something to make when he realized The Sand Bar was coming up. They had the best burgers and even though it was more of a sit-down place, he was sure he could order his food to go.

Feeling satisfied with his decision, he pulled into the turning lane and saw the parking lot wasn't overly full and he figured he should be able to get in and out pretty quickly. Then he pulled in and spotted a familiar car.

With a small trailer hitched to the back of it.

Courtney's still in town?

Pulling into a parking spot, he was out of his truck and stalking through the front door, his expression fairly murderous. The hostess took one look at him and stepped back before she could even welcome him and he barely spared her a glance while he scanned the room.

There she is.

Sitting alone in one of the small corner booths sat Courtney. She had a drink in front of her and a small basket with some sort of appetizer in it that he was determined to see for himself. He took a minute to compose himself so he didn't come off as some kind of aggressive jerk before walking over to her.

"Mind if I join you?" he asked smoothly as he slid in across from her. Her eyes went wide and he smiled. "Ooh... fried pickles. I love these." Popping one in his mouth, he continued to grin at her.

It was obvious he had surprised her and he had a ton of questions, but when she remained silent, he figured he'd have to be the one to lead the conversation.

Again.

"I would have thought you'd be checking out all the

places to eat in Raleigh tonight. Did you change your mind?"

Fidgeting in her seat, she shook her head. "Just getting a late start." She cleared her throat. "I had some things to take care of and I wanted one last burger from The Sand Bar before I left."

He nodded. "They are the best."

"Yup."

"But...it's not like you're never coming back to Magnolia again."

"Yeah, I know. It was just..." She stopped and shrugged. "I was just in the mood for it."

Another nod. "So what kind of things did you have to do? And this is going to make you get to Raleigh pretty late. Do you have a reservation at a hotel or anything?"

"Um...no. No reservation. I was just planning on driving and stopping at the first decent one I saw."

"And the reason you're leaving so late?" he prompted.

"I wanted to go see Scarlett and then I thought I'd spend the night at my grandmother's, but she had some friends from out of town staying with her already, so..."

So she had no place to go. He was going to suggest Scarlett's but figured she had her reasons for not going there.

The waitress came by and took his order and when Courtney stared at him with mild annoyance, he couldn't help but tease her a little. "What? Did you think I was going to go sit at another table? What would be the point in that?"

"How about I was enjoying sitting here by myself?"

Unable to help himself, he laughed out loud before resting his arms on the table. "Sweetheart, you and I both know that's a lie. You hate being by yourself–you especially hate eating by yourself. If you ask me, it's a good thing I came in here and sat with you."

And yeah, her eyes went wide right before they narrowed at him.

"You think you know me so well," she said with a hint of snark, "but you don't. I was just fine sitting here alone. I was thinking of all the things I'll need to do when I get up tomorrow. It's going to be very hectic. And now you're interrupting that!"

Leaning slightly across the table, he said, "You've got a three-hour drive, Court. You have more than enough time to think. Try again."

"Ugh...why are you like this?" she cried, slamming her hand on the table. "And why are you even here? I've never seen you in here before!" She paused and gasped. "Are you like...following me or something?"

Leaning back in his seat, he crossed his arms over his chest and saw the way her gaze landed on his tattooed arms. "I'm not following you. Trust me. I got the hint yesterday morning." He liked the way her cheeks flushed at his words. "I eat here a lot so I could say the same thing about you–I've never seen *you* here before either."

"This is ridiculous," she muttered. "I should have just grabbed some McDonald's on the road."

Reaching over, he plucked another fried pickle chip from the basket and popped it in his mouth. "Yeah, but you didn't. So why don't you just relax and we'll enjoy our dinner before you get on the road." And before she could argue, he asked about her parents and if they had left this morning as planned.

The change of subject seemed to do the trick because she visibly relaxed. She told him about how the first part of their trip was taking them to the western part of the state before they started off across the country. They were going to be gone for three months and he had to wonder how they could just take off from their jobs for such an extended period of time. Their food arrived before he could ask and then she began sharing some of the stories of their paranormal encounters.

And she had a lot of them.

Before he knew it, they were both done eating and he was paying the bill.

"Dean," she protested, "you don't have to do that."

"Yeah, I know. Just consider it a going-away present or something." He slid from the booth and waited for her to do the same. They walked out to the parking lot and over to her car. The idea of her pulling the trailer on a hitch her father installed still didn't sit well with him, but he hoped she would be okay.

Looking down at her–he towered over her by at least six inches–he thought of all the things he wanted to say. All the things he told himself he should have said to her yesterday were on the tip of his tongue, but...he didn't say any of them. He couldn't.

"Thank you for dinner," she said. Glancing over at her car, she sighed. "I should get going. It's already later than I thought."

With a curt nod, he stepped back and felt the first drops of rain hit him. Courtney's expression fell.

"Dammit, now I'm going to be stuck driving in the rain," she said with dismay. Opening her car door, she tossed her purse in and looked at Dean one last time. Her shoulders sagged and her eyes looked a little sad. "Dean, I..."

He nodded again. "Yeah," he said gruffly. "I know." Walking closer, he held the car door open for her while she climbed in. "Be safe, Court."

Wordlessly, she nodded and he closed the door for her.

And watched her drive away.

It wasn't until she pulled out of the parking lot and her taillights were out of sight did he move. The rain was starting to come down a bit harder and he was close to being soaked, but it barely registered with him. Letting out a long breath, he walked over to his truck and climbed in as he called himself every name in the book.

Again.

How many chances would he piss away without talking to her about the things that were important?

"Apparently, all of them," he said with disgust. Pulling out of the parking lot, he headed for home. It was still early and he was restless and considered going to Scarlett's again and doing some demo. All of his tools were still in the truck and it wasn't like he had anyone or anything waiting for him at home. With the decision made, that's where he went.

At the house, he carried the tools in and walked around inspecting the place. He took his time to try to envision what he wanted to do first and how he wanted it all to look when he was done. Scarlett had given him the go-ahead to do whatever he wanted. As much as he liked the idea of not having to follow anyone's plans, he hadn't given much thought about what he was going to do here. Most of the furniture was gone and he knew his sister had emptied all the cabinets and drawers in the kitchen so it seemed like the perfect place to start.

Placing his safety goggles on, he picked up the sledgehammer and almost felt giddy at the idea of smashing something. The sledgehammer was up over his head when his phone rang. Having learned his lesson yesterday about not ignoring calls, he placed the hammer down and pulled out his phone and saw it was his father calling.

"Hey, Dad! What's up?"

"Hey, Son. Are you busy?"

"A little. I'm getting ready to tear down the kitchen cabinets at Scarlett's place. How come?"

"I'm out with Tommy and Kyle up in New Bern and we just got a call about a car needing a tow."

"Dad, there are plenty of other tow trucks in town. Why can't someone else do it?"

"Because it's Courtney," he said. "I hate the thought of her waiting for some stranger to pick her up. She drove through some deep water and lost control of the car and the trailer. If you take the flatbed with you, you should be able to get both on there without a problem. I know it's raining and all, but..."

"I knew she shouldn't have left tonight! I knew it!" he growled.

"If you knew it, why didn't you stop her?" his father demanded.

"Dad, please. You know you can't stop a woman when she's made her mind up."

"Would you have let your sister drive in those conditions? Even if she got mad?"

"Of course I wouldn't! But we're not talking about Scarlett. We're talking about Courtney!"

"And she's family!" Domenic shouted. "She's like a daughter to me and another sister to you and your brothers! Now are you going to go help her or not? She's about ten miles past the bridge, near all that new road construction. I'll text you her phone number so you can call her if you can't find her, okay?"

"Yeah. Thanks."

"And Dean?"

"Yeah?"

"You be careful too."

"No worries, Dad. I'm on my way."

5

Of all the rotten luck.

Sitting in her car–which was sitting in a muddy puddle on a dark stretch of the road–Courtney prayed Mr. Jones would get here quickly. She knew he needed to go pick up the tow truck, but she hated being out here alone in the dark.

Why didn't I just stay at a hotel in town for the night? Why did I have to be so damn stubborn?

She didn't have any answers and right now, all she wanted was to curl up in a ball and cry. And on top of it all, why did she have to have such a nice dinner with Dean and why did he still not seem the least bit fazed by the turn in their relationship? There was a small part of her that wished he would suddenly realize he was in love with her and beg her not to go.

Wishful thinking was the worst.

Especially in this scenario.

It was like everything she wanted was right there within her reach and yet still impossible to get. How unfair was that?

For thirty minutes, she scrolled through her phone checking Instagram and Facebook, liking posts and seeing what everyone else she knew was doing. It was an okay way to pass the time, but all she wanted was to call Mr. Jones and see if he was almost there.

As if on cue, headlights appeared in her mirror and she straightened in her seat when they were close behind her. Then a large flatbed truck slowly drove passed her and carefully backed up to the front of her car. A wave of relief washed over her and she quickly stuffed her phone back in her purse and grabbed her things and waited for Mr. Jones to tell her what she needed to do.

Only...that wasn't who got out of the truck.

It was Dean.

Pounding the steering wheel, she cursed her rotten luck.

Why? She wanted to cry with frustration. Why did their paths have to keep crossing now?

He was next to her door before she could force herself to move. Sighing wearily, she opened it. The rain was pouring down and he was already soaked.

And somehow still managed to look sexy as hell, damn him.

"I thought your dad was coming," she said as she climbed out of the car.

"He was up in New Bern with my grandfather and Kyle. I was closer," he said before nodding toward the car. "Grab your stuff and go sit in the truck, but leave the keys."

Grabbing her things, she started to walk and noticed he was right beside her. "What are you doing? Shouldn't you be...you know...moving the car?"

With his hand low on her back, he guided her over to the passenger side of the truck and helped her in before running around and getting in on the driver's side. "Here are the controls for the heat. Feel free to warm it up as much as you want. There are a couple of bottles of water here too, so help yourself. This may take a little while because I have to try to get the trailer up there too since it's no longer attached."

And yeah, he sort of leveled her with a glare at those words.

"Okay, you were right. There. You happy now?" she said with a huff. "I should have let you or your dad install the hitch or at least inspect it before I picked up the trailer."

"Sit tight," he said, hopping out of the truck.

Unable to help herself, she twisted in her seat and tried to watch what he was doing. The rain and darkness really hindered her view. Dean sort of disappeared behind her car and for the better part of fifteen minutes, she couldn't see him at all. When he finally reappeared, he walked toward the cab of the truck and seemed to hit a switch or something because she could hear a loud hum right before she noticed her car moving forward onto the bed. Her eyes went wide when she saw the trailer moving up as well and figured he must have rigged the hitch again and got the two connected.

It took several minutes for everything to come to a stop and a few more minutes after that for him to secure everything. When he finally climbed back into the truck, he was drenched.

"I'm so sorry," she said.

"For what?" Wiping his dripping wet hair back, he looked over at her.

"For making you come out in this mess." She shook her head. "I should have just gone to a hotel or something tonight and left in the morning."

"No, you should have let someone who knows about cars make sure this setup was safe," he corrected.

Carefully, he pulled back onto the road and they had to drive a mile or so before there was a shopping center where he could safely turn around in the parking lot. Once they were heading back toward town, he spoke again.

"If it's all right with you, I'm going to drop your car and trailer at the shop and we'll look at it in the morning. I think we can both agree that it's too late for you to get on the road now, right?"

She nodded.

"We've already got cars slotted for first thing in the morning, but I should be able to look at yours by lunchtime and you can be on the road by one or two if that works for you–barring any damage from the trailer falling off."

She nodded again and they were back to driving in silence.

Turning her head and watching the scenery go by, she wondered where she was going to stay and how she was going to get there. Dean would obviously have to drop her off and pick her up, but that still left her wondering where she was going to stay. Pulling her phone out, she began looking at availability for a room for the night.

There was the new B&B in town–the one Mason's aunt owned and where Scarlett and Mason's rehearsal dinner was–but it was late and she didn't feel right calling to see if they had a room available. Plus, they were a little pricier than what she wanted to spend. Next was Magnolia on the Beach–a small, local motel that wasn't usually full. She pulled up their site and began entering her info.

"What are you doing?"

Courtney looked up at him. "Um…I need a place to stay tonight so I was seeing if Magnolia on the Beach had any rooms."

Without taking his eyes off the road, Dean reached over and took the phone from her hands.

"Hey!" she cried. "What did you do that for?"

They pulled into the parking lot for Jones Automotive and it wasn't until he parked the truck in the back lot that he spoke. Twisting toward her, he seemed to be searching for exactly what to say. "You don't need to go to a hotel."

She knew exactly what he was saying and it made her heart soar.

"No one's at Scarlett's old place and I still haven't started tearing things out so you should be okay to stay there tonight."

And just like that, her heart sank.

"Oh," she said quietly and hoped her disappointment wasn't too obvious.

"What else do you need from your car? Any luggage or anything to get you through the night?"

It took a minute for her to organize her thoughts because what she wanted to scream was that she needed–wanted!–him. He was all she needed to get through the night, but she couldn't make herself say it.

"Um...yeah. There's a black suitcase in the trunk and a hot pink duffel bag. Those two should do it."

Luckily he didn't comment or make a snarky remark about why she needed two separate pieces of luggage for one night. Dean climbed out of the truck and Courtney soon followed. If anything, the rain was coming down harder and she put her purse over her head to try to protect herself a little. Glancing around, she spotted Dean up on the flatbed where he was retrieving her luggage. Once the trunk was shut, he handed her the duffel bag before jumping down with the suitcase. Using the key fob, he made sure her car was locked and quickly ushered her over to his truck.

Her clothes were soaked, her hair felt like it was plastered to her head, and she cursed how bad she must look.

Thank God it's dark...

He pulled out of the lot before jumping back out to lock and secure the gate. When he came back in, he let out a loud sigh. She knew exactly how he felt and she knew as soon as she got to Scarlett's, she was going to take a hot shower and maybe have some tea and...

"Shit," she muttered.

"What's the matter?"

"The kitchen is completely empty. That bottle of water I drank yesterday when you came over was the last thing in there." She paused. "I hate to ask, but..."

"Why don't you just come home with me," he suggested, his eyes never leaving the road.

"Um...excuse me?"

This time he did glance her way. "Look, it's late and we're both soaked to the skin. I don't feel like going to the grocery store, and I'm sure you don't either. It's ridiculous for you to pay for a hotel room or to stay someplace where there's no food or anything to drink, so...stay by me."

If he hadn't made it sound like a completely practical–and platonic–offer, she'd be a little more excited. How was she supposed to go home with him and not...you know...jump him?

But considering he didn't think it was such a big deal, Courtney had no choice but to react the same way. "I guess that makes the most sense. Thanks."

He nodded and neither spoke again until they pulled up to his house. "I'll grab the bags," he said and she thanked him like a polite stranger.

This is weird. This is weird. This is weird...

At the front door, he opened it and let her go in first. They both kicked off their shoes before moving any farther into the house, but Dean walked right by her and took her bags into his master bathroom.

True, it was the only bathroom with a shower and he must have figured she'd want to wash up after being out in the rain. Shrugging, she slowly started to follow him and heard the shower running. At the door to his bedroom, she paused and wondered if he was going to shower first. Turning away, she looked around and was unsure of what to do with herself. Her clothes were wet so she didn't want to sit on his couch, and she didn't think it was polite to go into the kitchen and make herself some hot tea either.

"Well now what do I do?" she whispered to herself.

"You're supposed to come take a shower with me," he said from directly behind her. She all but jumped out of her skin at the sound of his voice.

"Jeez! You're like a ninja!" she said breathlessly, turning to face him. Then she got a look at him and saw he'd taken his shirt off and...damn. So much of Saturday night was spent in the dark or with nothing but moonlight coming into the room that she was a little awestruck at the sight of him. Her gaze scanned over him from head to toe and back again. That's when she noticed the grin on his face and she couldn't help but return it with a shy smile of her own. "You sure about this?"

"The thought of getting you in my shower and soaping you up has been on my mind since Saturday night. I had planned on doing that with you Sunday morning, but...you were gone."

Damn.

Feeling the boldness that only he brought out in her, she

slowly peeled her t-shirt up and over her head before tossing it to the floor. "A shower sounds really good."

Dean took her hand in his and slowly led her back to his bedroom and through to the bathroom where it was already steamy. He closed the door behind them before pressing her up against it and kissing her and she immediately reached out to him like he was a lifeline for her. His kiss was instantly deep and consuming and it made her feel empowered that he was as frantic for her as she was for him.

When he broke the kiss abruptly and lifted his head, his gaze was hot and needy and so damn sexy. "Is it wrong that I'm glad that your car broke down?"

She laughed and raked her hands through his hair. "Not at all because I'm pretty damn happy it happened too."

He kissed her again as he led her closer to the shower, his hands working on the button of her jeans. "Hey, Court?" he asked against her lips.

"Yeah?"

"Let me peel these wet clothes off of you so I can get you wet in a lot of other ways."

The things this man said to her…

"Yes, please," she groaned, letting him do whatever he pleased.

Those two little words filled Dean with relief.

Asking her to join him in the shower was a big risk; after all, they hadn't directly addressed their sex-fueled night since it happened. There had been a very real possibility of Courtney telling him he was crazy and slapping his face.

He said a prayer of thanks she didn't do either of those things.

Now as he peeled her jeans down her legs and was eye level with a pair of turquoise blue panties, he added a prayer for self-control.

Courtney Baker was beyond temptation. The way she looked, the softness of her skin, and the way she responded to him were perfect. Hell, if he had to create the perfect woman, she would be it.

So why had he waited so long to make his move?

For starters, he had no idea she felt the same way. But if the way she was gripping his hair and panting as he stripped her was any indication, he was fairly confident now that she did indeed feel the same as him.

Helping her step out of her jeans, Dean's hands gripped her hips before moving around and gently kneading her rear. Looking up at her, he saw her head was thrown back and she looked so damn sexy. Leaning in, he kissed her thighs and then lingered a little on the turquoise lace before slowly coming to his feet and kissing her lips. Her arms wrapped around him and he knew he could stand here like this for hours.

But he had other plans...

Forcing himself to break the kiss, he stepped back and slid his jeans and boxer briefs off before reaching out and helping Courtney with her bra and panties. When they were both naked, he led her into the shower and under the hot spray. It seemed a bit surreal that just hours ago he had stood right here and dreamed of her and now here she was.

They took turns soaping each other up and he enjoyed letting his hands roam all over her curvy body as much as he enjoyed when her hands were all over his. They kissed, they touched, and it was beyond erotic. He knew he'd never forget this night, and when she dropped to her knees in front of him, he swore he'd died and gone to heaven. It had been so long since he'd been involved with anyone that he had forgotten how much he loved making love to a woman.

The water began to cool and he carefully helped her back to her feet before turning the water off. Kissing her deeply one more time, he moaned as the air around them began to chill. "Damn," he whispered against her mouth. "I was really enjoying being in here with you."

Her smile was slow and a little shy– which he thought was adorable considering what she had just been doing to him. When he saw her shiver, he knew he needed to get them dried off quickly. Opening the glass door, he grabbed one of the towels and wrapped it around her. Once she held the towel around her, he grabbed the other for himself before taking her by the hand and stepping out.

It seemed odd how he felt the need to keep touching her–holding her hand in his kept their connection and it was something he was finding essential. Facing her, he gently took the towel from her hands and dried her off.

"Dean," she said quietly but with a slight hitch in her breath. "You don't need to do that. I can dry myself off."

Using the towel, he tugged her in close. "I beg to differ. I really enjoy touching you, Court. Can't seem to get enough of it."

"That's good because...I really like it when you touch me."

Dropping the towel to the floor, he motioned toward the bedroom and once he had her next to the bed, she hopped up on it and lay back.

And that was like hitting the launch button.

All the touching and teasing in the shower had led to this moment and he was more than primed and ready to go. Dropping his own towel to the floor, he crawled up on the bed and covered her body with his and damn if it didn't feel even better than the last time he had her here like this.

He was about to kiss her when he stopped himself. Staring down at her, he knew there were some things he needed to say. "No sneaking out in the morning," he said gruffly.

Beneath him, Dean saw her swallow hard. "Kind of hard to leave without a car."

That hadn't stopped her the last time...

"You know what I'm saying. If you don't want this..."

"I do."

"Or if you have any regrets, say something now because..."

"No regrets, Dean. I swear."

And he believed her. Between the look in her eyes and the conviction in her voice, he knew she wasn't lying and knew she was going to be here beside him when he woke up.

As well as beneath him for most of the night.

Unable to wait another moment, he settled in as her legs wrapped around him and he loved her all night long.

When his alarm went off the next morning, Dean swore he had just fallen asleep. He slapped his hand over the snooze button and pulled Courtney tightly against him, her back against his chest.

It felt good.

Really good.

The kind of feeling he wouldn't mind waking up with every morning.

Shaking his head slightly, his eyes drifted closed and he

worried he was getting too attached too fast. Granted, he and Courtney had known each other for years, but...it was too soon to think of this as something serious, wasn't it? And then there was his sister to consider. There was no way Scarlett was going to be happy that the two of them were sleeping together.

So where did that leave them?

Last night, sometime around three a.m. when they were lying facing each other, they agreed that they needed to talk about what they were doing. At the time, they had been half asleep and sharing soft caresses and even softer kisses. It was a great way to fall asleep. Now in the light of day, however, he realized there wasn't going to be much time for them to talk because he needed to get to work.

As if on cue, the alarm went off again, and this time he forced himself to roll away from Courtney and turn it off. Stretching, he wondered if he should wake her up or let her sleep. Opting to let her sleep, he got up and got himself ready for work. Not that it took long–jeans and a t-shirt were his work uniform and his hair required very little attention. He looked at her sleeping soundly in his bed and smiled. He liked seeing her there and he hoped sometime later today they could talk and figure out what it was they were doing and where they saw it going.

Out in the kitchen, he made himself a cup of coffee and went in search of his phone. It was probably still in the bathroom so he quietly walked back to get it. This time as he walked through the bedroom, Courtney stirred. He stopped at the foot of the bed and simply watched her coming awake. She was all tousled hair and sleepy eyes, but when she saw him, she smiled.

And for the first time in his life, Dean considered calling in sick to work.

"Good morning," she said, her voice a little raspy.

"Good morning to you too. Did you sleep okay?"

She nodded as she sat up and stretched, baring her breasts to him.

Yeah, I should totally call in sick.

"You heading to work?" she asked.

"Actually, I was considering calling in sick today so I could stay in bed with you. What do you think?"

Blushing, she pulled up the sheet to cover herself. "As much as I would love that, you can't do that to your dad."

He loved that she was concerned for his father–loved that it was her first thought.

"I've never taken a day off so...he owes me one. Or several dozen. Take your pick," he teased.

"Dean, you can't do that. Plus, you need to look at my car," she whined, but in a cute way.

They never did talk about it last night when he picked her up. "Okay, so you drove through some standing water and lost control of the car and trailer, right?"

She nodded.

"The car started up fine when I tested it last night. Did you hit anything?"

"No, the water was higher than I thought and I guess I was going a little fast, and the next thing I knew, I was swerving and heard a loud snap and then the trailer seemed to fishtail really bad. I pulled over to the shoulder as fast as I could because I knew it was going to drop. You saw it–it was practically turned sideways when you got there."

"Yeah, you're lucky you heard it and stopped when you did. If you had dropped it in the middle of the road, it would have been a real hazard to anyone driving by."

"I know," she said quietly. "I'm sorry I didn't listen to

you about it. I really didn't think it was going to be a big deal."

"Well, once we get the car up on the lift, we'll make sure there's no damage to the undercarriage or the frame. Plus, we'll give it a tune-up and oil change because I'm sure you haven't done that in a while either."

She blushed and looked down at the blanket and it was all the answer he needed.

"Are you going to be okay here by yourself? Like I said last night, I probably won't get to it until later this morning or around lunchtime. If you want, I can come back at lunchtime and you can take my truck or...you can drive with me to work and drop me off so you can use it if you need to."

Yawning loudly, she shook her head. "Lunchtime is fine. If you don't mind, I think I'm going to grab a few more hours of sleep." And without waiting for an answer, she lay back down and pulled the blankets up over her shoulders.

He walked around to the side of the bed and placed a kiss on her forehead before walking out of the bedroom and closing the door behind him. Within minutes, he was walking out the door and doing his best not to go back inside and say to hell with work and curl up beside her.

6

"Oʜ, my gosh! This is the best news ever! I am so glad you didn't go! And you're here and now Mason can go outside and scream because I'm making him crazy!"

After Dean had come home at lunchtime and told her he still hadn't gotten to her car, he offered her his truck to use for the afternoon.

Then he made love to her on the kitchen counter.

He could demolish her car and she wouldn't mind if this was how she got to spend part of her day.

She drove him back to the garage and decided to surprise Scarlett. And apparently, it was a good thing she did.

Laughing, Courtney sat down on the bed beside her best friend. "I hate to break it to you, but I did go. I just didn't make it very far."

"What do you mean?"

She explained about the rain, the water, the trailer unhitching, and finally, Dean picking her up.

"Wow! Sounds like you had quite a night! Why didn't you call me and come stay here?"

Damn. She hadn't thought of that.

"Um...you know, you've only got the one bedroom and I knew you needed your rest."

"So where did you stay?"

And...she *really* didn't think this through.

There was no way she could say she stayed at Dean's. That would be weird. So...for the first time in their friendship, Courtney lied.

"I stayed at your old place."

Scarlett's eyes went wide. "Seriously? Why would you do that? I'm sure it's a mess with Dean working on it. You could have gone to a hotel! Hell, you could have stayed at Dean's! Anything would have been better than my old place!"

Things were quickly spiraling out of control and she knew she needed to reel it all back in.

"Well...he offered, but...I don't know. That would be weird, right? It would be totally weird. Super weird," she murmured and realized how fast she was talking. "So yeah, it just seemed like your place was the most logical. Plus, I was soaking wet and a mess from being out in the rain and... I don't know...at the time it just made sense."

"I'm going to kill my brother," Scarlett said, a scowl on her face.

"Why?"

"Because he shouldn't have let you do that!" Then she paused. "Wait...how did you even sleep there? My dad went over there yesterday with Kyle and took all the rest of the linens and stuff. And the bed. I told them to take it all. Where did you sleep?"

"Um..."

"Oh, man...did you have to dig through the trailer to get bedding so you could sleep on the couch?"

"Yes!" she said quickly, thankful Scarlett was giving her the excuses she needed. "That's what I did. I dug through the trailer before Dean dropped me off."

Scarlett was quiet for a moment. "How did you know you'd need them?"

"What?"

"I mean, when you slept there with me Friday night, everything was still there so...how did you know you'd need pillows and blankets?"

"Oh...um...you...you mentioned it Friday night, remember? You told me your dad was going to clear out the rest of your personal stuff." She let out a nervous laugh. "I mean, how else would I know that there wasn't going to be anything there for me to sleep on, right?" Another laugh. "So um...how are you feeling today? Can I get you anything? Want me to go get some ice cream or cupcakes?"

In a pinch, Courtney knew she could always distract Scarlett with food and she prayed that was going to work right now.

"Ooh...cupcakes! That would be amazing! Mason's mom sent over a ton of food, but most of it is healthy stuff and I was dying for something sweet and yummy!"

"Somebody say sweet and yummy?" Mason asked as he walked into the room with a smile.

"Ugh...don't be such a dork in front of Courtney," Scarlett teased.

"I don't think I was being dorky; I was simply responding when I thought you called," he replied sweetly.

Rolling her eyes, Scarlett chuckled before looking at Courtney. "See how much fun married life is? You should seriously try it."

"Right. Because men are just banging down my door and proposing. Please," she said with a snort.

"Maybe if you weren't so picky you could find the perfect guy for you!"

"Scar, we were talking about cupcakes. Can we stick to the topic?" Standing, she grabbed her purse. "Which do you want–red velvet or death by chocolate?"

"Why can't I have both? I am eating for two, you know." She rubbed a hand over her belly for emphasis.

Mason cleared his throat.

"What? What's the matter?" Scarlett asked innocently.

"Two cupcakes? Seriously? Remember what Dr. Jackson said about overdoing it with sweets?"

Glancing away, Scarlett picked imaginary lint off the blankets. "And I've been really good. I just thought it might be okay to have some with my best friend who is sad and homeless."

"Hey!" Courtney cried.

"Sorry, but...you know, you kind of are right now." She shook her head. "I'm going to call Dean and tell him to bring blankets and stuff over to the house for you. And I'll ask my dad to bring the bed back."

"Scar, you know I'm not staying. As soon as my car is fixed, I'm leaving. Dean's got the car in the shop right now. It should be done by the end of the day." She smiled down at her friend. "Now, I'm going to grab us some cupcakes, okay?" Then she looked at Mason. "And I will grab some for you too."

He smiled with satisfaction. "I like the red velvet and the cookies and cream, please."

"You got it." With a smile and a wave, she walked out of the bedroom and out of the house. Dean's truck was ridiculously large and she practically needed a step ladder to get into it. She wasn't sure how wise it was to be driving all over town in it, but she had panicked and now she had to go get cupcakes. Hopefully when she got back, Scarlett wouldn't grill her again about where she's staying and what she's doing.

Hell, you could have stayed at Dean's!

Yeah, that statement completely stumped her. It was possible that she wasn't really thinking, but...it just seemed odd. In all the years that they'd been friends, never once had Scarlett encouraged Courtney in any way, shape, or form to do *anything* with her brothers. It wasn't like she was forbidden to talk with them or hang out with them when they were around, but...she had no idea how her friend would react if she actually told her she spent the night at Dean's.

And there was no way she would ever tell her *how* she spent the night or what they did.

Repeatedly.

And what she really hoped they'd do again before she left.

Ugh...I'm hopeless...

Sleeping with Dean wasn't getting him out of her system or helping her move on. If anything, she wanted him now more than ever! If he gave her even the slightest encouragement or even hinted that he'd like to see where this relationship was going, she'd stay. Sure there was the whole no job, no place to live thing, but somehow she'd make it work.

But only if he wanted to.

And again, she really hoped he wanted to.

Talking with Dean was never an issue. Hell, she could talk to him about almost anything. She'd had lots of practice with that. But they never–ever!–talked about feelings. And the thought of doing that now was a little scary. In her experience, men didn't particularly enjoy talking about their feelings, but...Dean wasn't like other guys. He'd always been more practical and more mature. Maybe he wouldn't mind it so much.

It was her own insecurity that was holding her back.

The last thing she wanted to do was open her mouth and pour out her feelings and send him running. They were already treading lightly and she didn't want this—whatever this was—to end before it ever really had a chance to begin.

She made the short drive to Henderson's Bakery and forced herself to think of something other than Dean.

Inside the bakery, she ordered a dozen cupcakes to take to Scarlett and another dozen to share with Dean.

Way to not think about him...

"Ooh...are you having a party or something?" Mrs. Henderson asked as she boxed up all the cupcakes.

"What? Oh, um...no. I'm bringing a dozen to Mason and Scarlett—you heard about them having to miss their honeymoon, right?"

Mrs. Henderson nodded. "I did. Her brother Dean was in here this morning to get muffins. He always picks them up on Tuesday mornings for the guys at the shop. Such a good boy."

"Um...," Courtney didn't want to point out that Dean was no longer a boy, but decided not to draw attention to that.

"Thankfully, Scarlett's okay. They can go on a trip after the baby comes. And trust me, by then, they'll need it!" Mrs. Henderson said with a laugh. She put the big pink boxes down on the counter and studied Courtney for a moment. "I thought I heard you were moving to Raleigh. Your folks turned the house into an Airbnb and you're moving, right?"

She nodded. "I had some car trouble, but hopefully it will be fixed by the end of the day."

"Why you would want to leave Magnolia Sound is beyond me. This town is so much better than any place in the state. Plus, you'll be landlocked! I know you, Courtney Baker. You're a beach girl. How are you going to handle living so far away from the shore?"

Taking out her credit card, she handed it to Mrs. Henderson to pay for the cupcakes. "Honestly, I have no idea. All I know is that I'm ready for a change and moving seemed like the way to go."

"Hmm..."

There was no way she wanted to ask what that "Hmm" meant, so she simply stood and smiled until she got her credit card back. Once she did, Courtney grabbed the boxes of goodies and wished Mrs. Henderson a good day as she walked out the door.

And cursed the giant truck.

"Need a hand?"

Turning, she smiled at Sam Westbrook. They had spent a lot of time together during all of the wedding planning and parties, but she still didn't know him all that well. Although right now she was more than happy for the help. "Thanks. I didn't think it through when I opted to get the large boxes of cupcakes."

Sam reached out and took the boxes from her while she unlocked the truck and ungracefully climbed in.

He handed her the boxes. "Is this Dean Jones' truck?"

She nodded. "It's a loaner while mine's being fixed."

"Ah. That makes way more sense than this being your usual ride."

"Yeah, my usual is a very sensible Toyota sedan. This thing is a beast. I hope I can back out of this parking spot without hitting anyone!" She laughed but it was definitely out of nerves.

"Tell you what, I'll guide you out, okay?"

"Thanks, Sam. I'd appreciate that. I'd hate to give Dean his truck back damaged."

"And I'm sure he appreciates that," he said with a wink. "Go on and get it started and I'll stand back and guide you."

She thanked him again and crossed her fingers that she wouldn't hit him in the process either.

Five minutes–and multiple stops and starts later–she waved goodbye to him and headed back to Scarlett's.

"What are you saying, Scarlett? Are you insane? Where's Mason?"

Having his sister call him at work wasn't anything new.

Having her call with a ridiculous and harebrained scheme was.

She groaned. "All I'm saying is...maybe find something wrong with Court's car so she can't leave. What's so wrong with that?"

"Everything is wrong with that," he countered.

"Why?"

"Because it's dishonest!" he cried. "And why would you want to do that to her?"

"This move isn't right for her!" she argued. "I was so wrapped up in all the wedding hoopla that I didn't realize how serious she was. For years she's been threatening to move away because her love life sucks and some guys are off-limits, blah, blah, blah. But for all her complaining, she's never done it so I thought she was just talking nonsense again. By the time I realized what was going on, it was too late. But now I've got nothing to do but sit around and think about it and I don't want her to go! You have to help me, Dean! You *have* to!"

He had no idea what he was supposed to do or say. If he completely agreed with her, she'd probably get suspicious. But if he didn't do this for her, she'd nag him forever.

"I don't know, Scar. I mean, don't get me wrong, her car isn't in the greatest shape, but I don't know what I'm supposed to tell her. What if she comes in here and talks to Dad? You think he's going to lie to her too?"

"Maybe. I don't know. All I do know is that...*gah*! Just do it, Dean! Why are you making such a big deal out of this?"

Before he could answer, she was talking again.

"And hold off on the renovations."

"Why?"

"Because I'm going to offer the house to Courtney rent-free while she looks for a job closer to town. That will eliminate one problem for her. And since I can't drive, she can use my car. She's going to need a way to get around." She let out a small laugh. "I can't believe you lent her your truck. You baby that thing."

Yeah, he couldn't believe it either. Normally, he didn't let *anyone* drive it, but this was Courtney and he felt bad about leaving her stranded.

Plus, it had given him an excuse to go home at lunchtime to see her.

And the sex on the kitchen counter definitely brightened his day.

"She was in a pinch and you know we don't keep a loaner car at the shop."

"Well, it was very nice of you. I just wish you would

have called me and just brought her here. I can't believe you let her go to my old place. What were you thinking?"

Um...what?

"Oh, uh...what was I supposed to do? You know how Courtney is. There was no way I could change her mind."

"You should have insisted. Hell, you should have taken her home with you!"

"*What?!*" he cried, more than a little shocked that his sister was even making this suggestion. "Are you saying you would have been fine with me asking Courtney to spend the night?"

"Of course!" she said with a laugh. "What's wrong with you? I know she's like a sister to you and you're the brother least likely to pounce so, yeah. I wouldn't have a problem with that."

Now she tells me...

"If it were Kyle, I would have had to break both his arms, but I know I can trust you."

"Uh...thanks," he muttered.

"Anyway, it's all a moot point now," Scarlett went on. "Once you handle the whole car thing and tell her she can't have it back because...I don't know...the frame bent from the trailer pulling and falling off and then tack on shocks and brakes and...you know, general maintenance that you might as well tackle while you have it. Trust me when I say Courtney knows nothing about cars. You could probably make up words and she wouldn't know the difference."

"You're being a really crappy friend right now. You know that, right?"

"I don't see it that way. As a matter of fact, I'm being a *great* friend because I'm making sure she doesn't make a big mistake. If we can keep her here until her parents get back, then we should be okay."

"That's three months, Scarlett! I can't possibly hold her car for three months!"

"Okay, yeah. I didn't think that through..."

"And what do her parents have to do with this? They were fine with her moving away."

"They were but at least then she can move back in with them if she needs to. Right now she's on a limited budget and needs to find a job. I'm giving us three weeks to make that happen."

"Three weeks? We just said her folks were going to be gone for three months!"

"They are, but if we don't do something fast, she'll leave. Like I said, it's up to us to make this happen and get her a job."

"Us? And now I'm supposed to find her a job too?"

"No, doofus. You're supposed to hold onto her car and make sure it's really okay. Not only doesn't she know anything about cars, she doesn't believe in maintenance either. We argue about it all the time."

He groaned.

"Think about it. When was the last time she brought her car into the shop?"

"Maybe she takes it someplace else," he reasoned.

"Dean, please," she said blandly. "She knows I'd kill her if she went to another garage. Plus, you're the only garage in Magnolia and she knows she can trust you and Dad not to screw her over."

"And yet, that's exactly what you're asking me to do! Think about it!"

"Nobody's screwing anyone."

Ugh...if you only knew...

"For all we know, we're saving her life because we're making sure she's not driving around in a death trap."

"Jeez, dramatic much?"

"Can you *please* just work with me on this? Sheesh!"

"Okay, okay, fine. When Courtney comes by later, I'll break the news to her and then we'll swing by and pick up your car, okay?"

"Perfect! And in the meantime, I'll send Mason over to the house with new pillows and blankets so she doesn't have to keep digging through the trailer for her stuff."

"*No!*" he cried.

"What? What's wrong with that?"

"Nothing, I just...I mean...I've got extra stuff. No big deal. There's no reason for Mason to have to go out. You shouldn't be left alone and I'm sure he doesn't want to be out delivering blankets and stuff. So yeah, no worries. I've got this." Then because he couldn't seem to stop his mouth, he added, "Or...you know...you can just give her the stuff when we come over later. No one needs to go out of their way. Which...you really don't need to do. Really. I've got this covered."

Scarlett was quiet for a moment. "What's going on with you?"

"Nothing. Why?"

"You're just suddenly being...overly accommodating. And babbling. Normally I have to argue with you a little more."

Great. How the hell did he explain himself?

"Um..."

"Admit it. Court's like a second sister to you and you're helping her because you care."

"Um..."

"Come on, admit it. There's nothing wrong with it. You know she's an only child so it's kind of cool that you and Hunter and Kyle are there for her. Like big brothers."

Why did she have to keep saying that?

"It's not the same, Scar. Can you just let this go? I'm doing all I can to help you with this crazy scheme. Don't look a gift horse in the mouth, you know?"

"Okay, fine. For whatever it's worth, thank you. This means a lot to me."

"No problem. But enough about this crazy situation, how are you feeling? Do you need anything? When I come back later with Courtney to pick up your car, do you want us to bring dinner or something?"

"That is incredibly sweet of you, but Mason's mom went overboard with having food brought over. But...maybe you and Court could hang out for a while and eat with us?"

"I know I can," he said, not wanting to agree on Courtney's behalf because that might look suspicious.

"I'll just ask Court when she gets back."

"Where'd she go? Did she take the truck?"

Laughing, Scarlett replied, "Dude, relax. She went to go grab cupcakes for me. Well...for us. Mason put in his order too. She should be back any minute."

"Okay, tell her I'll text her when it's time to pick me up. And if it's okay, I'd like to go home and change before coming over."

"Why? What's the big deal?"

He let out a long breath. "Because I'm filthy and Mason's place is all...you know...nice. I'm not going to sit on his furniture with grease-stained clothes."

"Oh, that makes sense, but the place is mine too, you know. You can stop referring to it as just Mason's."

"Whatever. I'll text when we're on our way, okay?"

"Fine..."

"Look, I've got to go. There's a lot to do around here and

I can't believe I've stayed on the phone this long already. I'll see you tonight, squirt."

"Later!"

Sliding his phone back into his pocket, Dean rested his head against the office wall and sighed. He honestly didn't mind going to see his sister later, and he didn't mind lending Courtney his truck. The problem was he didn't like lying to her. Them. It was all for the greater good–on many accounts–but he never liked to lie. Ever. Even when it was for his own benefit.

Like now.

"Everything okay, Dean?"

Great. Now his father was going to start asking questions.

Straightening, he forced himself to smile. "Yeah. I was just talking to Scarlett." And then he told him all about her crazy plan regarding Courtney's car.

For a minute, his father simply stared at him. "I'm not sure I like lying to Courtney, but I see where your sister's heart is at."

He nodded.

They stood like that for several minutes before his father finally said, "Well, I think for today we tell her the truth–that we haven't had time to look at it. Tomorrow we'll get it up on the lift and see what kind of damage there is." Then he shook his head. "It's not like I'm hoping for damage so we won't have to lie, but...I think we just prolong telling her the actual truth."

"Either way, it's lying, Dad."

Domenic nodded. "I know, but it really is for a good reason. Courtney's like a daughter to me and I hated the thought of her moving away, especially when it wasn't for the right reason."

Frowning, Dean asked, "What do you mean?"

He waved him off and turned to go back out to the work bay.

"Dad?"

With a long breath, his father turned around. "Courtney's always looking for something bigger, something more. She's looking for the great love of her life and when she didn't find him here in Magnolia, she thought she'd go look elsewhere."

This was all brand-new information.

Although...didn't Scarlett say something similar to him just minutes ago?

"How do you know this?"

Shaking his head with a small snort, he said, "Dean, I've spent enough time around Scarlett and Courtney and neither one of them ever held anything back. And believe me, sometimes I wish they would have." He shuddered. "Personally, I think when Scarlett and Mason got together, it hit Courtney hard. Her best friend found her true love and where did that leave her?"

Inwardly groaning, Dean wondered how they had ended up talking like this—about the love life of his sister and her best friend.

"Okay, maybe that had something to do with it, but...she lost her job, Dad. She needs to find a new one and there aren't any here in Magnolia. What is she supposed to do?"

He shrugged and turned to leave again. "Maybe have a little faith. Not everyone loses a job one day and finds one the next." He looked over his shoulder back at Dean. "And do you really think another dentist isn't going to set up a practice here in town? The good people of Magnolia will make sure of it."

And then he turned into the garage bay and out of sight.

Dean took a minute to sit down behind their desk and just let everything they talked about settle in.

So Courtney's disillusioned with the men here in town. Did that include him? Was he even a consideration–you know, before the weekend?

Then he thought about their conversation from the night of the rehearsal party.

"Then I guess that makes you one of the idiots," she grumbled before trying to walk away, but he stopped her.

"Excuse me?"

"You heard me. Then you're an idiot too. Probably the biggest idiot."

Raking a hand through his hair, he sighed. This was getting complicated, and the only way he was going to feel better was to talk to her and see where her head was. Even though he still didn't feel good about lying about the car, he knew the extra time was going to help in figuring out what he was doing.

What they were doing.

And if they were going to keep doing it.

7

"So...wait...you didn't get a chance to look at the car at all?"

Dean shook his head. "I'm really sorry. There were a few cars ahead of yours that we had...you know...complications with."

Her shoulders sagged. "Oh."

And yeah, she was kind of disappointed, but...not as disappointed as she should have been. After all, this was supposed to be her big adventure–her big move! Her chance to finally break free of small-town living and possibly meet the man of her dreams.

Except...she already did and he was standing in front of her with greasy hands, a stained t-shirt, and a lopsided grin on his face.

"I really am sorry, Court."

"It's okay. I understand. I wasn't expecting preferential treatment or anything. You told me there were other cars ahead of me so...it's fine. Really." She paused and looked around the garage. Mr. Jones was still puttering around and a few of the other mechanics were gathering their things and saying goodnight. "So, um...can I borrow your truck again tomorrow?"

"Didn't Scarlett talk to you?"

"About what?"

For a minute he looked mildly uncomfortable. "Um... she's lending you her car. We're supposed to go over and pick it up and have dinner with them. At least...I'm supposed to have dinner with them. I didn't want to make the assumption that you'd want to go too."

And she couldn't help the silly smile tugging at her lips. He was so adorable and unsure of himself right now and it was so unlike him. For as long as she'd known him, nothing seemed to get him flustered. But suddenly, one little dinner invitation has him completely off his game. If they weren't standing in the middle of the garage with Mr. Jones ten feet away, she'd kiss him.

"It's not like I've got any other plans," she said lightly. "All day long I'd been thinking...wait. How did Scarlett know my car wasn't done before me?"

His eyes went wide. "Oh, um...she called here after you left her place to find out for herself. You know how nosy my sister can be."

That had her relaxing.

And laughing. "That she is." Looking around, Courtney had no idea how long they were supposed to stand here or when they were supposed to be back at Scarlett's. "So...you ready to go?"

"Yeah. Definitely."

She handed him his keys as they both called out a goodnight to his father. Outside, they started to walk toward his truck when he stopped.

"What's wrong?"

"Do you want to get anything else out of your car or

trailer? I know you only took the necessities last night, but..."

Waving him off, she started walked toward the truck again. "I think I've got enough with me for another night. It's no big deal." She was almost beside the vehicle when she realized he wasn't with her. Turning, she said, "Dean?"

There was something in his expression that she couldn't read–something like...guilt.

That's odd...

He caught up to her and helped her into the truck before walking around to the driver's side and climbing in. "What's in the box?" he asked, but he was already grinning.

"I got cupcakes for Scarlett and decided to grab some for you too," she admitted shyly. "I just thought..."

"You know I want to kiss you right now, right?" he asked, his voice doing that low, sexy thing she was really coming to love.

All Courtney could do was nod.

"I didn't think it was a good idea to...you know..."

Reaching over, she placed her hand on his jean-clad thigh. "Dean, you don't have to explain. I understand."

His gaze was intense as he continued to look at her, and when he finally looked away, he started the truck and quickly pulled out of the parking lot. They talked briefly about her visit with Scarlett on their way to his house and she found she was a little nervous about going back there with Dean. No one knew her better than Scarlett, and Courtney feared she wouldn't be able to hide her feelings in front of her. Especially now since things were...different between the two of them. How could she possibly act casual when in her mind all she could think of was how this was like a double date?

Something she and Scarlett always talked about doing when they found their perfect guys.

And they had, only...Courtney couldn't openly claim hers.

She sighed as they pulled up in front of Dean's house and he glanced over at her. "You okay?"

"What? Um...yeah. Just wondering how this is all going to go."

Twisting in his seat, his expression a little grim, he said, "Okay, Scarlett thinks you stayed at her old place last night and she's going to assume you're staying there again."

She nodded.

He raked a hand through his hair and let out a long breath. "Here's the thing, Court, I hate lying to her–I do – but I'm also...you know...it's like the whole thing with kissing you in front of the shop. We haven't..."

Holding up a hand to stop him, Courtney felt as helpless as he sounded. "I get what you're saying. I don't think I'm ready to tell Scarlett about last night or Saturday night. Honestly, it's none of her business."

"I agree, but like we said earlier, she's nosy." He paused. "We're not strangers either. We've known each other for so many years so there's nothing odd about us hanging out together at Scarlett and Mason's, right? I mean, we've hung out before and no one said anything."

She gave him a look that said, "Really?"

"Okay, yeah. Not the same," he said miserably. "So...can we do this? Can we go there and relax and enjoy ourselves?"

"I want to say yes, but...it feels weird. And your sister has some serious skills at detecting when something's not right."

"Then you don't want to go?"

Did she? Thinking about it for a moment, she realized she was being crazy and paranoid. It may be a completely innocent dinner, but in her mind, she was going to pretend it was all normal and the double date they always talked about having.

Finally, she nodded. "I think we'll be fine." Then something hit her. "Why are we here then? Why didn't we go directly to Scarlett's?"

Dean held up his hands. "Because I'm filthy and wanted a chance to wash up and change before heading over."

Was it wrong that she liked him dirty? That the way he looked right now was as much of a turn-on as the way he looked in a tuxedo?

"Keep looking at me like that, and neither of us is going to make it to dinner," he growled before his hand cupped her nape and he hauled her in close and kissed her. It was all wet and wild and she wanted to crawl over the center console and climb all over him.

And the way he kept tugging her closer, it seemed like that's what he wanted too.

It had been a long time since she'd made out in someone's car and it seemed a bit ridiculous to be doing so now when there was a house less than ten feet away. Forcing herself to break the kiss, she said, "What time do we need to be to Scarlett's?"

"Um...like...forty-five minutes?"

She offered him a sexy smile. "That doesn't leave us a lot of time. Let's get inside and get you a little dirtier before you get cleaned up."

They all but raced to the front door and stumbled inside in their haste to make the most of the time they had.

And they were still thirty minutes late to dinner.

Dean never considered himself to be overly suspicious, but he had a feeling his sister was on to them. She was watching them both like hawks and he was tempted to just stand up and shout that they had slept together so she'd stop staring.

It was maddening.

"So, Mason," Dean forced himself to say to break the tension he was feeling. "Anything new planned for the town? Got any new businesses coming our way?"

"The town's looking at a couple of proposals–one for a new grocery store, another for a chain restaurant–but we're really looking to entice other businesses here that aren't food-related."

"Like what?" Courtney asked.

Mason chuckled softly and looked over at Scarlett as if asking for permission to answer. And when she nodded, he did. "Actually, we're looking to get more medical practices to come here, including dentists. When Dr. Curtis closed his doors, we didn't realize how much it was going to affect the entire community. So we've got a committee working on figuring out incentives to bring more medical offices to Magnolia."

"Oh, my gosh!" she cried. "That would be amazing! Do you think it's going to work?"

He shrugged. "I honestly don't know. We've never tried anything like this before. Your office closing really opened our eyes to the kind of things that need to be a priority for the town. I mean, sure we can all drive another twenty or thirty minutes away to go to the dentist, but why should we? We're a small town but not small enough that we don't deserve to have the kinds of doctor's offices that the bigger towns have, right?"

Dean had to wonder if it was just a coincidence that this was the first time he was hearing about the search for more doctors for the town. Was this really a thing or was his sister to blame?

Or thank.

He glanced over at Courtney who looked very excited about what Mason was talking about–she was even asking questions and offering to help in any way she could. He took that as a good sign.

Then he glanced over at Scarlett and saw she was watching him and grinning.

Shit.

He stared back at her for a solid minute while Mason and Courtney continued to talk before he finally snapped, *"What?"*

She shrugged. "Just...observing," she said sweetly.

"Well...stop. It's annoying." They'd played this game for years so maybe he was looking for trouble where there was none, but he still couldn't help but be on his guard a little. Hell, maybe they shouldn't have come to dinner together– especially after their romp in the shower when they got back to his place. Courtney had sworn she liked him dirty and hated helping him get clean and that had turned him on beyond belief.

Just like everything she did.

Dean knew, as a guy, that he enjoyed sex.

A lot.

But sex with Courtney was far better than anything he'd ever experienced before. It didn't take much to get either of them going and he knew that for as long as she was staying in Magnolia Sound, he was going to want to keep their relationship going. There was so much more that he wanted to know about her and he wanted the time with her to learn. And if he wasn't mistaken, she maybe felt the same way too.

Yes, having Courtney stay in Magnolia was definitely something that needed to happen.

Especially if his sister didn't know about it because he had a feeling if she did, it would ruin everything. He frowned at her. "Seriously, Scar, stop it."

She just smiled wider and Dean opted to put his attention back on what Mason was saying. He enjoyed hearing about how the town was growing and all the things that were planned. For a while, he didn't think Magnolia was going to bounce back after the hurricane that hit it almost two years ago, but now as he drove around, he saw more and more examples of growth and revitalization.

Even in the north end of town, which had always been considered an eyesore.

"So when's the big grand reopening for the Mystic Magnolia?" he asked. "Gramps talks about it a lot, but I have to admit that I haven't paid much attention."

"Dean!" Scarlett cried. "That's kind of rude!"

He just waved her off. "There was a lot of information that he was always spouting about and I just figured once the place reopened, I'd know," he reasoned. "I've gone in there a couple of times and grabbed a bite while they were testing recipes, but...you know...no one had any definitive dates yet."

"Yeah, we hit a couple of snags, but I'm hoping we'll be up and running by the middle of next month," Mason explained. "Don't get me wrong–we're open, but we're still working out the kinks. Once everything is smoothed out, we'll hold a big celebration." He paused and took a sip of his beer. "I thought about going in there today, but opted not to think about work. Technically, this is still my honeymoon. Such as it is."

Beside him, Scarlett moaned. "Ugh...we should totally be sipping tropical drinks and listening to the sound of the waves!"

"Um...sweetheart," Mason said with a smile, "we live on the beach. If you want, we can eat dinner out on the deck and I'll make you a tropical drink."

She pouted. "You will not..."

"Virgin tropical drinks," he said with a wink before he stood and walked over to the kitchen. Dean immediately followed. It was the only way to get his sister to stop staring at him.

"Actually," Mason called out, "why don't you and Courtney go sit outside while Dean and I make up some platters of food for dinner? You know it's overwhelming for one person to sort through all the stuff my mother sent over."

Dean watched as the girls went outside, closing the sliding glass doors behind them. "Are you sure that's a good idea? I thought Scarlett was supposed to be on bed rest."

"She's allowed to walk around the house–and I carried her from the bedroom to the sofa so she's good." He grinned. "So, what's going on with you and Courtney?"

Dean just about choked on his own saliva. "What?"

Chuckling, Mason pulled several aluminum pans from the refrigerator and set them on the kitchen island. "I've never seen the two of you hang out together and now you're lending her your truck and bringing her to dinner." He shrugged. "Just seems a little out of the ordinary, that's all."

Great.

"Yeah, well...weird circumstances and all. We've known each other since forever so..."

"That's what I figured," he replied, placing more pans on the counter. "But can I give you a little advice?"

"I guess..."

"Relax a little. You were looking pretty tense while we were all sitting and talking–like you'd rather be anywhere but here."

You have no idea...

"Sorry. It does feel a little...I don't know...weird. I don't think we've ever done anything like this before."

"Dude, we've hung out together..."

"No, I know, but that was with the whole family. This just feels...different. Like it's just the four of us and..." He groaned and walked around, taking lids off of the pans for something to do.

Mason nodded and was quiet for a minute while he helped Dean uncover the food. "Is it because Courtney has a crush on you?"

This time he did choke.

And cough.

And sputter.

Mason walked over and gave him a couple of swift pats on the back even as he laughed softly. "You okay?"

It took a minute, but Dean finally straightened and nodded. "Yeah, thanks."

"So I take it you didn't know?"

"Wait, how do *you* know?"

"I've seen the way she looks at you–the last couple of months and all through the wedding planning whenever we all got together. Of course, I mentioned it to Scarlett and she neither confirmed nor denied it, but...from where I was standing, it was obvious."

How had he been blind for so long if other people saw what he didn't?

He shook his head again. "You're crazy. I never noticed her staring at me."

Mason clapped him on the back again before walking around and grabbing plates from the cabinets. "I'm shocked you didn't with all the time you spend watching her."

This just keeps getting worse...

Rather than respond, Dean studied the food and tried to figure out what they were supposed to do with it all. There were easily a dozen different dishes to choose from and he had no idea if they were supposed to take it all outside or make sampler plates of everything.

"How many people did your mother think she was feeding?" he finally asked.

"Yeah, she got a little carried away. Still, it's nice not to have to worry about cooking for the week."

Hard to argue that logic.

Together they made up four plates of assorted food and carried it out onto the deck. Luckily Mason didn't push any further on the topic of him and Courtney and once they all sat down to eat, conversation flowed in other directions as well. Between Scarlett's bed rest, their canceled honeymoon, the construction on their new home, and general town gossip, there was never a loss for discussion topics. It wasn't until Dean looked over and saw his sister yawning that he realized how late it had gotten.

Standing, he began gathering plates.

"What are you doing?" Scarlett asked around yet another yawn.

"Cleaning up so you can go get some sleep. You look exhausted." And when she went to comment, he stopped her. "Not in a bad way," he corrected. "More like you're pregnant and need your rest way."

"Good save," Mason said with a laugh as he stood and

helped with the clean-up. Within minutes–and with every-one's help–everything was put away and they were saying goodnight.

Standing back, he watched as Scarlett gave Courtney the keys to her car and then hugged her. He shook Mason's hand and hugged his sister before walking with Courtney out to the cars.

"So, um..." she began.

They were standing next to Scarlett's car and for the first time since they'd gotten here, Dean felt like he could breathe. But he also wasn't sure what to say. Things like "See you at home" sounded a little too familiar and personal, but then again, something like "See ya later" or "See ya around" just seemed wrong.

"Yeah," he said softly, scrubbing his hand along the back of his neck. "So you've got a car to use now."

She nodded. "Scarlett was very excited to let me use it." Silence.

"Um...she also seemed excited that you were going to stay at her place," he said.

Another nod. "Oh...yeah. She was."

"You know," he began carefully, "you don't have to..."

"Wait!" Mason called out, jogging out to the driveway with his hands full. He handed Courtney one of the covered foil pans.

"What's this?"

"Seriously, there is way too much food in there and we know we're never going to finish it all. Scarlett wanted you to have some since there's no food in the old place." Then he paused and chuckled softly. "Although I'm sure by now that you've gone to the grocery store."

Even in the dark, Dean could see her blush.

"I um...I did," she said, staring down at the tray in her

hands before looking back up at Mason. "But this is great. Thank you."

Then he handed her a large bag. "And here's some extra pillows and blankets for you. Scarlett wanted to make sure you're comfortable." He stepped back and smiled.

"Oh, uh...thanks. I appreciate it." She hugged him again and they both stood back and watched him go back into the house.

Courtney turned to face him and sighed. "This is ridiculous, right?"

"What, about the food?"

Rolling her eyes, she said, "No! The fact that we're both acting weird."

Oh. That.

"Look, if you want me to go and stay at Scarlett's, that's fine. You don't have to feel bad about it. Clearly, I'm going to be okay. I have a car I can use and now this." She held up the pan and bedding for emphasis. "I can just run in and get my things and..."

"Court, just...relax, okay? No one's asking you to leave."

She blinked at him several times in confusion. "You're not?"

He shook his head. "No. But I do think we need to talk because...you're right. We're both acting weird and it's crazy. So..." Pausing, he smiled as he reached up and caressed her cheek. "Let's go home."

And it didn't sound nearly as weird as he thought it would.

8

HER HEART WAS HAMMERING like mad ever since she got in the car and followed Dean...home.

It was crazy how hearing him say that word made her feel all warm and gooey inside.

Reel it in, Court. He probably didn't even realize he said it.

Granted, he hadn't asked her to pack up her things and leave, so she took that as a good sign. Still, that didn't mean he wouldn't once they had this conversation.

The thought of leaving bothered her more than when she packed up her room at her parents' house. That was odd, right? She shouldn't have gotten so attached to being here after only a couple of nights.

You've been crushing on him and dreaming of this for years...

True. But...this wasn't a dream. This was really happening. She was really here in Dean's home; she made love with him in his bed–and his shower and kitchen counter–and now that they were sitting on the sofa in his living room, she couldn't help but wish this was all theirs.

And that she didn't ever have to leave.

Dean had offered her something to drink, but she declined. All he had was beer, soda, and water, and what she really wanted was a glass of wine to calm her nerves.

"So...tonight was a little...awkward, huh?" she began, figuring one of them had to speak.

"Yeah. Just a little."

She waited for him to expand on that, but he didn't. The only way they were going to get anything accomplished was for one of them to just blurt out the obvious.

"Okay, I think it's time we talked about...this," she began. "We slept together and...I know we both probably thought it was going to be a one time, one night kind of thing, but then...it wasn't. We're both adults and I think we're allowed to acknowledge that."

"I agree," he said firmly, looking more like the serious and intense man she had known for so long. "However, I don't think I want to announce that to...you know...everyone."

"You mean Scarlett," she corrected.

"For starters."

As much as it pained her, she knew what she needed to ask. "Are you...ashamed of this? Ashamed that you slept with me?" And yeah, her voice trembled slightly.

She braced herself for his response and was ready to argue with him if need be.

Reaching out, Dean took one of her hands in his and gently squeezed it. "I'm not ashamed of what we did, Court."

"But...?"

"But..." He let out a long breath. "I guess I'm not ready to deal with how everyone else is going to see it. And honestly, it's no one's business but ours."

Okay, that wasn't really a great answer or the one she was looking for. She was definitely going to need more information. "And I agree with you on that, but...I guess we don't really need to discuss what we've done as much as we need to discuss what we're doing. Or going to do."

He nodded and she could see how uncomfortable he was. She was too but this was something they needed to do.

"You realize that I don't have to stay here, right?" she asked. "Because I have a place to go to. And once you get my car fixed, I...I'm leaving."

That didn't even sound a little bit confident...

He studied her long and hard. "So what are you saying? That you want to go to Scarlett's? That...we did what we did and now we're done?"

Wait...did he sound...hurt?

"Do you want to be done?"

Growling, he jumped to his feet. "Dammit, Courtney, why are we talking in circles like strangers?" Raking a hand through his hair, he began to pace in front of the sofa for several moments before he stopped and looked down at her. "Look, are you interested in me at all or was Saturday night and last night and this afternoon, just a way to kill some time or...or to settle some sort of curiosity?"

She wanted to be offended, but couldn't.

Standing up, she was toe-to-toe with him. "I guess I could ask you the same thing!"

"One of us is going to have to actually answer a question here!" he said, his voice growing louder with each word.

Maybe it was bratty of her or maybe it was just her super stubborn streak, but she didn't want to be the one to answer first. She knew her reasons, knew she kissed him first because it was something she'd always wanted to do. But if Dean were to admit it was only curiosity or that he'd never noticed her before, she swore she wouldn't be able to handle it.

Because yeah, sometimes the truth *did* hurt.

Stepping away from him, Courtney stormed to the bedroom and began gathering her things. As she moved around the room, she wanted to yell at herself for not leaving earlier in the day on Monday, for stopping to eat at The Sand Bar instead of getting on the road, for calling Jones Automotive when her car broke down...on and on she thought of all the bad decisions she'd made.

And that was just on Monday. She didn't even want to think about how different everything would be if she just hadn't kissed Dean at the rehearsal or gone home with him after the wedding.

Tossing her dirty clothes into her suitcase, she cursed the fact that now she knew what it was like to be with him. If she had just left things the way they were and never crossed that line, she would have moved away and eventually gotten over her feelings for him. But now? Now she knew there was no way she'd ever forget and there certainly was no way any man would ever compare.

Ugh...I make the worst decisions...

Yeah. She knew this and yet she went and did what she did anyway.

"What the hell are you doing?"

Looking over her shoulder, Courtney did her best to look calm–like it wasn't killing her to be leaving. "Getting my stuff together," she said blandly, turning her attention to all her stuff cluttering up his bathroom. She walked over to it. "Now that Scarlett thinks I'm staying at the old house, I figured I should. Plus, my car should be ready tomorrow, right?"

It wasn't until she was in the bathroom collecting her

things that she noticed he'd moved to the doorway. He didn't say a word. He simply glared at her.

With her arms loaded, she went to step around him.

But he wouldn't move.

Sighing loudly, she glared back at him. "Seriously? Can I please get around you?"

"No."

Part of her wanted to throw her stuff to the ground and fight while the other part wanted to sit on the floor and cry. What was she thinking, getting involved with someone like him? He was older and more mature and so different from any guy she'd ever been with. Her pouting and temper tantrums usually helped her to get her way, but it was clear that wasn't going to work with Dean.

"Look, what do you want from me?" he asked after a minute. "I'm trying to have a...a conversation with you and you just decide to get up and pack your shit? Why would you do that?"

Okay, she could throw out a bitchy comment and finish packing so she could leave–that would be the easy thing to do–or she could do something she'd never done before.

No manipulation.

No pouting.

No tantrums.

Straightening slightly, she looked him in the eye. "I guess it just hit me how...that maybe...I've never done this before, Dean. I have no idea how to talk to you." Courtney was amazed at how calm she sounded considering she felt like she was going to throw up.

"What are you talking about?" he asked, sounding calmer than he was just moments ago. "We've never had a problem talking to each other."

She rolled her eyes. "Oh, please. That's when it's about

nothing personal or when Scarlett's there with us or we're talking about her. We've never just...you know...had a conversation that was specific to us." She paused and shifted uncomfortably. "Okay, I really need to put some of this stuff down before it all falls on the floor."

Dean stepped in close and took it from her and placed it back on the bathroom vanity. Once he was done, he took her by the hand and led her back out to the couch. They sat and looked at each other and Courtney realized they were right back to where they started. She was about to comment on it when he spoke.

"I'm not going to lie to you," he began solemnly and her heart sank. "For a lot of years, I only saw you as my sister's friend.

Don't get up and run away...don't get up and run away...

"But lately...things started to feel different." He paused. "It's not like it was a spur of the moment or an instantaneous sort of thing, but...all I know is that I started feeling different around you and I kept telling myself it was wrong."

"Why?" her voice barely a whisper.

"Let's be real, Court. I'm older than you and any time you ever came around the house when we were all younger, you gravitated toward Kyle. I was almost like one of the parents when we were growing up, and you were one of the kids. It felt wrong to think of you in any other way."

If he was being honest, she knew she owed it to him to be the same. "I've had a crush on you for years," she said quietly, opting to look down at her hands in her lap rather than at him. "I never told Scarlett. Heck, I never told anyone." Now she did look up. "And I figured you'd never look at me as anything other than a kid. Which...you just said you did."

"Courtney..."

"No, I get it. I do. And I don't hold it against you. I mean, how could you know?"

She wished he would reach out and touch her–even just a caress on her hand–but he didn't.

"I always thought I'd outgrow it," she went on. "I've dated other guys–probably more than I should have–and I kept telling myself I'd get over it. Over you."

His expression softened but he didn't say anything.

"Part of the reason I want to leave Magnolia is...well... because I'm *not* getting over it. I figured the best thing for me to do was to move. You know, out of sight, out of mind."

"You shouldn't have to move away," he said, his voice gruff. "I don't *want* you to move away."

Wait...what?

"But..."

Now he did reach out and take her hand. "I know this sort of started weird–well, not weird, but...in reverse. Maybe we could try hanging out and doing things together other than...you know...just sex." Then he gave her a lopsided grin. "Although, I'm all for that continuing too."

She knew her face was flaming red. "So you want to...date?"

"Yeah. I do."

Ohmygod! Ohmygod! Ohmygod!

Her heart felt like it was going to beat right out of her chest, but she managed to smile and say, "I'd like that."

Then he leaned in and kissed her because...they'd talked enough for one night. They could start dating tomorrow.

"Let's go work on Scarlett's place!" she said excitedly. Dean had asked her if she wanted to do anything special today–it was Saturday and he had the whole day off–and this was what she wanted to do. Why? Because she knew how badly her friend wanted to sell the house and how she felt bad for holding up the renovations.

So yeah...dating Courtney was...different.

It had only been a couple of days, but...things were good. Really good. There was a certain level of ease because they had known each other for over twenty years, and yet... he was learning so much about her.

Sometimes he'd sit and listen to her talk and feel like he never knew her at all. For so long she was simply this snarky friend of the family who was a little dramatic, a little loud, and, sometimes, really immature.

Not that he would ever admit that to her.

Now he was discovering a woman with a wicked sense of humor who isn't afraid to laugh at herself–or him–and someone who genuinely cares about the people she loves.

Every day she went over and had lunch with Scarlett and made sure to always bring her some of her favorite treats or a new book or her guilty pleasure, gossip magazines.

Women.

But it was her date suggestion for today that really surprised him.

"Are you serious?" he finally asked. "I thought...I don't know...that we'd go someplace–maybe grab some lunch or go down to Wilmington for the day."

She was smiling serenely as she sipped her coffee. Waving him off, she said, "Nah. We've both been there a million times. Let's work on the house! We can be like one of those HGTV couples and tear the place apart while we bicker about my crazy design ideas and your need to stay on budget! It will be epic!"

That wasn't quite the word he'd use, but...it definitely could be fun. Plus, he really did want to get started on it. He and Courtney watched quite a bit of HGTV during the week and even though he never mentioned anything to her out loud, he did get a few ideas for things he wanted to do at Scarlett's.

"Um...I'll need to get you some gloves and safety goggles," he began. "Have you ever done any demolition on a house?"

"Nope, but I am a quick study, I swear!" Placing her coffee mug in the sink, she turned and looked up at him and was practically bouncing on her toes. "C'mon, I'm dying for something to do! I'm so bored!"

That made him laugh. After he told her there was more damage to her car than they originally thought–and it really wasn't a lie–she had settled in and accepted that she wasn't going to Raleigh just quite yet. Besides spending a couple of hours a day with Scarlett, she also went and met with some of the people at town hall to discuss ways to possibly gain a new dentist for Magnolia. And if that wasn't enough, she volunteered over at Happy Tails, the animal rescue his sister was so passionate about.

The woman was never still; how could she be bored?

After finishing his own coffee, he told her how to dress to best protect herself and then went out to his shed to see if he had the supplies she would need. When she met him back there a few minutes later, her excitement hadn't lessened one bit. If anything, the fact that they were gathering tools got her even more worked up.

"This is going to be so cool," she said, placing the safety goggles on. Her long hair was pulled back into a ponytail and she had on black leggings, an oversized t-shirt, and sneakers. "Do you have a flannel shirt I can borrow?"

"A flannel shirt?"

She nodded. "To tie around my waist to give me the whole construction chick vibe."

Laughing, Dean hauled her in close and kissed the top of her head. "Far be it from me to keep you from looking fashionable."

After getting her a shirt, they climbed into the truck. "Do I get a toolbelt?"

"Court, you seem a little more fixated on how you look than the work we're going to do. Trust me, you don't need a toolbelt."

"Will you be wearing a toolbelt?"

"Yeah..."

"So why can't I wear one?"

They hadn't even pulled out of the driveway yet and he was already exhausted. Twisting in his seat, he looked at her. "For starters, I don't have one small enough for you and it seems a little crazy to go out and buy one for a single day's work."

"I only get to work today? Why?"

"How about we just take it one day at a time, okay?"

"Fine. Whatever," she murmured, crossing her arms with a pout.

Pulling out of the driveway, he chuckled. "You forget my sister is the queen of pouting when she doesn't get her way. That tactic doesn't work on me."

He heard her small curse and grinned.

She didn't say another word until they were both standing in Scarlett's kitchen. "Okay, we're going to start by taking the doors off the cabinets, okay?"

"Are you reusing these cabinets?"

"No. Why?"

"Then why can't we just smash them? It seems like a lot of extra work to take the doors off if we're not saving them."

She had a point, but...

"Look, I don't have a dumpster here yet so I'm trying not to make more of a mess than we need to."

"Ugh...I thought this was demolition, not let's-neatly-take-the-house-apart. On HGTV, they take a sledgehammer to the kitchen and call it a day!"

"Do you see a camera crew here?"

She shook her head.

"Then can we please try it my way?" he asked wearily. "I promise to let you smash one of the walls we're taking down, okay?"

Her shoulders slouched but she agreed. "But it better be a big wall!"

He agreed just for the sake of getting them started.

Within minutes Courtney was using the drill to take the doors off and Dean was disconnecting the plumbing under the sink. Once they were both done, they worked together to remove the countertops before carrying them and the base cabinets out to the living room.

"Why are we leaving it all in here?" she asked. "Why can't we put it all outside?"

"Because there's rain in the forecast and wet wood is a bitch to try to move. We'll make a big pile of debris and then when the dumpster gets delivered, I'll haul it all out there."

"Okay. Gotcha."

After that, Dean pulled the upper cabinets off the wall and tossed them into the living room and stood back and studied the almost-empty space.

"You're keeping the appliances?"

"Yeah. How come?"

Shrugging, Courtney replied, "Well, I guess it depends on what you're going to do in here and how much money you want to spend. They're white and...I don't know...they look old. We should see if we can find a deal on some matching stainless steel ones–you know, like maybe ones that have a small scratch on them or something to get them at a discount–and maybe consider adding a dishwasher."

Rubbing a finger over his chin, he nodded. "I thought about it. Mason told me to just give him all the receipts, but I was trying to be mindful of the cost."

"Trust me on this, good appliances will help them sell this place. You can make the kitchen look gorgeous and updated, but if you put the old appliances back in, it's going to look awful."

He had to agree.

"Okay, so we'll call the town and arrange for them to come pick up the stove and refrigerator."

"Sounds good."

After that, they worked on tearing down the non-load bearing wall that divided the kitchen and living room before tearing up the old linoleum flooring up. It was only in the kitchen and the rest of the house had the original hardwood, so it only made sense for the cheap stuff to go.

"You going to tile the kitchen?" she asked, wiping the sweat off of her forehead.

"Yeah. That's the plan. Why?"

Another shrug. "I've seen shows where they match the existing floor and sand it all down and then stain it for a better flow. This place is small enough as it is and having a break in the flooring is going to be distracting."

Dean lifted his shirt and used it to wipe the sweat from his face. "I know what you're saying, but...how much do you really think this house is going to sell for? I don't want to upgrade it out of a reasonable asking price."

"Have you looked at the comps in the area?"

Unable to help himself, he chuckled. "You really watch way too much of that channel. You know just enough to be dangerous."

She smiled sweetly at him. "Let's put a pin in the whole floor thing for now and I'll do some research later on and see what we're competing with. Deal?"

"Deal."

"What's next?"

Pulling out his phone, he saw they'd already been at it for almost four hours. If it were just him here alone, he'd keep going, but he didn't want to exhaust Courtney. Plus, until some of the clutter was gone, there wasn't much more they could do.

"Ooh, can we demo the bathroom now?" she asked excitedly. "Scarlett always hated that bathroom and I know it's small, but I think we can do a really cool shower in there." Her big green eyes shone with enthusiasm. "What do you say? Can we yank out the shower, toilet, and vanity? Please?"

"I think I've created a monster," he muttered, raking a hand through his hair. "I was thinking we'd call it a day and…"

"No!" she cried. "Come on! This is so much fun, and after the bathroom, we can call it a day. Then we'll go back to your place and shower and maybe go grab some dinner out. What do you say?"

"You want to go out to eat?"

"Sure. Why not?"

He shrugged. "This was a lot of hard work. I just

thought maybe I'd grill some steaks for us or something, and we could watch a movie and just...you know...chill."

It wasn't like they were hiding out, per se. But they were just being a little choosy about where they went out together. Tonight, however, he knew they'd both be exhausted from all the demo and staying in sounded really appealing.

She moved in close to him and wrapped her arms around his waist. "I have to admit, I was looking forward to going out and maybe getting something a little farther up the coast, but a good steak certainly has its appeal, too."

He mimicked her move, wrapping his arms around her. "I happen to grill an excellent steak."

Humming with approval, she went up on her toes and touched her lips to his. "You happen to be excellent at many, many things, I'm finding."

Was it wrong how much he loved hearing that? "Oh, yeah? Like what?"

"Hmm...let's see...you're really good with your hands," she said, her voice a little breathless and sexy.

Dean let his hands skim down and cup her rear. "And what else?" he teased, his own voice going husky.

"You're very strong..."

He lifted her until her legs wrapped around his waist. "Go on."

"You are extremely caring and generous and sexy..." She began to nibble along his jaw. "And you always smell so damn good."

"I like where this is going." Looking around, he tried to find a spot where he could either put her down or lean against something so he could kiss and touch her properly. There was the bedroom. The furniture was gone, but..."

"There is one category, however, where you're a little disappointing."

Say what now?

Pulling back slightly, Dean looked down at her and was certain his expression was slightly horrified. "Um...excuse me? How am I disappointing?"

And then that impish grin that he knew so well crossed her face. "Well, I used to think you were a stellar mechanic, but since it's taking so long for my car to get fixed..."

He moved her until her back was against the wall and silenced her with a kiss. It was a little wild, a little brutal, but he took a little offense to her comment. He knew he wasn't a slacker and that there was nothing wrong with his skills as a mechanic. The problem with her car was just a ruse to keep her here. He wanted to tell her that–wanted to defend himself–but doing so would make her leave sooner.

And there was no way he was going to let that happen.

And it had nothing to do with his sister's request and everything to do with him and how much he didn't want Courtney to leave.

Something he should probably address with her sooner rather than later.

The unfortunate part of having known each other for so long was that...he *knew* her. Courtney dated a lot of guys–something she openly admitted–and he knew she had a fairly short attention span when she dated. He had no way of knowing it would be any different with him, and yeah, it was something that was niggling at the back of his mind this past week. Part of him was afraid to rock the boat and end this before he was ready.

Enough depressing thoughts! You have a sexy woman clinging to you! Focus!

His lips left hers and burned a trail down her cheek, her

neck, and down over her breast–gently biting it through the fabric of her t-shirt. She was grinding against him and making all the sexy little sounds she always did.

"Do you know how many times I dreamed of having you kiss me whenever we were both here?" she said breathlessly. "You'd walk in when I was hanging out with Scarlett and I used to wish you'd come over and kiss me just like this."

"Yeah?" he growled against her. "Did you ever dream I'd be doing this?" Lifting her shirt, he kissed her bare skin. It was warm and smooth and tasted so damn good that he could go on kissing her forever.

She sighed as his mouth moved from one breast to the other. "I dreamed of this and so much more. You were always very dirty in my fantasies," she admitted. "I wouldn't mind you being very dirty right now."

It was all the encouragement he needed. In the blink of an eye, he whipped her shirt up over her head and began to tug at her yoga pants.

"What a coincidence," he murmured, his mouth moving up along her throat. "I plan on being very dirty with you right now."

No words were spoken after that. It was all breathless sighs and it was damn near perfect.

9

On Wednesday afternoon, Courtney hung up her phone and sighed. She was sitting on the sofa in Dean's living room and seriously just wanted to cry.

Nothing was going right.

Nothing.

Here she was almost two weeks since she was supposed to leave for Raleigh and her car wasn't ready yet, she had no leads on a local job, and she was tired of lying to Scarlett. It was all becoming a little too much for her to handle but she didn't want to have a breakdown in front of Dean. She called him at lunchtime to ask about her car and he said he was busy and would talk to her when he got home.

Actually, he said he'd talk to her later because he was standing in the office with his father.

Yeah, the lying was getting old, and if she just knew when she was leaving, it would be okay–like if they only had another couple of days together, she could almost excuse their lying to everyone. But if her car needed to be junked and she was going to have to stay in Magnolia for another couple of weeks until she could buy a car, then she needed to rethink so many things and deal with the fallout.

But...she didn't want to just have to stay for another couple of weeks. Honestly, she was re-thinking her entire relocation. It didn't seem like Dean was just killing time with her—otherwise he wouldn't have let her all but move in with him. Of course that didn't mean he was looking for something serious or permanent, but he also wasn't booting her out the door, moving her over to Scarlett's, or helping her look for places to stay. That had to mean something, right?

Every day they spent together had her feeling like she never really knew him at all. So many things she had thought she knew were just...wrong. It didn't seem possible for her to be learning so much about him. After practically growing up around him, Courtney felt like she knew just about all there was to know.

But she was wrong.

The man who essentially was the rock for his family, the one who took care of everyone and always seemed like he had everything under control...well...he didn't seem to have anyone taking care of him. He was always doing for others and she didn't see anyone returning the favor.

Not that she thought his family was doing it on purpose, but...they all looked to him to fix things in their lives and in the week and a half that she'd been here with him, no one called just to see how he was.

They only called to ask for help and favors.

And again, maybe she just didn't know any better because she was an only child. Maybe this was the way things were between siblings, but...it still left her feeling a little bad for him. More than once she had seen the weariness on his face after hanging up the phone and it made her wonder if he was wishing he didn't have to be the go-to guy for everyone.

That was one of the reasons she was happy she was here.

The little domestic bliss their situation had created fulfilled her in a way she never thought possible. Whether it was picking up groceries or doing the dishes, Dean was always beyond grateful. He thanked her for every little thing she did and seemed surprised by it all at the same time. Just last night she had done a load of laundry for them and folded it and put it away and he had been at a loss for words.

He thanked her for hours on end.

Who knew laundry could be so sexy?

It wasn't all about the sex, though. It was a definite perk, but she genuinely enjoyed spending time with him–just talking and watching TV and hanging out. They were going to go back to Scarlett's this weekend to do more work on the house and she was beyond excited about it. All week long she had gone online looking for design inspiration and checking prices so they could get the best deals on the items they were going to need. She wanted to call Scarlett and tell her all about it, but...she didn't. She talked to her friend almost every day but was always careful to veer the conversation toward how Scarlett was feeling and how the progress on her and Mason's new house was coming.

When had her life gotten so complicated and exhausting?

And on top of all that, every day she looked for jobs and there were a few that weren't as far away as Raleigh, but most were still an hour's commute.

"Ugh...I so don't want to do that drive every day."

Yeah, nothing was going right.

Her next option was to get a job doing something other than being a dental hygienist to hold her over, but...that bothered her. After all her schooling and having a job she loved—and yes, she totally loved working in a dentist's office—the thought of taking on some other job seemed like a waste of time.

But you're running out of money...

Right. That was another thing. Pretty soon she was going to have to start charging everything because her savings would be gone. When she planned her move to Raleigh, she felt good about the money she had put aside to fund her fresh start. Now with the car repairs and not working, that money was possibly going to be gone fast.

Groaning, she threw her head back against the sofa cushions. "And now all I want to do is go shopping to make myself feel better." Another groan. "Something's got to give here. Soon."

Turning her head, she looked at the oversized clock on the living room wall and realized Dean would be home any minute. He was extremely regimented and she found that he walked through the door every day at five-thirty or within five minutes of it. It was kind of cute. The garage was only ten minutes away but clearly the man had a routine. Back when Dr. Curtis' office was open, she never found herself coming home from work at the same time every day. After work, she always stopped to talk with her co-workers or ran errands. She wondered if he normally did those things and she was the reason he wasn't.

Hmm...

Rather than sit and think about that, she went to the kitchen and checked on the chicken and biscuit casserole she placed in the oven earlier. It would be ready soon and she looked up when–right on cue–Dean walked through the door.

And yeah, he took her breath away.

"Hey," he said with a small smile as he tossed his keys on the kitchen island.

"Hey, yourself," she replied, not wanting to seem too anxious. "So? Any news on my car?"

His smile quickly faded and she swore she heard him groan.

That can't be good...

"It's bad news, isn't it? You can tell me. I can handle it."

"Why don't we talk about it over dinner? I'm going to go grab a shower."

Courtney didn't even let him take a step. "So...what's wrong with it?"

"Court, come on. I've been under cars all day. I really just want a hot shower and clean clothes..."

"And you'll get all of that after you tell me what's going on with my car."

Raking a hand through his hair, he sighed. "Fine. Okay. It's the uh...rear axle. It's cracked."

"And you're just seeing that now?"

"Yes."

Courtney stared at Dean hard for a minute in disbelief. "You've had the car for almost two weeks. How come you're just finding this problem now? I thought it was almost fixed!" For the life of her, she wasn't sure why she was so upset. No car meant she couldn't move to Raleigh.

And it meant she was staying with Dean.

That part was perfect, but she was beginning to wonder about what was going on with her car.

And then it hit her.

"Oh, my gosh...I get it," she said quietly, solemnly. "I know what this is about."

If anything, Dean paled.

"You...you do?" he asked, his voice equally quiet.

She nodded. "Yeah. I do." Pausing, she tried to think of the best way to say what she wanted to say without coming off as...bitchy.

"Courtney," he began before she could speak again. "Let me explain. It wasn't..."

But she held up a hand to stop him. "You're worried because this is turning into way more work than either of us expected and it's going to cost a lot, right?"

"Um..."

"Look, I appreciate that you're trying to protect me, and I know because I'm still unemployed you're wondering how I'm going to afford to pay for it all since I'm already practically mooching off of you by staying here..."

"Uh, no. I just..."

"But I want you to know that I don't expect you to give me some sort of crazy discount or deal because we're dating." Then she laughed softly and reached for one of his hands. "Not that I'd say no to a little discount and maybe the possibility of making payments, but..."

"No," Dean said again. "That's not it. I need to tell you..."

But she wasn't listening. He had just come home and he was dirty and a little sweaty and...yeah, who knew engine grease and the smell of gasoline were such turn-ons? And yet, every day she found herself practically tackling him as soon as he walked in the door.

"And I need to tell you how much I need you," she cooed, taking him by the hand and leading him through the bedroom and into the bathroom. She knew how much he liked taking a shower as soon as he got home and she really liked helping him with it.

Honestly, she'd never been so clean in her entire life, but it was totally worth it.

"Court..."

"Shh." Placing a finger over his lips, she reached in and turned the water on. "You are amazing and I want to show you how much I appreciate you."

He groaned and she took that as a good sign.

Quickly stripping, Courtney reached out and helped Dean with his clothes, and before she knew it, he was kissing her under the steamy spray. God, how she loved this! For all the years she'd known him, she always saw him as someone who was in control. Since the night of the wedding, however, she was coming to learn how much she loved making him lose it. There was a wildness to him–a ferocity when they were making love–that she was completely addicted to. Hell, if her car wasn't such a mess already, she'd be tempted to sneak down to the garage and start pulling parts out herself so she'd have an excuse to stay.

Probably something I really need to start thinking about...

Although, in all fairness, it was hard to even remember her own name when Dean's hands were soaping up her body.

This would eventually fade, right? This need, this... this...craving she had for him and that he clearly had for her too. This was all just because it was temporary. It had to be. Once she had her car back and was preparing to leave, they'd be okay.

Or...she hoped she would.

Eventually.

His mouth was working its way down her body and she knew she was lying to herself again.

There was no way she'd ever be okay after this. Dean Jones had ruined her for all other men and as he dropped to his knees and hooked one of her legs over his shoulder, she couldn't find the will to care.

The next day, Dean looked up from his seat in the office when he heard the door close. It was his turn to handle the billing and as much as he appreciated the peace and quiet and not having to be bent over an engine, he hated staring at the computer while he entered in numbers. The interruption was exactly what he needed. His brother Hunter was standing against the door staring at him.

"What's up?" he asked gruffly, leaning back in his chair.

Hunter rarely showed up unannounced, mainly because his life was so busy. Between his job as a fireman for the Magnolia Sound fire department, he also had a toddler. So for him to be here, there had to be a reason.

Dean motioned for his brother to take a seat and he did. "So?"

"So what's going on with you?" Hunter asked after a minute.

"What are you talking about?"

"Dude, come on. The door's closed and it's just me. What's going on?"

For the life of him, he had no idea what Hunter was talking about. Maybe it was a lack of sleep and exhaustion from putting in hours both here at the garage and at Scarlett's place over the weekend, but...Dean wasn't afraid to admit he was clueless—which is exactly what he said to his brother.

With a smirk, Hunter crossed his arms over his chest and shook his head. "Okay, fine. I was over at Scarlett's earlier today. She told me she put the plans for her old place on hold because Courtney's staying there."

"O-kay..."

"Then she told me how she asked you to stall on getting Court's car fixed so she'd be forced to stay in town."

"Yeah. But I don't feel good about that. I almost told her the truth a couple of days ago, but..."

"But you didn't, right?"

He nodded.

"So I asked if Court's found a job yet and Scarlett tells me no." Shifting slightly in his seat, he adds, "Then I mentioned how I know of a position opening up in the public health department that might be a good fit."

Dean instantly perked up and straightened in his chair. "Really? Here in town? That would be awesome!"

Hunter smiled. "That's what I thought, too." He paused. "Anyway, so Scar tries to call her and it goes to voicemail and I just figured she'd talk to her later. I hung out for a little bit more and then left." Another pause. "On my way home, I decided to stop at the Publix and pick up some burgers to make for dinner and I see Courtney getting in her car."

His brother was the worst at telling a story. It always took forever.

"I couldn't get to her in time so I decided to just follow her back to Scarlett's house."

Oh. Shit.

The smirk got a little cockier.

"But Court didn't go to Scarlett's place," Hunter said. "Do you know where she went?"

Resting his arms on the desk surface, Dean's face rested in his hands.

"Want to tell me why our friend Courtney's bringing groceries to your house?"

"Uh..."

Leaning forward, Hunter's smile grew. "And being how you weren't home and she just let herself in..."

"Okay, okay, okay," he snapped, straightening again. "Enough." Raking a hand through his hair, Dean stood and felt like punching something.

Preferably his brother, but...that wasn't an option right now.

After taking a moment to mentally count to ten, he looked at Hunter. "Yeah, so...Court's staying at my place." And then the whole story came out–from the kiss at the rehearsal dinner, to her spending the night after the wedding and...everything since.

Within reason.

His brother stared at him for a solid minute without saying a word and Dean couldn't take the silence. "Well? Aren't you going to say anything? Tell me how wrong I am or...or that I'm some kind of hypocrite?" he demanded.

Hunter relaxed in his chair and said, "Do you think you're a hypocrite?"

"Of course I do!" he cried. "Hell, at the wedding, I gave Kyle shit for even looking at Courtney, and then I went and..."

"Did a whole lot more than look?" Hunter finished for him, his grin still in place.

"Exactly!"

More silence.

"Okay, so obviously no one knows about this, right?"

Dean nodded.

"And why is that?"

He knew his eyes went ridiculously wide. "Why? Are you serious? Can you imagine what everyone's going to say?"

"Um...maybe 'Good for you' or 'It's nice to see you so happy'?"

"No one's going to say that and you know it," Dean said miserably, sitting back down in his chair.

"Okay, I'll play along," Hunter said mildly. "What do *you* think people are going to say?"

"Let's see, first there will be the whole indignation thing and how dare I mess around with the girl who's like family to us."

Hunter merely nodded.

"Then there's going to be all the comments about how I'm too old for her or she's too young for me or some crap like that."

"Dude, it's six years, not sixty."

But Dean wasn't listening. For almost two weeks he'd been torturing himself with all the things that could go wrong if they went public with their relationship. It was making him crazy and as much as he hated that his brother now knew what was going on, he was kind of relieved to have someone to talk to.

"And don't even get me started on Scarlett. Do you think for even a minute that she's going to be happy about this?"

"If you're serious about Courtney and not messing around with her, I would think Scarlett would be fine with it. If anything, you'd probably be her first choice of which brother to date her best friend."

He couldn't help but snort with a bit of disgust at that. "You can't be serious. Scarlett's always been protective of Courtney and hasn't liked any guy she's dated. I don't see how I'd suddenly be her first choice."

"Neither do I. I was just saying out of me, you, and Kyle, you'd be her top choice. Not out of all the guys in the world."

Glaring across the desk, he said, "You're kind of a dick."

With a shrug, Hunter stood. "I've been called worse."

"Wait, you're not leaving, are you?"

Another shrug. "I need to go pick up Eli. Melissa called and said she was going to be working late."

"That happen a lot?"

And that's when his brother's cocky smile finally fell. "More than it should," he admitted. "Hell, I just wish she'd quit jerking Eli and me around. I'm doing this whole co-parenting thing like she wanted, but sometimes it's like I'm the only parent. Eli's an afterthought to her and it pisses me off."

"So why don't you do something? Can't you fight for full custody?"

"Dean, how would I handle full custody? My schedule is all over the place. I mean, it doesn't change much, but I do 24-hour shifts and then I'm off for two days and then I'll pull three 12-hour shifts in a row. How would I take care of Eli? Who would watch him when I'm gone overnight?"

"Damn. I didn't think about that. But you know we'd all help out. Dad loves having Eli sleepover."

"I don't know..."

"Look, you don't have to decide right now, but just...you know...think about it. We're all here for you."

"I just hate that things turned out this way. I look at Scarlett and Mason and I'm just..." He paused and shook his head. "I'm so damn jealous. That's what I wanted–what I thought Melissa and I were going to have."

"Hunt, maybe if you guys went for counseling..."

"Been there, done that, paid the deductible. A relationship can't work if only one person is invested. She's not."

"I'm sorry."

"Yeah, me too." He let out a long breath.

"So what are you going to do now?"

"I'm taking it one day at a time. That's all I can do. My son comes first, and if that means I have to deal with Melissa jerking me around, then that's what I'll do."

"But how is that good for Eli?" Dean cried, hating how his nephew was stuck in such a crappy situation.

"Because at least when he's with Melissa, she takes care of him! A child deserves to have both parents in his life and just because Melissa doesn't do all the things I wish she did–or just because she doesn't love me–I know when Eli is with her that she's physically there with him. I'd rather that than a full-time babysitter."

"Are you sure she's taking care of him? Or is she pushing him off on someone else because she doesn't feel like being a mother?"

Hunter's eyes narrowed to mere slits. "Low blow, Dean."

"Again, I'm sorry. I just think you need to be aware that...things may not be what they seem where Melissa is concerned. I know you can't be there 24/7 to watch, but... just maybe...dig a little and make sure Eli's safe. That's all I'm saying."

They both went silent for a minute.

"What are you going to do with Courtney? Is this serious?"

Damn. He was hoping they'd moved on from that.

"It's too soon to tell," he said evasively. "She's still talking about moving and I don't want to be the guy forcing her to stay. And then there's all the stuff we just talked about. I'm not sure I want to draw that much attention to us. You know I hate that shit. Being the center of attention is totally not my thing."

"You're good at staying in the background," Hunter said, his voice a little grim. "Maybe it's about time you focused on you and what makes you happy instead of worrying about the rest of us."

"What the hell does that mean?"

Hunter walked over and clapped him on the shoulder and said, "Think about it" before he turned and walked out the door.

He knew he needed to get back to work, knew he couldn't hide here in the office forever, but the entire conversation with his brother made his head spin.

And not just the part about him and Courtney.

Dean was ten when his mother died, but she had been sick for a year before that. As the oldest, it was his job to help out with his siblings. He was old enough to understand what was going on, but Hunter, Kyle, and Scarlett weren't. Every day he did his best to play games with them and distract them from what was going on and it was something he never outgrew. He wanted to protect them from all the bad things that were happening to their family–to keep them happy and smiling and positive for as long as he could. And after their mother died, he did his best to help everyone overcome their grief–even his father and grandfather. He did it by making sure everything was taken care of–made sure his brothers did their homework and that Scarlett always had someone to read to her. It meant that he didn't have much of a social life as he became a teenager and even an adult, but...his family always came first.

To hear Hunter talk about his struggles, it took everything in his power not to go and organize a stakeout to find out if Melissa was taking proper care of Eli. If he found out she wasn't, Dean wasn't sure what he'd do. He wasn't a violent man, but just the thought of something happening to that sweet boy filled him with rage.

Maybe he could go talk to Hunter's boss and see if he could possibly cut his brother some slack and give him better hours for a little while. He knew Hunter wouldn't want to rock the boat, but sometimes you had to.

And then there was Courtney.

Always Courtney.

There was a part of him that was very protective of her too. The thought of her moving away bothered him because he knew it wasn't something she truly wanted to do. She never came outright and said it, but she said enough about the things she loved here in Magnolia that he knew Raleigh wasn't going to ever feel like home for her. He wanted to go down to town hall and talk to whatever committee Mason mentioned was scouting for medical practices and tell them to hurry up! Then he wanted to put something in their contracts that Courtney would be guaranteed a job.

Yeah, that wasn't practical, but it didn't mean he didn't want to do it.

He wanted to make sure her car was safe for her to drive and to find ways to always keep a smile on her face because...hell, she had a great smile. Her entire face would light up and those gorgeous green eyes would sparkle. He particularly loved it when she smiled at him. It occurred to him just how much she never really did that before the wedding. She always held a part of herself back. But now that he was getting to know her without all the protective walls that she put up around herself, he realized just how much he'd been missing.

Maybe he wasn't the guy Scarlett would pick for her best friend, but...so what? It wasn't her call to make.

And maybe their age difference wasn't ideal, but there were plenty of people with way more years between them.

So where did that leave them?

Well, it was Friday night and she asked if they could grab a pizza and go work on Scarlett's place. She found some tile for the bathroom that she wanted to show him and she had arranged for the dumpster to be delivered.

That's how she wanted to spend the weekend, being amateur house flippers.

Hell, there were worse ways to spend the weekend.

Still, he kind of liked how she wasn't as high maintenance as he once thought she was. Oh, he knew she could be, but she didn't mind getting her hands dirty either. Maybe at some point this weekend he'd bring up his conversation with Hunter and see how she reacts. For all the talking they do, they both seem to do a fine job of avoiding the topic of their relationship.

And he really hoped it was just because she was as nervous about rocking the boat as he was.

10

"Cancel your moving plans! I found the perfect guy for you!"

Courtney choked on the cupcake she just took a bite out of. "Um...what?"

Scarlett was smiling from ear to ear. "Yesterday, Mason took me for my doctor's appointment and the ultrasound tech guy was super cute!"

"I heard that!" Mason yelled from the other room, but Scarlett just waved him off.

"Anyway, he was super cute, single, and he lives in New Bern so, you know...not too far away. A forty-five-minute drive, tops! But best of all, I showed him your picture and he gave me his number to give to you! Isn't that great?"

"Are you crazy?" she cried. "Why would you show my picture to a complete stranger?"

"I told you she would be mad!" Mason called out.

"Oh my God," Scarlett groaned from her spot on the couch. "I wish I was in the bedroom so I could slam the door on him."

"He's not wrong, Scar," Courtney said after she took a

minute to compose herself. "I am mad! What were you thinking?"

"That you're always bitching about how there are no nice guys here in Magnolia that you're interested in! I thought I was doing a good thing!"

"I don't need you acting as some sort of...you know... pimp," she said wearily. "Look, I get that your heart was in the right place, but..."

Scarlett reached out and took one of Courtney's hands in hers. "I don't want you to go," she said earnestly. "For so long you've been saying how you wanted to meet a great guy who would make you want to stay here."

"That's not quite what I've said..."

"And I know things are rough right now with the job situation and all, but I know that's going to get worked out. You know you can stay at my place as long as you need and your parents won't be gone forever, so you have more than enough people who love you who are willing to help out until you get back on your feet."

The sound she made was part growl and part groan. "I'm tired of needing help, Scarlett! Everyone else has their shit together and I'm still floundering! It's bad enough that I can't find a job; I don't need you pimping me out to strange guys!"

"Okay, for starters, Evan was not a strange guy. He was super nice and super cute..."

"You realize we're still on our honeymoon, right?" This time Mason walked across the living room on his way to the kitchen, a scowl on his face.

Scarlett rolled her eyes but kept talking. "I'm telling you...he seemed like a great guy–blonde hair, blue eyes...he totally had the surfer guy look. And he had a great tan!"

With a quick glimpse at Mason who looked ready to

smash something, Courtney sighed. How could she possibly explain that she wasn't interested in anyone–especially a surfer guy–because she had Dean? No matter how much the two of them danced around the topic, the only thing they seemed to agree on was how they weren't ready to let Scarlett know.

But...what if that was the only way to get her off the campaign of finding her the perfect guy?

"I even scoped him out on Facebook," Scarlett was saying as she scrolled through her phone. "You know, so you can see for yourself. And if you don't think he's good looking, then I'll let it go."

"I can tell you already that I'm not going to find him attractive," she replied carefully, leaning forward to coax Scarlett to put her phone down.

"What? Why?"

"For starters, I've never liked blondes. You know that."

Shoulders sagging, Scarlett let out a sigh. "I know, but..."

"And surfers annoy me."

"I said he *looked* like a surfer, not that he surfed."

She leveled her friend with a glare. "Look, I get that you want this for me and I love you for it, but...now just isn't the right time, okay? My car is a mess and I have no idea how I'm going to pay for it. I don't have a job and pretty soon all the money I put aside for the move will be gone. And then where will I be?"

"Um, here with people who love you?"

It was hard to stay mad or even annoyed when she knew this was Scarlett's way of trying to help.

"And I love you too, Scar. You know that." She paused and smiled. "Now if you had said you met the perfect guy and he was the head of human resources in something like...

I don't know…another dental practice or the public health department…"

"Oh, my gosh! That totally reminds me! Did Hunter talk to you?"

That was an odd question. "No. Was he supposed to?"

"Well, yeah. He told me that he heard about a position at public health that might be a good fit for you. I told him you were staying at my old place and I just figured he'd go talk to you."

She shook her head even as she willed herself to stay calm. If Hunter went to Scarlett's place, he'd see a ton of construction debris and would know there was no way anyone could be living there. How was she going to find out if he was there or not? The only solution was to mention it to Dean later and see if he heard anything.

Crisis averted for now.

"So I know it's not in a dental office," Scarlett went on, "but it's local and you wouldn't have to move."

"How did Hunter know about it? I've been searching for jobs for weeks and haven't seen anything posted anywhere about it."

"I think he said it wasn't formally put out there yet. You know how he does those fire safety talks at the local businesses? Well, it was his turn to do the talk over at the public health building. He said he was talking to a group of people and someone asked if he knew anyone who might be interested. You should totally talk to Hunter and get the contact info."

Nodding, she said, "I definitely will." Then it occurred to her that maybe she should go talk to Hunter personally and see what he knew rather than involving Dean–especially if she didn't have to. "Do you happen to know if he's working today or if he's off?"

"No idea. His schedule is always so weird to me. Between the wonky firehouse schedules and the whole co-parenting thing with Melissa, I don't know how he keeps track of it all."

"That's got to be hard."

"I wish he'd find a woman who cared about him and Eli and settle down." Her eyes went wide for a minute before she schooled her features again. With a discreet clearing of her throat, she asked, "You ever think that Hunter was good-looking?"

"Oh my God! Stop!" Courtney cried. Grabbing her purse off the floor, she stood. "You're killing me today. First you want to set me up with a complete stranger and now you want me to marry Hunter? What is going on with you?"

"What? It's like I can't win here! Fix you up with a stranger, and I'm wrong. Fix you up with someone you've known practically your entire life, and I'm wrong! Maybe I should ask what's going on with you? And what's wrong with Hunter?"

With another groan, Courtney's head lolled back before she answered. "There is nothing wrong with Hunter. He's a great guy! But he's like a brother to me! There is like zero attraction there."

"And what about Kyle?"

Her heart skipped a beat. If she was going through all her brothers, that must mean...

"Nah," Scarlett said before Courtney could answer. "Kyle's kind of a doofus and I'd break his arms if he hit on you. I've seen the way he is with the women he dates. I don't want you on the receiving end of that!" She laughed.

And what about Dean?

"What about Dean?" Mason asked with a smirk as he walked back through the room. He didn't stay to hear Scarlett's response and Courtney was a little curious as to why he would be the one to bring it up.

Scarlett's first response was a snort. "Dean? No way. His relationships never last long because he doesn't put any time into them."

Okay, not quite the response she had expected.

"So why is Hunter okay but not Kyle or Dean?"

"Do you want to go out with Kyle or Dean?"

"Could you just maybe answer my question?" Courtney asked with mild annoyance.

"Hunter's always been a good guy. Loyal. Faithful. Even when he shouldn't have been. He and Melissa have been together since forever and I know he takes relationships seriously. The other two?" She shook her head. "Like I said, Kyle's too much of a player and Dean? Well...he's too busy taking care of everyone else that he puts zero effort into a relationship. Hell, I can't even remember the last time he had a girlfriend! And besides, he's too old for you."

"He's only six years older, Scar. That's hardly a big difference. Especially at our age!"

Scarlett's eyes narrowed and her voice took on that deadly calm tone that Courtney knew was never a good sign. "Wait...have you like...*thought* about this?"

"Thought about what?"

And yeah, her voice totally cracked.

"Scar, leave Courtney alone," Mason came back into the room and sat down beside his wife. "No one's dating your brothers and no one's going out with strange men who make a living rubbing warming gel over pregnant women's bellies, so relax." Wrapping an arm around her, he pulled her close and kissed her on the forehead.

She took that as her cue to leave.

With a thankful smile at Mason, she said a quick goodbye and all but ran out the door.

And then cursed herself the whole way home because that was the total prompt that they needed to just deal with the situation–to poke the proverbial bear–and move on! It was like having a ticking timebomb in the room that was just waiting to go off.

And I went and reset the damn timer.

"What are we doing here, Dean?"

With a slice of pizza halfway to his mouth, Dean froze. "Well, I was thinking we were going to start with the bathroom floor. The tile you picked out is great. I thought maybe..."

But Courtney was shaking her head. "I don't mean the work on the house, I mean...us. You. Me." She paused and he watched her swallow hard. "So...yeah. Us."

Tossing the slice back into the box, he let out a long breath. This conversation was way overdue but he didn't expect them to talk about it quite like this. He studied her face and as she watched him, he could see the unease there. Letting out a long breath, he leaned back against the wall. "I'd say that we're...you know...dating."

She nodded. "Yeah, I get that, but..." She paused and began to pace. "It's getting harder and harder to keep it a secret, and, honestly, I don't know if we should anymore."

"Oh?"

Another nod. "I don't like lying. At all."

"Me either."

"Then why are we?" she cried, stopping in front of him.

"Seriously? Court, we've talked about this. Repeatedly!"

"Yeah, yeah, yeah...Scarlett. I know, but..." She sighed. "She tried to set me up on a blind date today."

"*What?*" he demanded, pushing off of the wall. "With who? And are you going to go?"

Her eyes went wide. "Is that what you think? That I'd go out with some random guy when we're dating?" She went back to pacing. "Wow. Just...wow."

He knew that "wow" and knew he needed to calm her down. Fast.

Stepping in front of her, he gently grasped her shoulders. "That's not what I think, okay? I just wasn't expecting you to tell me something like that. What was my sister thinking?"

"She's thinking she doesn't want me to move!"

And that's when it hit him...

"Wait, so...you're still planning on moving?"

Courtney went still, her green eyes going wide again. "Um..."

"We keep putting off talking about these things, and that ends. Now," he said firmly as he began to pace.

"Dean..."

"No, I'm serious! This isn't who I am—I'm not a guy who lies or keeps things from people and I've never shied away from talking about things—no matter how uncomfortable it may make me! Hell, just today, I had to talk to Hunter about possibly suing Melissa for full custody! Do you think that was an easy conversation to have?"

"You talked to Hunter today?"

He nodded.

"Okay, I know this is a really awkward time to interrupt

your speech but...did he mention anything about a job with the public health department?"

"Uh, yeah. Why? How do you know about it?"

"Scarlett told me, but she didn't have any details, just that I should talk to Hunter."

He groaned and wished there was someplace they could sit because it was really awkward to do this in the middle of piles of construction debris.

"What? What's the matter?"

"Hunter saw you going into my house."

"When?"

"Does it matter? He wanted to tell you about the job and saw you leaving Publix and figured he'd follow you back here and then..."

"I went to your place," she finished for him. "So...okay. Um...how did you explain it?"

"I told him the truth," he admitted. "There was no way I could lie to him."

She paled. "And...what did he say?"

It was like they were focusing on all the wrong things. Reaching out, he took one of her hands in his. "It doesn't matter what he said, Court. Hell, it doesn't matter what anyone says. We are in a relationship, right?"

She nodded.

"Are you looking to date anyone else?"

She shook her head.

"Neither am I." He took a steadying breath and said the thing they both had been avoiding. "And I'm done hiding. So I say we ditch this pizza, go home and get cleaned up and then go out someplace here in town. No more driving down to Wilmington or up to New Bern. Here. And it doesn't matter who sees us."

Her smile was a little slow and a little shy. "Are you...are you sure about this? Because you know people are going to talk."

"People are always going to talk, and if anyone wants to say anything to our faces, then we'll deal with it, right?"

She nodded and then a nervous giggle escaped. "Oh, my goodness. We're really doing this. We're going to go out as a couple and…"

"And have a great night," he said with confidence before leaning in and kissing her. "Now I know we were having pizza, but how about Italian? Like a real dinner. We can go to Michael's. I know how much you like the alfredo."

Blushing, she nodded. "I really do."

"So is that a yes?"

"That's a yes. Let's do this!"

Within minutes, Dean was in his truck and Courtney was in her car leading the way home. He took the pizza with them because they could heat it up for lunch tomorrow. There was no point in throwing it out when neither had even taken a bite.

As they drove, he couldn't help but smile. It felt so good to have finally talked to Courtney about them. And he meant what he said–he didn't care what anyone had to say. It wasn't anyone's business. Was he expecting there to be a lot of pushback? Not really. Mostly it was going to be from his family, but all he had to do was remind all of them that he was the most responsible of the bunch and he wasn't messing around with Courtney. He cared about her. In fact, he cared about her a lot.

Now that he thought about it, he realized that forcing her not to tell anyone what was going on between them might have hurt her feelings. And that was the last thing he ever wanted to do. So he vowed to make it up to her. Dean knew he wasn't an overly demonstrative man–he was always the levelheaded one—but for her, he'd be willing to go all out and make a fool out himself if necessary.

But hopefully it wouldn't come to that.

When they got back to the house, Courtney took her shower first and he was a little disappointed she didn't invite him to join her. Not that they only showered together, but...he really enjoyed it when they did.

But tonight was going to be different.

They had turned a page and he needed to remember how this was going to be a big step for both of them. He wanted to make it special—memorable—and that meant he could wait to make love to her until after they got home.

Although...there wasn't much he could do on such short notice to make this a really romantic date. It was too late to get reservations to a nicer restaurant and too late to get her flowers, so...where did that leave him?

Raking a hand through his hair, he paced the length of the living room and racked his brain for ideas. They had already decided where they were going for dinner, but what about after that? He wasn't really into hanging out at a bar or club.

But maybe she did.

Okay, if that was something she wanted to do, then Dean knew he'd do it.

That meant he had a few hours to come up with a better and more appealing idea.

A few minutes later he heard the shower turn off and figured he'd go take his. Walking into the bedroom, he pulled a clean pair of jeans out of the closet along with a shirt that actually buttoned. It wasn't often that he had to dress up—not that jeans and a nice shirt would be considered dressing up, but for him it was. Still, he figured it was better than donning another t-shirt.

Another few minutes went by and Courtney still hadn't come out of the bathroom and that's when it hit him.

He'd never had to share a bathroom with a woman before.

Well, he had shared a bathroom with Scarlett when they were growing up but by the time she hit the teen years, he had already moved out.

Was she going to stay in there until she was ready? And how long was that going to take? Ever since he brought her home with him, he hadn't been around when she got ready to go out anywhere. Sure, he'd been here when she got ready to go work on Scarlett's place, but that wasn't something he'd really consider "going out."

Should he knock on the bathroom door and ask how long she'll be? Go and make himself a sandwich and watch some TV? Why was this so complicated? Placing his clothes down on the bed, he was about to walk out of the room when the bathroom door opened. Courtney was wrapped in a towel and her hair was too. Even without an ounce of makeup on, she was beautiful. All he could do was stop and stare.

She, of course, gave him a bright smile as she breezed around the room grabbing what she needed. "I'm glad we're going someplace casual. I don't have anything dressy in the suitcase. All my nice clothes are in boxes on the trailer or in storage back at my parents' place." She rummaged through her suitcase and pulled out a few things before she straightened and looked at him. "The bathroom's all yours. I'll finish getting ready in here while you do your thing."

"Really? Are you sure?" It almost seemed too easy.

Nodding, she walked back into the bathroom and came out carrying her makeup bag, some brushes, hairspray, and her blow dryer. "I'm going to get dressed in here and then finish up in the other bathroom. No biggie."

He wanted to question it because so many of his friends who were married or living with their girlfriends complained about how they never got time in their own bathrooms. But...who was he to argue? He already knew Courtney was different and this little show of consideration just made him like her even more.

"Great," he replied, reaching for his pile of clothes. "Thanks. I should be done in fifteen minutes, but don't feel like you have to rush on my account."

She simply smiled and went about doing her thing, and when he stepped out of the bathroom fifteen minutes later, she was waiting for him in the living room.

Her hair and makeup were done and she was wearing a pair of black skinny jeans and an off-the-shoulder black and white polka dot top. All he could think of was how she looked amazing.

At the stunned look on his face, she laughed. "Admit it, you thought I was going to take much longer to get ready."

"Well..." No way was he going to admit it and potentially ruin their night.

"It's okay," she said, picking up her purse from the sofa. "There are times I take way longer, but I was motivated to get done quickly."

"Court, I told you you didn't need to rush."

Walking over, she kissed him on the cheek. "Believe it or not, it wasn't for your benefit. It was for mine." And before he could comment, she added, "I'm starving!" Then she laughed. "C'mon! Let's go!"

Living in a small town meant it didn't take long to get to the restaurant or to be seated. Their waitress was a woman named Lila who graduated with him way back when. She smiled at them both but didn't seem the least bit interested in the fact that he and Courtney were out together. And over the course of the meal, they each saw several familiar faces who they either waved to or chatted with briefly and none of them seemed shocked or horrified that they were out together.

Could it be we're the only ones freaking out over this?

Over dinner they talked about the work they wanted to get done on Scarlett's house and then talked about the potential job opening at the public health department. It wasn't exactly what she wanted to be doing, but she was keeping an open mind. He was proud of her for being smart about it. She had a fairly specialized job and it appeared to be one that there weren't many openings in.

Especially not anywhere close to Magnolia.

Dean knew he took it for granted how much easier his trade was. Even if his father's garage closed, he knew there was always a need for a good mechanic.

He just hoped he never had to test that theory.

Either way, as he listened to her talk about the different possibilities of positions she was trained for in the public health department, he realized just how intelligent she was too.

Something he never noticed while she and Scarlett were growing up.

There was a time when he even wondered if she'd graduate high school because she was forever skipping classes and going to the beach or getting her hair or nails done. He lost track of the times he had warned his sister that she better not be doing the same things her friend was.

And then he realized just how much of a parental role he really had taken on and how it was a wonder all his siblings didn't hate him.

"Why would your siblings hate you?" Courtney asked, confusion written all over her face.

He hadn't meant to say that out loud, but now that he had...

After briefly explaining his train of thought to her, he hoped he hadn't insulted her.

With a bright laugh, she smiled at him. "Oh my goodness! Yes! Scarlett used to complain about you all the time and how it was like having two dads!"

"It wasn't that bad..."

But all she did was smile and nod.

"Come on, I'm the oldest and I was the one who had to babysit and be responsible for all of them! So maybe from time to time I *may* have acted like one of the parents, but..."

"Nuh-uh. You acted like that all the time. It's like you couldn't even help yourself. Always quick with advice on how to correct everything we were doing wrong," she said, still chuckling. "Kyle used to imitate you and it was so spot on!"

Okay, now this was getting a little out of control.

"Yeah, yeah, yeah, that's great," he murmured before smiling at Lila as she came to collect their dishes. "Can we skip all the ways that I'm a terrible person and go back to telling me about job possibilities?"

Reaching across the table, Courtney rested her hand on top of his and gave him a sympathetic smile. "I'm sorry. I really wasn't making fun of you or even implying that you're a terrible person." She squeezed his hand. "You were our rock. You were the one who we all counted on to be there. And yeah, maybe sometimes you were a bit of a jerk and super bossy, but the rest of the time, you were just this great guy who was always looking out for us. So...I think that makes you a pretty awesome person."

Now he could practically feel himself blush. "You don't have to..."

"Hey," she interrupted softly. "I know I don't have to say it, but I am saying it because it's true."

They stayed like that, Dean linking his fingers with hers, and just enjoyed the moment. It was nice how neither of them felt the need to make pointless conversation.

"Would either of you like dessert?" Lila asked when she came back over. "We've got the best chocolate chess pie and cheesecake–but I'm sure you both know that already."

Dean smiled and caught Courtney doing the same. "I think I'll go for the cheesecake."

"And I'll take the chess pie, please."

"Y'all just balance each other out," Lila said with a big smile. "I love when couples each order something different so they can share. You're adorable."

It wasn't such a bad thing to hear at all.

Maybe everyone would feel that way.

11

On Monday morning, Dean found himself staring at Courtney's car which was currently on the lift. Other cars needed to be worked on—ones that he knew he could work on quickly and get them back to their owners in less time—but he'd put this off long enough. It was time for him to ease his conscience and get the car fixed and then let her decide whether she was going to stay in Magnolia or go on with her move.

"Dean, I just got off the phone with Mrs. Alden and..." His father stopped beside him and followed his gaze up to Courtney's car. "How come that's on the lift? Mrs. Alden needs her car back by noon. I thought that was what you were starting with today."

Nodding, he took a slow sip of his coffee. "I just thought we should get this done. It's not right that we've kept it here this long." Over the weekend, they brought the trailer over to his place so Courtney could easily get to any of her things she needed and that's when he realized that he couldn't have this lie between them anymore.

"Well, we talked about it and agreed it was an okay

thing to do if it was helping Courtney. From what your sister's been telling me, she lent Courtney her car and she's possibly got a lead on a local job. We have other cars that have priority here today, Dean. If this is bothering you that much, you can work on it after hours, but for right now, I really need you to start on Mrs. Alden's Hyundai."

"Dad..."

"Nope. I'm serious," Domenic said firmly. "I appreciate your conscience and all that, but we're busy right now, and friends and family don't get preferential treatment. At least not today, so...get this car down and get Mrs. Alden's up there. You know how snippy she gets when she has to wait too long."

His father walked away but Dean didn't exactly spring into action. He stood there and finished his coffee and tried to work out the rest of his day in his head. They had a full lot of cars waiting for work and that meant a full day. If he did want to work on Courtney's car, he would have to work late. And working late meant...

Not being with Courtney.

Not that they were one of those couples who couldn't bear to be apart, but he found he liked going home to her at the end of the day. He liked walking in the door and having her there to greet him and kiss him and–usually–shower with him.

Yeah. Best part of his day.

Working late meant missing out on that. Maybe if he just spent...

"Why is Courtney's car up on the lift?"

Turning, he saw Scarlett standing behind him looking all kinds of annoyed. She glared at him, arms crossed and resting on her pregnant belly.

"I'm serious, Dean," she snapped. "What are you doing? I thought we agreed not to work on it yet!"

"No, we said we would tell her things were wrong with it. I never said I wasn't going to work on it," he explained calmly. "And what are you even doing here? Aren't you still on bed rest?"

"No, that stopped a week ago. Now I just need to take it easy and not have stress. But now, thanks to you, I have it!"

"*Me?!* What did I do?"

"Are you trying to make Courtney leave town? Huh? Are you? Because once this car is fixed, she's leaving!"

"You're overreacting. Again."

"No, I'm not..."

"You've said no like three times already. Why are you here again?"

Rolling her eyes, she dropped her arms to her side. "Mason and I decided we're going to get away for a few days since we didn't get to go on our honeymoon. We're going down to Hilton Head. It was a spur-of-the-moment decision and we thought we should stop in and tell you guys that we're going so nobody worries."

"Oh, well...good for you. I hope you have fun."

Scarlett rolled her eyes again. "Please. It's hard to have fun when I've got this beach ball body going on. Every move I make feels awkward."

He couldn't help but smile. "Personally, I think you look great. Pregnancy really agrees with you."

Her eyes narrowed. "Thanks."

Looking around, he asked, "Where's Mason?"

"Oh, he wanted to go across the street to talk to Gramps and make sure things were okay over at the Mystic Magnolia."

"I really wish they'd change the name of the place.

With the whole new design and menu, I just thought they'd give it a new name."

"Trust me, there were a lot of discussions about it, but... Grandma named it way back when and everyone feels like it's finally going to be the kind of place she originally envisioned, so..."

"I guess that makes sense."

"You're not going to tell Court that you're working on her car, are you?"

Was he? He still wasn't sure, but instead of telling his sister that, he simply shook his head. "Honestly, I'm not working on her car. Dad just asked me to take it down from the lift and start on Mrs. Alden's car."

"Ugh...that woman can be a nightmare. You better do as he says."

"I was already planning on it."

"Then why is Courtney's car up there?"

He shrugged. "I just felt bad about...*Ow!* What the hell!"

She punched him in the arm as he spoke.

"We talked about this!" Shaking her finger at him, she continued. "She's going to look into the job with public health this week so just *stick* to the plan and keep her car here! If she gets the job, then we're all good and we can know we did the right thing!"

And for some reason, he couldn't let her go on. "It wasn't our call to make, Scarlett," he said with more heat than he intended. Her eyes went wide. "We had no right to play God and keep her here if that wasn't what she really wanted!"

"She doesn't want to go. Trust me. This is just Courtney being Courtney! She would have moved and hated it and ended up coming back here eventually."

"Then why stop her?" he cried. "If you knew she was going to come back, why go through all this?"

"Because why should she have to go through and make a mistake when she didn't have to?" she yelled back. "She's just being dramatic and–in typical Courtney fashion–had to blow the entire situation out of proportion! People get laid off all the time and they don't have to move across the state to find a job! If she hadn't made the announcement that she was moving, her parents never would have turned their house into an Airbnb and she would have had a place to live! And possibly a car to drive! This is really all her fault and..."

"That's enough!" he shouted and the entire garage went silent. With a muttered curse, he took Scarlett by the hand and led her back to the office. Once the door was shut, she yanked her hand away. But before she could utter a word, Dean was talking. "What the hell is wrong with you?"

"Me? What's the matter with you?" she demanded.

"I'll tell you what's wrong with me; it pisses me off to hear you talking about someone who you claim is your best friend! The way you were talking was pretty insulting, Scar! And for the record, you haven't made the greatest decisions in life either! Maybe Courtney felt overwhelmed! Maybe she didn't feel like she had a choice but to move! And who knows? Maybe it was a rash decision, but it was her decision to make! No one stopped you when you wanted to start working on cars! And no one stopped you when you started riding motorcycles! And no one stopped you when you started making luxury dog houses for rescue dogs!"

"Hey! No one's supposed to know about that!"

"Oh, yeah? Well too bad! I've seen them and they're adorable!"

They both started laughing at the same time and Scarlett walked over and hugged him. "You're right," she said after a minute. "And you know what? Court's always been supportive of all the things I do and I wasn't being supportive of her." She looked up at him with a sad smile. "I'm a crappy friend, right? At the rehearsal dinner, I told her she was the worst friend and it turns out that's me."

He kissed the top of her head and led her over to a chair to sit down. "You're not a crappy friend." He paused. "Okay, in this scenario you kind of are, but...your heart's in the right place. Just...you need to trust her to make the right decision. And even if it's not? If things don't work out? Then just be there to support her and be her friend."

Tears welled up in his sister's eyes and for once, he wasn't worried. Pregnancy hormones had made her cry at the drop of a hat for months so all he did was smile down at her.

"You gonna be okay or do I need to call Mason and tell him to hurry back?"

She wiped her eyes. "I'm fine. You know how emotional I am."

He nodded. "Can I ask you something?"

"Sure."

"When you and Mason started dating, did people think it was weird?"

"Um...some. A few, I guess. Why?"

Ugh...why did he even bring it up?

"It's just something I've often wondered about. I mean... I can see now how great you two are together, but in the beginning, it seemed like...I don't know...awkward."

"You mean because he's from one of the wealthiest families in town and we're one of the poorest?"

"Scar, we're not the poorest, so stop that. You and Mason just seemed like you had nothing in common, that's all. You ride motorcycles and work on cars, while he looks like someone who doesn't like to get his hands dirty at all."

"Hey! That's my husband you're talking about so tread carefully."

Crossing his arms as he leaned against the desk, he let out a long breath. "I didn't mean it in a bad way. Just pointing out the obvious, that's all. And I guess I've always been curious about how you handled it. Hell, you didn't even tell any of us–your own family–until it had been going on long enough for you to get pregnant."

"Yeah, well...that happened a lot sooner than either of us ever thought, so..."

"Not the point I was going for," he said dryly.

"Okay, yeah. It was a big sore spot for me. I was afraid everyone was going to look at us funny or say something snarky because he was so out of my league. But it was my hang-up, not his. If anything, Mason was all for us going out and just being...you know...normal. I fought him on it but the only one who really had an issue was his mom."

"Really? Like...no one? None of his friends?"

"Well, you guys were all jerks in the beginning too."

"That's because he knocked you up and we had no idea you were even dating! It wasn't because we didn't think he was someone appropriate for you to date!"

She looked at him funny. "That's an odd thing to say. Appropriate? Really? And for the record, you guys never liked any guy I dated."

"Because you're our baby sister. That's the way things are," he said with a grin. "But honestly, Mason's a great guy and it's obvious to anyone who meets the two of you that you're crazy about each other." He shrugged. "So that makes me happy."

She smiled up at him. "Me too. Although, not that it

would have mattered. I was in love with Mason and wanted to be with him, so while I would have hated it if you and Dad and Hunter and Kyle didn't like him, I still would have been with him."

"Really?"

"Hell yeah. I'm the one involved with him, not any of you."

Huh. Maybe he needed to rethink the way he was looking at his relationship with Courtney. It would be easy to simply blurt it out right now to Scarlett and get it over with, but being that it didn't just involve him, he knew he should talk to Courtney first.

There was a knock on the office door, and Mason walked in. "Everything okay in here? Dom said you guys were arguing."

Dean helped Scarlett to her feet and stood back as she walked over and hugged her husband. "We're fine. I was being a brat and–in typical Dean fashion–he had to reprimand me."

Mason wrapped his arms around her before grinning at Dean. "Being a brat, huh? And you're over it now?"

Pulling back, she gave him a sassy grin. "For now. I'm sure you'll tell me I'm doing it again later, but we'll deal with that when it happens."

Laughing, Dean walked over and clapped a hand on Mason's shoulder. "Yeah, good luck with that!"

"Tell me about it."

"Hey!" Scarlett cried. "I'm right here! You can't make fun of me like that when I'm standing right in front of you!"

"Babe?" Mason said, his expression going serious. "You're being a brat."

"Oh, you!" She smacked him playfully as they all turned and walked out of the office.

Yeah, Dean knew his sister was with the right man for her and he was thrilled to see her so happy. He had no doubt that she'd want the same for him.

Even if it was with Courtney.

"How long are you guys going to be down in Hilton Head?" he asked.

"We'll be back on Friday," Scarlett replied. "How come?"

"Just curious. Maybe we can get together when you get back? You haven't seen my place since I finished the renovations. How about you come for dinner Saturday night? I'll grill some steaks and we'll hang out."

The words were barely out of his mouth when his sister flung herself at him and gave him a fierce hug.

"Um..."

"I love that," Scarlett said, going up on her tiptoes to kiss him on the cheek. "I love that you're inviting us over and we get to hang out."

"We just hung out not that long ago, remember?" he said with a low chuckle.

"Yeah, I know, but...sometimes I worry about you, that's all. Like I envision you working here all day and then being all alone all weekend. I'd like to think that you still have friends you hang out with–or maybe you're dating someone." She stopped and gasped. "Oh my God! Is that what this is about? Do you have a girlfriend you're going to introduce us to?"

Doing his best not to react, he gently grasped her shoulders and turned her toward Mason. "Just wanted to hang out with you and hear about the trip," he said evenly. "Now go have fun and try not to get rushed to the hospital again, okay?"

She groaned but didn't argue.

She was also completely spot on about why he was inviting them over. She just didn't know it yet.

———

On Wednesday afternoon, Courtney needed to take out a little aggression and decided to head over to Scarlett's old place to do some work. Granted, there wasn't a lot of stuff that she knew how to do, but they were at a good place in the renovations to do some cleaning. After stopping at Target for cleaning supplies, a couple of bottles of water, and a king-size bag of M&M's, she walked into the house and let out a primal scream.

When she was done, she plopped down on the floor, pulled the bag of candy out, took a handful, and quickly ate them before taking a long drink of water. Her heart was racing and she was still trying to catch her breath and all she wanted to do was scream again.

The job at public health was already gone. They had given it to somebody in-house. Then there had been another job that would have been an hour-long commute. She had applied just because it would keep her closer to Magnolia Sound and Dean, but that position had already been filled as well. And that was on top of the few non-dental jobs she had applied for and didn't get. It was killing her that she couldn't even get hired as a cashier at the supermarket and she was running out of options.

Not that she shared it with anyone.

Not even Dean.

Scarlett was out of town and there was no way Courtney was going to call her and interrupt her belated honeymoon. Her parents weren't answering their phones because they were at some big convention today and it all just hit her how much her life sucked at the moment.

If she did happen to bring any of this up to Dean, he'd just tell her not to worry and it was all going to get better. He'd probably tell her she could pay off the car repairs and how she didn't have to kick in for groceries if she didn't want to or he'd help her with anything she needed, but...she was so tired of needing. Tired of things just not going her way.

They're going your way with Dean...

Yeah, yeah, yeah, she knew that, but she knew eventually she was going to have to get her shit together and get a job and start paying her own way again. It was one thing to accept help when it was short-term, but the way things were going, short-term wasn't going to be very short. Muttering a curse, she stood and brushed off her yoga pants and began pulling out cleaning supplies.

Over the weekend, they had gotten the tile down in the bathroom and installed the new pre-fab shower and a new vanity. With all the grout finally dry, it was safe to clean and mop in there so that's where she started. She put every ounce of energy into making the room sparkle and when she stood back an hour later, it did.

Wiping her forehead, she walked over and looked in the lone bedroom. All the furniture was gone and it was the one room in good shape. They were going to paint in here this weekend or...maybe she could paint it now.

"Hmm..."

True, she was certainly no painter and never even tried to paint a wall herself, but...how hard could it be?

"Knock, knock!" Someone called out, and Courtney stepped out into the living room to see who it was.

Hunter.

Shit.

Mortified because she looked like a complete mess—and then embarrassed because she knew he knew about her relationship with Dean—she couldn't quite force herself to look directly at him. "Oh, hey, Hunter. What's up?"

He walked into the house and looked at the work that had been done. "Wow, you guys have made some progress. I heard the kitchen cabinets were coming this weekend. I'm supposed to come help Dean install them." He walked into what was left of the kitchen and let out a low whistle. "New appliances are coming too, right?"

"Uh, yeah," she said quietly, combing the hair away from her face that had escaped her ponytail. "I thought the kitchen would look better and the house would potentially sell for more if he put new appliances in. Stainless steel ones."

He nodded. "Good call. I was thinking of asking Sam Westbrook if he could come take a look at the property and give us an estimate on clearing some of it. I know Scarlett never really cared about landscaping, but if she wants the place to sell for a decent price, she really needs to think about the curb appeal."

And for some reason, this conversation suddenly put her more at ease. "That's a great idea! I always told her she should do a little something in the front. Nothing major—just a couple of shrubs in front of the porch and a little mulch so it all didn't look so..."

"Barren?"

"Exactly!" They both laughed for a moment. "So, what brings you here?"

He shrugged. "Honestly, I just wanted to see what we were in for on Sunday so I could be a little prepared. I was surprised when I saw your car out front. What are you doing here working alone?"

She looked down at her feet and tried to think of the best way to explain without getting into too much detail. "Not much else to do today," she admitted. "None of the job inquiries are panning out so I figured I'd see what I could do around here. Plus, I really can't stand daytime television so this seemed like a good way to kill some time."

"Yeah, I heard about the public health job, Court. Sorry. I really hoped it would have worked out for you."

Another shrug. "It's not your fault. I appreciated you even thinking of me for it." She sighed before she could stop herself. "I just don't know..."

The next thing she knew, she was crying.

Dammit.

"Hey," he said softly. Stepping in close, Hunter awkwardly wrapped his arms around her and hugged her. "It's all gonna be okay. I didn't mean to upset you, I swear."

It took her a few minutes, but she did stop crying. And when she did, she looked up at Hunter and tried to smile. "You didn't upset me. The reason I'm here by myself is because I was already upset. I needed someplace to go and scream and get out my frustrations." She sighed. "I guess I've been keeping a lot bottled up."

Releasing her, he took a step back. "Yeah, well, you've kind of had a lot to deal with."

She nodded.

"Have you talked to Dean about this?" he asked carefully.

"Some. I don't want to bog him down with my problems. He knows what's going on so...why keep talking about it? Besides, that's always been his role, you know? People go to him with their problems and he fixes them." She walked over to her purse and pulled out some tissues to wipe her face. "I don't want to do that to him anymore. I don't want him to think he has to keep doing that for me. He does enough of that for everyone else."

Hanging her head, she realized what she'd just said and to who.

Looking over her shoulder, she said, "Hunter, I didn't mean..."

He held up a hand to stop her. "Don't worry about it. I know exactly what you meant, and for what it's worth, I agree. We've all turned to Dean for way more than we should have." He paused. "You know, when he told me about the two of you, my first thought was how I was glad he was finally doing something for himself, that he was finally dating again. I know he's worried because it's you and what everyone's going to think but...personally, I think you're good for him."

"You do?"

He nodded. "I do. Mainly because I know you and I know you're going to push him when most people don't. You're going to call him out when he goes into big brother or parent mode and remind him that he doesn't have to do that anymore. We're all grown up and he can stop hovering."

She laughed because it was true. "I don't think he even realizes he's doing it most of the time, but yeah. I want him to start doing more for himself. Is that wrong? Like...is it mean to ask him to let other people work their own problems out?"

"Not at all. He's going to ultimately do what he wants to do. Like this house. I think it's great how he's helping Scarlett out, but let's be honest. She and Mason have enough money that they could have hired someone or they could have just sold the place as-is. I'm sure some DIY couple would've had a field day with it."

"Actually, I've been having fun being one of those DIY couples with Dean. Crazy, right?"

Shaking his head, Hunter looked around the room. "I kind of like the fact that he's not here doing it alone. That maybe he's not looking at this only as a favor he's doing to help his sister out." He paused. "For all you know, he's having fun being part of a DIY couple with you too."

She thought of some of the things they'd done together in the midst of this mess and started to blush.

Hunter groaned. "Ugh...the look on your face tells me you're both enjoying it in ways that I don't even want to think about!"

"What? You said you didn't have a problem with me and Dean dating!"

"And I don't. I just don't want to think about what the two of you do when you're alone and I certainly don't want to witness any excessive PDA." He shuddered dramatically. "Keep that shit to yourselves."

"I'll try to remember that," she said solemnly, even though she was smirking. After a minute she said, "Come on, I'll show you how the bathroom came out and then you can help me figure out how to paint a room."

"Paint a room? What room?"

"The bedroom. It was next on my list."

"Wait, why? Why do you want to do that by yourself?"

"Like I said, I'm bored and I'm on a roll today. If I can get the bedroom painted and cleaned up, I'll feel like I've really accomplished something." She paused and smiled at him. "Will you help me? Please?"

"Fine," he drawled. "It's my day off, but whatever."

That immediately made her stop. "Oh, my gosh,

Hunter, I'm sorry! You probably need to go get Eli or something, right? Don't mind me. I can totally get this painting thing going on my own. Go on!"

With a chuckle, he walked past her to the bedroom. "What color are you painting it?"

"We're going with the same soft gray we're using on the rest of the house. Dean mentioned possibly doing a feature wall with shiplap, but the whole room needs to be painted first."

Hunter looked around the room. "You got painter's tape?"

She nodded.

"You got drop cloths?"

She nodded again.

"Brushes and rollers?"

"Trust me. We've got it all. But you really don't need to do this. Your son is way more important than painting this room. If I can't do it today, there's plenty of cleaning that still has to get done."

"Melissa has Eli today and I would have told you if I had to go. Why don't you go tackle some of the cleaning while I prep the room?" He looked around again. "When I'm ready to start painting, I'll let you know, and if you want to, I'll show you how it's done."

"Really?"

"Yup."

With a little squeal of excitement, she all but tackled him in a bear hug. "Thanks, Hunter! You're the best!"

He laughed when she released him. "Don't tell my brother that!" Then he just laughed harder. "On second thought, do tell him that and let's watch as his head explodes!"

12

"I can't believe you did so much without me."

"It wasn't a big deal. And Hunter helped."

"Still, I thought we were only going to work on this on the weekends."

She shrugged. "I needed something to do. With both Scarlett and my parents out of town, I'm kind of feeling a little lost. Besides, we both know the place really needed to be cleaned up before we could go any further. And you're already so busy at the garage that I didn't think it was a big deal for me to put in a little extra work here."

It was Saturday morning and they were having their bagels and coffee on the floor of Scarlett's house. "I just don't expect you to do it all by yourself, Court."

"Like I said, Hunter was here on Wednesday and helped out with painting the bedroom. He showed me what to do, so I felt fairly confident doing the hallway and the rest of the living area. It wasn't a big deal. You've done all the rest—the floors, the drywall, and most of the heavy demolition. I told you, we're a team with this."

He really liked the sound of that.

"I wish the cabinets were in already," she continued.

"How come?"

"Then we could have brought Scarlett and Mason over after dinner to show them. I mean, the cat will be out of the bag so they'll know I haven't been living here. Why not show them how much we've accomplished?"

"We still can. I think if we spend today doing the rest of the cleanup and paint the new wall one more time, it will be in good shape. I do want to be home by three so we have time to shower and get cleaned up before they come over."

"I don't think we'll need three hours for that."

He gave her a lecherous grin. "You know how we both enjoy a good shower." Hell, just thinking about it was enough to make him want to rush to get home.

"Mmm..." she hummed. "You do have a point. Everything else is good to go there. I did all the shopping yesterday, the steaks are marinating, and the house is spotless. They are going to be very impressed with all the work you've done there too. You sure you don't want to do more of this? You've clearly got a knack for flipping houses!"

"Nah, too much pressure. As much as I'm enjoying this, I'll be glad when we're done so I can have my weekends back."

"Oh."

"Why? You thinking of changing careers and becoming one of those home designers?" he teased.

Another shrug. "I don't know. Maybe. It's not like I can find a job doing anything else."

And there was something in her tone that stopped him. She'd been a little...off...for a few days and whenever he asked her about it, she just changed the subject.

"What's that supposed to mean?"

Sighing, she tossed the rest of her bagel down and

looked at him. "It means I can't find a job, Dean! I've tried to be optimistic but...it's just not happening! And what's worse is that I even got turned down to be a cashier in the grocery store! What am I supposed to do?"

Throwing his own breakfast down, he crawled over to her and pulled her into his lap and held her while she cried. His hands gently rubbed up and down her back and it killed him to hear her cry like this. He knew things weren't going well for her with the job hunt, but she hadn't let on that it was bothering her until now.

"Hey," he said softly. "It's going to be okay, Court. I swear. We'll get through this."

Lifting her head, there was a look of utter devastation on her face. "You don't get it, Dean. There's nothing you can do to fix this. There's nothing here for me."

"I'm here," he said, his voice a bit harsher than he intended.

She kissed him softly on the lips. "I know that, but...I have to work. I can't keep going like this. My savings is going to run out. In a million years, I never thought I'd be in this position! My car isn't fixed, I have no place to live, I mean...how much more can I possibly take?"

Okay, she was spiraling and he needed to calm her down. "Listen to me," he began, giving her a gentle shake. "I get that you're freaking out and no one's telling you that you're wrong for feeling like this. But you need to know that you're not alone. You're going to find a job. We both know that. So what if it's taking a little longer than you thought? Who cares?"

"I do!"

Rolling his eyes, he kept his grip on her. "Courtney, your car is going to be fixed and you already have a place to live. With me," he said, his voice going gruff. "I love having you there and no one's pushing you out the door! If you're that upset about not working, hell, we can give you a job at the shop! We've got a ton of billing that needs to get done on the computer and there's always the need for someone to answer the phones...it's not glamorous and it certainly isn't your dream job, but if working means that much to you, it's yours!"

Her eyes went wide but she didn't say a word.

"Or if that's not something you want to do, we'll ask around at every business in town if that's what it takes. We'll go door to door! Just...don't cry. Please." He caressed her cheek. "I hate to see you this upset. It kills me."

"Dean..."

"I mean it." Resting his forehead against hers, he let out a long breath. "We'll make it work. I promise."

She let out a shuddery breath. "You don't get it. And maybe I'm being stubborn but...I want a job in my field. That's what I went to school for and I love it! The thought of giving up and never doing it again isn't an option."

"No one's saying you'll never do it again. I'm just suggesting finding something short-term, that's all." He stood with her in his arms and helped her stand on her own two feet. Reaching up, he cupped her face in his hands. "You're going to get through this, I promise."

"But what if the only option is to move?" she asked sadly and just the thought of it gutted him.

Hell, he didn't want to even think about it. How could she even still be considering it after the last several weeks?

"One day at a time," he said, kissing her cheek. "Come on, we've got some work to do here so we can brag to Mason and Scarlett about what an awesome job we're doing and how we should totally have our own HGTV show."

As he hoped, that made her smile.

It wasn't a great deflection, but he seriously didn't know what else to do or say. Come Monday, he was going to bring her to work with him and give her something to do before calling in every favor to every person he knew in hopes of finding her a job. Then he was going to get on his brother-in-law to try to speed up the process of bringing a new dental practice to town. One way or another, Dean was determined to help her.

"I think I'm going to throw up."

Dean's eyes went wide. "Seriously? Do you think the sandwiches we got were bad? I feel fine, but..."

"No, no, no...it's not lunch that's making me sick; it's nerves. I am so nervous about seeing Scarlett tonight. I mean...you're going to answer the door and invite them in, and I'm going to be standing here in the middle of the living room shaking like an idiot."

Slowly, he wrapped his arms around her and pulled her in close. "First, nothing you do makes you an idiot. And it's perfectly normal to be nervous. My sister has been our biggest obstacle and we have no idea how she's going to react."

Courtney took several deep, cleansing breaths before she moved out of his arms. "What if she freaks out?" she demanded, feeling the first waves of an anxiety attack come on.

"Well, I think we should expect a little bit of a freak-out, but once we talk to her and remind her how we didn't freak out on her when she started dating Mason..."

"You kind of freaked out on her. I didn't."

He sighed loudly. "I only freaked out because I heard she was pregnant and never even knew they were dating."

"Still, I think you need to prepare that she'll throw that back at you."

"I don't know...we talked a little about that the other day and..."

"Wait. You talked about what?"

"About what it was like when she and Mason started dating and how other people reacted to them."

"Why would you bring that up?"

The smile he gave her was all charm and confidence. "Just laying the groundwork, sweetheart."

She had to give him credit; it was a brilliant idea.

"And what did she have to say?"

"Basically, she said the only one who really gave her grief was Mason's mother. She also said that if any of us had had a problem, it wouldn't have fazed her because the only one in the relationship with Mason was her."

"Seriously?"

He nodded.

"Wow."

"I know. She pretty much just handed us our response, so even if she freaks out, we're good."

"Well, let's hope she doesn't freak out too much. These steaks look like they're going to be fantastic and I made all her favorite sides–loaded twice-baked potatoes, green bean casserole, and a Caesar salad. Plus, we've got an antipasto platter for an appetizer and cupcakes for dessert."

"Jeez, that's a lot of food."

"Trust me, it's the best way to distract your sister at this point." With a laugh, Courtney turned to grab herself something to drink when Dean's cellphone rang. Glancing over her shoulder, she watched as he looked down at the screen and frowned. "If that's Scarlett calling to cancel, tell her I'm eating all the cupcakes!"

Again, she knew food was not only a good distraction, but also a good motivator.

Dean answered the phone and took a couple of steps away from her.

"What?" he cried. "Are you kidding me?" Silence. "Do you want us to come or..." He nodded. "Yeah, okay. I'll call them and we'll be there soon." With his back to her, she noticed him take several deep breaths even as he hung his head.

"Dean? Is everything okay?"

"You're not going to believe this," he said wearily as he turned to face her. "Scarlett's in labor."

"What?" she cried, mimicking his reaction from just moments ago. "How is that even possible? It's too early! Are they sure it's really labor?"

He nodded and walked into the kitchen and began putting all the food away. "Mason said her water broke two hours ago. They're at the hospital and she's already dilated to six centimeters." He stopped what he was doing and looked at her. "That's a thing, right? Like that's supposed to happen?"

Unable to help herself, she laughed. "Yes, that's a thing." Then it hit her. "Oh my God! She's having the baby!"

Dean looked at her funny. "Um, yeah. That's what I've been saying. I need to call my dad and everyone and let them know and then we'll head to the hospital."

"Okay, you go make the calls and I'll finish putting the food away," she told him, shouldering him out of the way. "I've got this."

He gave her a quick kiss. "Thanks."

Fifteen minutes later, they were getting ready to walk out the door. "Should we eat something first? I mean, I know we don't have time to grill the steaks or anything, but maybe just a snack?"

"How about we pack up the antipasto and bring it with us? We can share it with everyone."

She made a face. "I don't think there's enough for everyone. I made it to feed four–well, four extremely hungry people so maybe it will feed more if we don't overdo it. Or if your brothers keep their hands to themselves," she added with a laugh.

"Hunter's on call at the firehouse so he won't be there and Kyle's out on a date so..."

"We're wasting time here," she murmured and turned back to the kitchen and began pulling out containers to put the assortment of meats and cheeses in. "Grab the box of crackers and I'll add some of that cheese spread we were saving and maybe some of the grapes and strawberries."

"Court, how many people do you think are going to be there?"

"I don't know! Us, your dad, your grandfather, Mason's family..."

"That doesn't mean we need enough food for everyone," he reasoned.

With a patient smile, she continued to package up the food. "Look, we were getting ready to have dinner and chances are so was everyone else. I'm not saying we have to feed them all, but this can be our contribution to the festivities."

"Festivities? We're going to be sitting around waiting for a baby to be born."

"Maybe we should stop for cake..."

"Courtney!" His voice was full of exasperation but she

didn't take offense. He was clueless as to why this was all such a big deal and it was okay. By the end of the night she knew he'd be just as excited as she was.

Placing all the containers in one of the reusable shopping bags he had in the pantry, she took the box of crackers from him and walked toward the front door. "You want to bring anything else with us? Drinks? A board game? Our Kindles?"

"How long do you think we're going to be there?" he asked, frowning.

"You poor, sweet, clueless man," she said, patting his cheek. "You really have no idea about these things, do you?"

"Court..."

"Weren't you there when Eli was born? There's no timetable!" she said with a laugh. "Babies come when they're ready."

"Clearly this baby is ready considering it's like seven weeks early." Then he paused. "Is this a safe amount of time? Are there going to be complications? Is there a chance..."

She could see it was all hitting him and he was starting to freak out. Reaching out, she took one of his hands in hers. "Hey," she said softly. "It's going to be okay. It's definitely early but Scarlett's pregnancy has been really good."

"Until a few weeks ago," he reminded her. "What if that caused a problem or hurt the baby? What if it's the reason she's in labor now? What if..."

Squeezing his hand, she interrupted, "Dean, we have to think positively! The doctors have been watching her carefully and she's been very cooperative and following their orders to take things easy."

"They never should have gone away this week," he

muttered, pulling his hand from hers and walking out the front door.

With no other choice, she followed, locking up behind her. When she climbed into his truck, she knew she needed to get him to calm down before they went anywhere. The last thing anyone needed was Dean flipping out at the hospital and starting a fight with someone. She reached out and snagged the keys from him before he could start the truck.

"What the hell?" he demanded.

"You need to calm down!" she said firmly. "I get that you're upset and worried about Scarlett, but we all are! This is one of those times when calm, cool, and collected Dean is most appreciated. We're going to a hospital and you can't go in there looking for a fight!"

"I'm not going to fight with anyone," he said with disgust. "You know I'd never do anything like that."

"Normally I would agree, but I've never seen you like this before and I have no idea what's going on in your head."

Letting out a long breath, Dean rested his head back against the seat. "Yeah, I'm usually alone when I freak out this way. Sorry."

Without thinking, she reached for his hand again. "I don't want you to apologize. If anything, I like knowing that you're not always in control." When he looked at her like she was crazy, she gave him a small smile. "You've said it often enough–you're the levelheaded one all the time. I often wondered how it was even possible. Now I know that you're just as human as the rest of us."

"It's not a bad thing, right?" he asked, his voice a little hesitant.

"It's actually a great thing." Leaning in, she kissed him

softly on the lips. "Now let's go to the hospital and wait for a baby!"

But he didn't pick up the keys right away. He looked down at their hands and sighed.

"What? What's the matter?"

"This was supposed to be our night to finally tell Scarlett what's going on and now..."

"Yeah, I think she's got more important things on her mind." She laughed softly again.

"But we're showing up there together and..."

"And we'll deal with it if anyone has anything to say," she quickly stated. "Although with so much going on and everyone focused on worrying about Scarlett and the baby, I highly doubt anyone's going to be paying much attention to us."

He kissed her again before picking up the keys and starting the truck. "We'll see."

"You're going to wear a path into that floor if you don't stop pacing."

Dean merely glanced at his father and kept walking. Was it normal for labor to take this long? And why hadn't anyone come out to update them lately? No one had seen or heard anything from Mason in over two hours!

With a low chuckle, Domenic Jones blocked his son's path. "Come on. Come walk with me outside. I can use some air."

"Dad, if we go outside, we might miss an update on Scarlett!"

That just made his father laugh again. He turned toward the cluster of sofas in the waiting room where everyone was sitting and talking. "If any word comes down, Dean and I will be outside," he called out. "There. Problem solved. Let's go."

Knowing there was no arguing with his dad, Dean simply followed him across the lobby and out the doors. It was dark outside and the air was cool, but he had to admit it felt good after being inside the hospital for over four hours already.

"These things take time, Dean," his father said once they were walking away from the front doors and down the walkway to a sitting area. "Trust me. I did this with four kids of my own and not that long ago with Hunter on the night Eli was born. There's no rushing a baby to be born."

"But she's so early, Dad," he reasoned. "You would think they would be doing their best to deliver quickly so they can make sure the baby is okay."

"Sometimes that puts more stress on both the mother and the baby. They're monitoring both of them and if they see something's wrong, they'll do whatever needs to be done. We just need to be patient."

"Yeah," he said wearily. "Not my strong suit lately."

"Oh, I don't know about that. I think out of the four of you, you're the most patient. Always have been. Sometimes I wish you'd be a little more impatient and take some initiative, just...not right now in this particular situation."

Frowning, he stopped walking. "What does that mean?"

A small smile played on his father's lips. "I noticed you arrived with Courtney. And food."

"And?"

"And I just think it's interesting," Domenic said. "I think something's been there for a long time and you've just been standing back, being patient, and not confident enough to do anything about it."

"Dad, you're not making any sense."

Rather than argue, his father just nodded and began walking again.

Seriously, did everyone notice how there was a...a thing...between him and Courtney that neither of them ever did? How was that possible?

One of the things Dean had always prided himself on was being attuned to how other people felt or to their needs–particularly with his family. But somehow he has missed out on the fact that Courtney had had feelings for him for years and how other people were aware of it.

"You're a smart man," Domenic went on. "And you're one of the most caring people I know. It's no wonder you're looking out for Courtney. She's a little lost right now and I think it's nice how you're looking after her."

Wait...

"Although, I have a feeling you're not really doing it out of brotherly concern..."

"I'm not her brother, Dad."

"Glad to know you realize that."

He stopped walking again. "Dad..." he said with exasperation. "If you've got something to say, can you please just say it?"

Domenic paused and turned around, a look of mild amusement on his face. "All I'm trying to say is that if you're happy and Courtney's happy, then I'm happy. It seems to me the both of you have seemed a whole lot..."

"Happier?" he asked, with just a hint of sarcasm.

"Well, yeah. For lack of a better word." Then without another word, he turned and started walking again.

Sighing, Dean followed. After several silent moments, he had to speak. "So you don't think there's anything wrong with what we're doing?"

"Depends on what exactly it is that you're doing."

"Dad..."

"I'm not asking for specific details, Son, so relax. What I am saying is that if the two of you are just messing around–even if it's mutual messing around–I can't say I'd be pleased."

He'd ask why, but Dean was pretty sure he already knew the answer.

"We're not messing around." He paused. "At least, I don't think we are."

"You're not sure?"

"Honestly, I'm not sure about anything anymore. I was so freaked out about how everyone else was going to react that I've sort of been on pins and needles, holding part of myself back just in case things couldn't work out."

"Couldn't?" Domenic repeated. "That's an odd word choice."

"You know what I mean. If everyone freaked out and made Courtney uncomfortable, there's no way we would could continue seeing each other."

"Why?"

"What do you mean why? Because it would be hard!"

"So?"

He groaned. "You don't understand..."

"I understand better than you think," Domenic clarified. "When I first met your mother, I wasn't exactly her family's first choice for her."

"How come?"

Shrugging, he went on, "Because your mother had dated Alan Wagner before we met."

"Who's Alan Wagner?"

Domenic chuckled. "To me he was nothing more than a pretentious jackass, but to your grandparents, he was someone who had a tremendous future who could give your mother a better life than she had growing up."

"Wow."

"Yeah. But your mother was smart and knew he wasn't the man for her." With a mirthless laugh, he added, "Although he did seem to be the man for a lot of other women around town."

"Ah. Gotcha."

"Anyway, that was something your grandparents didn't know about him, and when I started coming around, they were very vocal about all the ways Alan could give her more than I ever could and how I was destined to stay in this small town and live paycheck to paycheck."

"Wow, Dad. I had no idea. It always seemed like you had a great relationship with them."

"That came with time," he explained. "But there were a few years where they made it very hard to be around them. Your mom used to cry all the time about it. I thought about walking away but...I couldn't. I loved her and she loved me and we used to just pray that they'd come to realize that."

"I guess they finally did."

He nodded. "They did. It helped a lot when Alan went to jail for racketeering and it came out what a womanizer he was."

Dean laughed out loud. "I'm sure that really helped."

"I'm not a spiteful man or one who takes pleasure when bad things happen to people but...I was really happy to see ol' Alan fall like that."

"I get that." He paused. "But it's not really the same with Court and me..."

"It is. You two are happy together, right?"

With a nod, Dean said, "We are."

"And if other people weren't happy for you–if they

thought you should be with someone else or she should be with someone else–they'd be vocal about it, right?"

"Right."

"See? Same thing. We got it from your grandparents. You thought you'd be getting it from me and your brothers and sister."

"Hunter knows and he was fine with it. I haven't mentioned it to Kyle but I imagine he'd just make fun of me for a while or joke around and tell Courtney she picked the wrong brother."

"And your sister?"

He sighed. "We planned on telling her tonight over dinner, but then Mason called and told us she was in labor."

"She always did have bad timing," Domenic responded with a laugh and after a moment, he asked, "How do you think she's going to respond?"

"I think she's going to freak out."

"You know her bark is worse than her bite. Scarlett talks first, thinks second. That's always been her biggest downfall. If I were you, I'd prepare for the bark and then just give her a little time. Although, you may have lucked out with the baby coming early."

"Why?"

"She'll be a bit distracted. I'm not saying go in there when the baby comes and open with announcing you and Courtney are dating, but...you know what I'm saying."

The sound of footsteps rapidly approaching had them both looking over their shoulders. As his brother Kyle quickly caught up to them, he knew it could only mean one thing.

"It's a boy!"

13

"Thanks for being willing to stay and hang out for a few minutes," Scarlett said as she kissed her newborn son's head. Courtney hadn't really thought about the reality of her friend having a baby, but now that he was here, she began to feel a little emotional.

"No worries," she said softly, not wanting to startle the baby. "Is everything okay?"

Looking up at her, Scarlett smiled. "I feel like I ran a marathon and then got kicked in the crotch, but other than that, I'm great."

Laughing quietly, she commented, "You really have a vivid way of painting a picture."

"I try." She paused, kissing the baby again before relaxing against the pillows and focusing on Courtney. "Listen, I have something I have to talk to you about."

Uh-oh...

"The last couple of weeks, there's been something on my mind, but between the bed rest and missing our honeymoon and...well, you know..."

Courtney nodded, afraid to speak.

Reaching out, Scarlett grabbed for one of Courtney's hands and squeezed it. "You know how much I love you, right?"

Another nod.

"I mean...you're my sister!" she explained emphatically. "Ever since we were assigned the same table on the first day of kindergarten and you asked me if I liked Beanie Babies, we've been inseparable."

"I know," she said, smiling at the memory.

"I had never met anyone as girlie as you," Scarlett went on. "I was fascinated by everything you did and said and wore. I think my family was so tired of hearing me talk about you and all the demands I made for more girly things." She laughed. "You were my first friend. My first *real* friend."

"Scar, you're going to make me cry." And sure enough, her eyes were beginning to sting with unshed tears.

"Welcome to my world. I've been crying for almost a whole year."

"Oh, stop," she said, her attention going to the tiny baby in her friend's arms. "All those tears were worth it. I mean, look at him. He's perfect."

Scarlett's smile grew. "He really is, isn't he? And I can't believe how big he is for a preemie. The whole time I was in labor, the nurses were preparing me for the fact that he could be small and have to go into an incubator and be monitored, but he's over five pounds and seems perfectly fine." She paused. "Although, they are going to keep him in the nursery tonight to monitor him. I just asked to keep him with me for a little longer."

"You probably should have let Mason stay with the two of you instead of shooing him out of here."

"He understands. He knew I needed to talk to you."

Damn. She thought she'd distracted her.

"Whatever it is, Scar, it can wait. You've had a long day and I'm sure Mason wants to be back in here with the two of you." She stood and squeezed her hand before letting go. "And have you given this little bean a name yet?"

"Sadly, no. We wanted to wait until he was here so we could look at him but there hasn't been a spare moment to really stare at him, you know?"

"All the more reason to get Mason back in here." She paused and smiled at how happy Scarlett looked. "I'll go get him." Leaning down, she kissed her on the cheek. "And I promise to come by tomorrow. Do you think you'll get to go home?"

"I think it all depends on this little guy. If he's staying, I'm staying."

"Okay, I'll check in with you in the morning and see what's going on." She walked to the door before she stopped and turned around. "Scar?"

"Hmm?"

"I'm so happy for you. I know you've only been a mom for like...an hour, but it's a really good look on you."

"Dammit, now I'm going to cry!"

"Like that wasn't going to happen anyway," she said with a wink. "Talk to you tomorrow. Try to get some sleep."

"I will. Thanks, Court."

"I love you, Scarlett," she said, her voice thick with emotion.

And with a watery smile, Scarlett replied, "I love you too."

Out in the hall, she took a minute to compose herself. There were so many emotions threatening to overwhelm her and she needed to get herself together before she walked out to the waiting room and faced Dean and Mason and whoever else was still here.

Sitting with Scarlett and seeing the baby in her arms had her longing for the same thing. How many times had they talked about doing this together–having their babies at the same time so they'd either be best friends or a couple who would one day marry each other? There was no way she was ready to talk to Dean about anything like that, but she couldn't help but wish that she was.

She'd never admit it but...all the times she and Scarlett talked about their kids, Courtney always pretended her child was Dean's.

Oh, if only...

Taking a steadying breath, she made her way back to the waiting room. Stopping before anyone could see her, she simply watched everyone as they talked and celebrated. Mason was hugging his sister Parker while he talked to their parents. Domenic was standing with them and he was just beaming. That made her smile as well. Next to them, Dean was talking with Kyle and whatever it was that Dean said made his brother laugh.

It was a good scene and she was so happy she hadn't missed it. If she had made it to Raleigh that night weeks ago, she wouldn't have been here for this.

As if sensing her, Dean looked over at her and smiled and just like that, her heart skipped a beat. He was everything she ever wanted and it didn't matter if it was too soon or if they didn't know how everyone else felt about them, she wanted him to know how she felt.

Tonight. I'll tell him tonight.

Forcing herself to relax and smile, she joined the group. Domenic stopped her as she walked over and hugged her.

"Congratulations, Grandpa," she said, hugging him back. "Another boy in the family!"

"I really thought she was having a girl," he said with a grin. "Or maybe it was just wishful thinking."

"Yeah, I was kind of hoping for a girl for her too, but once she found out she was having a boy, I realized a boy would be perfect."

His eyebrows shot up. "You knew?"

Blushing, she nodded. "Yeah. She swore me to secrecy."

Chuckling, he shook his head again. "You two...why am I not surprised?"

Dean walked over with Kyle and when he put his arm around her right there in front of everyone, she melted a little. It felt so good not to hide their relationship anymore. It gave her hope for them.

And if she could just find a damn job, life would be perfect.

"You ready?" Dean asked and she nodded.

It took over fifteen minutes to say goodbye to everyone and collect all their things before they were finally seated in Dean's truck. Resting her head back against the seat, Courtney let out a happy little sigh.

"Everything okay?"

Nodding, she turned her head and smiled at him. "Yeah. This was a good day."

"Agreed." He paused. "I was so worried about the baby coming early, but it seems like he's okay."

"Well, he's still a preemie and even if his weight is good, they might want to keep him a couple of days to make sure he's okay."

"I have a feeling my sister will freak out if she has to go home without the baby."

"She's already announced that if he's staying, she's staying."

Laughing, he said, "Typical Scarlett."

"I know, right?"

They drove for several minutes in silence before Dean asked, "So what did she want to talk to you about?"

"I'm not really sure. I kind of think she was hinting that she knows about us..."

"What?"

Nodding, she said, "I know. But she was rambling and I think still a little loopy from the drugs they gave her during delivery, so..."

"Why do you think that's what she was hinting at?"

Her gaze narrowed slightly. "Does it matter? We were going to tell her tonight anyway."

"No, I know that. I just think it's odd that she would bring that up, that's all. She just had a baby, so why would that even be on her mind?"

"Like I said, I think she was loopy so I have no idea what she was really going to say. I'm probably looking deeper than I need to."

"Maybe."

It bothered her how freaked out he seemed. Earlier–before they had gotten the call about Scarlett being in labor–they were totally in sync about what they were doing and now he sounded like he did a few days ago. It was beyond frustrating.

But she wasn't going to focus on that.

She wasn't going to let it get to her.

Instead, she reached over and let her hand caress his denim-clad thigh. "I know it's too late to grill the steaks, but are you hungry? Basically we only ate a little of the antipasto for dinner and some sad coffee. Should we stop at a drive-thru and grab something?"

"Nah. There's plenty to eat back at the house. We can whip up some sandwiches or something." He looked at her with a boyish grin and for some reason, it made her want to reach out and kiss him, touch him.

As soon as they were in the driveway ten minutes later, that's exactly what she did.

Dean hauled her in close and it took several awkward maneuvers to get herself settled in his lap, straddling him. Her hands cupped his face as he squeezed her ass. Courtney couldn't help but grind against him as she poured everything she had into kissing him–praying he'd be able to tell how she felt. The thought of breaking the kiss to talk to him wasn't the least bit appealing because kissing Dean was like a religious experience and beyond addictive.

Shifting slightly, his hands snaked under her shirt, cupping her breasts. This time she did break the kiss to simply get air. "That feels so good," she panted.

"It would feel even better if we were inside and I had you sprawled out on the bed," he murmured, his breath hot against her throat.

Next thing she knew, Dean had the driver's side door open and was sliding them out. Her legs wrapped around him once he was standing and she was the one to slam the door shut. "Hurry," she whispered, peppering kisses along his jaw before nipping at his ear. "Please."

Almost instantly, they were through the front door–with Dean kicking it shut behind them–and striding toward the bedroom. Pulling back slightly, Courtney whipped her shirt up over her head and tossed it aside, not caring where it landed. Her back hit the mattress seconds before Dean's body covered hers. His mouth claimed hers and then it was madness all over again.

Something she loved.

Her hands raked up into his hair as she wrapped herself around him, holding him as close as possible even as she cursed the fact that they were both still dressed.

Well, except for her shirt.

With his hands roaming all over her bare torso, she wondered if it would always be like this or if the need and urgency would lessen over time.

It had to, right?

She'd never been in a relationship long enough to know. Plus, she'd never been in a relationship where she felt this strongly.

Hell, she'd never been in love.

And yeah, she knew without a doubt that she was in love with Dean Jones.

She had *always* been in love with Dean Jones.

As if sensing her thoughts, Dean broke the kiss, lifted his head and looked down at her. His expression was intense. "Every time," he said gruffly. "I swear, every time you touch me, kiss me, I'm ready to lose control."

She couldn't hide her smile. "I love it when you lose control."

His own smile was slow and sexy as hell. "What if I said I didn't want to lose control just yet? What if I said I wanted to take my time and make love to you all night long–slowly." He kissed her. "Sweetly." Another kiss. "Until you can barely remember your own name."

With a slight shiver, Courtney's hand moved from his hair down over his shoulder and chest before dropping to her side. "I'm totally on board with all of that," she whispered, her eyes drinking in the sight of him.

"Good," he said with a curt nod, right before he slowly leaned in to kiss her again.

After that, everything changed–their movements became less frantic. Touches became soft caresses. Kisses lingered rather than devoured. It was all slow and sensual and unlike anything they'd ever done together.

And it was erotic on a whole different level that she never knew existed.

She lost track of time and her focus was solely on Dean and the pleasure he was giving her–and on giving it back to him.

Much later, when they were tangled together, breathless and exhausted, she felt him place a soft kiss on her cheek before he dozed off. She waited, holding her breath to make sure he was asleep before whispering, "I love you."

Then she fell into a deep and satisfied sleep.

"What are you doing?"

Dean didn't even look up. He was focused and knew he'd put this off long enough. "I'm fixing Courtney's car. It's time."

Beside him, his father nodded. "I agree. Scarlett's going to need her car back now that the baby's here."

"That's not the only reason I'm doing this, Dad. I never should have agreed to this stupid plan. I had no right to lie to Court this way." He tightened the last bolt and took a step back. The car was up on the lift and he just finished securing the trailer hitch.

Guilt had eaten away at him all day yesterday and had him getting up earlier than usual so he could get into the shop before anyone else arrived. It was still dark out when he left his house, but considering he hadn't slept much, he didn't mind.

"Something happen?" Domenic asked, his tone mildly concerned.

Yeah, something had happened. Courtney had said she loved him.

Logically, he knew she was half asleep and more than likely thought he was asleep, but he wasn't. He'd been right on the verge when he heard her softly spoken words and they kept him up for longer than he thought possible–especially considering how exhausted he had been.

Still, he didn't want to jump to conclusions.

Yesterday, while she went up to the hospital to visit his sister and the baby, he worked on Scarlett's place. Both Kyle and Hunter showed up to help him finish installing the new flooring in the kitchen, as well as the rest of the cabinets. Both tried to talk to him about Courtney, but Dean was a bit of a hard-ass and told them to focus on getting the house done.

So they did.

Sort of.

They both took turns ribbing him about his feelings, but he didn't take the bait.

Now the inside of the house was just about done–all that was left was to touch-up some spots on the walls with paint and a good cleaning. After that, they only had to take care of the exterior and some landscaping. Hunter had mentioned getting Sam Westbrook's company in to handle the landscaping and Dean suggested to Mason that they hire a company to paint the siding and replace the rotten wood. Not that he couldn't do it, but he knew it would go faster at this point with an actual paint crew.

It felt good to know the job was almost done and

although it wasn't a particularly big job–and it wasn't on the same scale as what he'd done to his own place–he was proud of himself for what he'd accomplished.

Well, with the help of his brothers and Courtney.

"Dean?"

Oh, right. His father had asked him a question.

Shaking his head, he wiped his hands on the rag he kept in his back pocket. "No. It's just been weighing on my mind, that's all."

"You sure?"

He nodded and let out a sigh of relief when his father walked away. While it might have helped to talk to someone about how he felt, right now he just wasn't ready to.

She loved him. At least...she had said that while she was half asleep. Still, if it were true, how did he feel about it? Was he in love with her? Was it possible to feel that way so soon? Okay, it's not like she was a stranger who he just started a relationship with; they'd known each other for years. Their history with each other went way back even if their romantic one didn't start until recently. That shouldn't matter, right? Their past, who they know, that shouldn't have anything to do with how they felt about each other. So again, was he in love with her?

For more than twenty-four hours he'd been obsessing over it and he still couldn't bring himself to answer that question.

"Dean! Charlie called in sick and we've got six cars slated to be done by lunch. You done working on Courtney's?" his father called out.

"Yeah. I'm taking it down now. Whose car am I doing next?"

"Jack Seddon's! It's the black Nissan. Keys are at the desk!"

"Got it!" he called back and walked over to lower Courtney's car down. Within minutes, he had it parked out back and figured he'd either call her at lunchtime or wait and tell her when he got home later.

Once he pulled the Nissan into the bay, he put all his focus on getting the work done. The car needed an oil change and a tire rotation. Neither were particularly challenging and he knocked it out in less than an hour. After that, he had to do a brake job on Mrs. Henderson's Chevy. They all fought to do any work for her because she always gave the mechanic who did the work a box of cupcakes. Today, he would gladly accept them and bring them home to share with Courtney–after he gave his father a couple too.

At lunchtime, he thought he'd have time to stop and call her, but his grandfather had shown up and asked Dean to join him for lunch across the street at his newly-renovated bar and grill, the Mystic Magnolia. A year ago, it had been a hole-in-the-wall bar on its last legs, then Mason Bishop stepped forward and offered to help redo the place and he breathed some new life into it.

Unable to say no to his grandfather, he joined him for lunch–along with his father, his brothers, and his nephew Eli.

"I can't believe there's going to be another boy at the table," Hunter said. "I really would have thought Scarlett was having a girl."

"Why? Because she's a girl?" Kyle asked with amusement.

"Well...yeah," Hunter replied. "Didn't you think that too?"

"No," Kyle said, laughing. "One has nothing to do with the other. Clearly, the male genes are strong in this family.

And I think it's cool that Eli will have a male cousin to play with. Right, buddy?" He smiled at his nephew who simply stared at him like he was weird.

"Have they named him yet?" his grandfather asked. "Last I heard Scarlett was still staring at him trying to figure out the perfect name." He shook his head. "In my day, it didn't matter what they looked like; you gave them a good, strong family name."

"Gramps, no one does that anymore," Kyle said.

"Courtney saw her yesterday and said they decided to name him Asher Ezekiel," Dean said before taking a bite of his burger. "Damn, Gramps, this is fantastic. You're going to give The Sand Bar a run for its money!"

Tommy Flynn beamed with pride. "That's what we're hoping for. I'm telling you, Mason's sister Peyton really has a gift. She's a fantastic cook and she's got a good head for business and what works. She redid our entire menu and trained the kitchen staff. She's been a real godsend."

"I thought I remember hearing that she owned another place here in town," Hunter commented.

"Her great-grandfather left her Café Magnolia in his will but she hasn't done anything with it yet. The place is holding its own and I think she's afraid to rock the boat. I was more than happy to let her test her wings here. Hopefully she'll gain some confidence and feel like she's ready to take control over there."

"Aren't you worried about the competition?" Kyle asked.

Shaking his head, Tommy said, "Nah. Totally different clientele. Even with all the changes we've made here, our menu is still your typical pub food–burgers, sandwiches, and all that. The café has a little more of an upscale vibe to it. Apples and oranges."

They all nodded.

"When's the big grand opening celebration?" Domenic asked. "It looks like you're already open but I thought you were going to do a big thing."

"We are. Next month. We're still fine-tuning everything here. I don't want to invite the press in and have all the attention on us until everything's perfect."

"That makes sense," Dean commented. "Although I've yet to see any issues. Everything you've let us taste is delicious and the place has never looked better."

Tommy's smile only grew. "This is the kind of place your grandmother envisioned. Back then, we didn't have the money to make it look like this. I know she would have loved this. Especially seeing all of you here enjoying it."

They all fell silent and ate for several minutes before speaking again.

"Just let us know if there's anything we can do to help," Domenic said. "You know we're all more than willing to lend a hand."

"I know," Tommy replied, "and I appreciate it. It's still a little mind-boggling how much the town's changing and how different everything's looking. I never thought I'd live to see the day when this end of town looks as good as the main drag. This was like no-man's land for so long."

"We've got Mason to thank for that," Domenic said. "He's a good man. He works hard and he's got strong roots to this area. It's nice to see him giving back to the community the way his great-grandfather did."

They all nodded.

"You ever think of expanding the garage?" Tommy asked. "You've got more than enough business and you have the property for it. Seems to me your lot's been full every day for the last several months. Or maybe you should consider a second location."

Dean looked at his father and grinned. It was something they'd talked about, but business had been exceptionally busy and they couldn't seem to find the time to do more than just casually talk about it.

"It's something I'd love to see happen," Domenic explained. "I figured I'd continue to run this shop and if we did a second location, that would belong to Dean." He shrugged. "Life's just keeping us all too busy to do anything more than just think about it."

In all honesty, Dean knew he'd love a shop of his own. He enjoyed working with his father, but he had some ideas of his own about how he'd like his own garage to be laid out and there were some new tools he'd love to invest in. But as his father mentioned, there just never seemed to be the time.

"Well, maybe now that Dean's done working on Scarlett's place you guys can sit down and hammer out the details," Hunter suggested. "I know Magnolia's not a huge town, but it's not like you guys would be competition. You'd just be setting up a second location to move customers through faster. Same-day service is a big perk when it comes to car repairs."

"And the cost of property is only going to go up now that the town is getting so many upgrades," Kyle said. "Maybe talk to Mason and see if he knows of any property you can look at."

"Why not just talk to a realtor?" Dean asked. "Mason's not in real estate."

"No, but you never know if he has some insight into what's being built here in town and where the best spot would be for you to set up shop," Tommy explained.

Just the thought of it excited him. How cool would it be to have a shop of his own? To be a full partner in the business with his father was something he always dreamed of rather than just working with him or for him. Of course, there would be loans to take out and a lot of hours to put in to get it all up and running, but he wasn't afraid of hard work–never had been–especially if all that work was leading to him doing something he always hoped to do.

"You know those warehouses down at the south end of town? The ones that used to be part of the old cotton mill?" Hunter asked and everyone nodded. "You guys should look into them."

"That's a lot more than we would actually need," Dean replied. "What would we do with the rest of them?"

"Maybe get some investors and see about making it into something more," Hunter said. "You know, you make space for a garage, put a few other businesses on the ground level and then see about converting the upper levels into either office space or maybe even apartments."

"You can't put apartments over a garage," Dean commented. "I don't think that would work."

"Still, there are tons of possibilities. And if you put the garage on the end so you'd have the entire side lot, you could still have plenty of options for the rest of the space. Put your office in the upper level–at least the space above the garage."

Domenic shook his head. "I don't think you can put a garage in a space with other businesses. They need to be freestanding. But there is a smaller structure down there next to the warehouses. I think that could work and be converted into a garage and then we look for investors for the warehouses and see them converted into businesses and apartments." He paused and took a drink of his sweet tea.

"But we still should talk to Mason and find a good realtor to talk to about it."

"Holy shit, are you guys seriously going to do this? Because...this sounds amazing!" Kyle said excitedly.

"Slow down," Dean said. "There's still a lot to do and this isn't going to happen overnight."

"Ugh...why are you always the downer?" Kyle whined.

"I'm not the downer; I'm just logical. No need to get our hopes up yet until we do the research. That's all I'm saying."

"You know, I really hoped Courtney would have helped you unclench a little."

Everyone laughed and Dean tried not to let it get to him.

"Okay, that's enough," Domenic said. "There's nothing wrong with Dean being cautious. It's a fine quality."

"Please, there's cautious and then there's moving at a turtle's pace," Hunter said. "And our brother here would get his ass handed to him by the turtle!"

More laughing.

"Guys..."

"Fine. We won't poke fun at him anymore. Out loud," Hunter added, winking.

Dean was used to it. None of them realized how much his cautiousness benefitted them all and that was fine. But he was going to research the old warehouses and look into what it would cost for them to renovate one of the spaces for a garage versus building one on its own piece of property. Once Mason had Scarlett and the baby home and settled, he'd set up a time to go talk to him about it. And tonight he'd run it by Courtney and see what she thought. He found he enjoyed getting her input on things and, more times than not, she made him think about things he never would have thought of on his own.

She balanced him.

Hell, she completed him.

And he wanted her input on this venture because it would affect her too. If he was going to do this, it would mean time away from her and demands on his time and his finances. It was one thing when he only had himself to consider, but now...he wasn't alone. There was still a good chance that she was going to find a job soon, but right now he was helping her out and wasn't sure he'd be able to keep doing that if his time and money had to go elsewhere.

Just thinking that had his chest squeezing. For the first time in a long time–possibly ever–Dean was thinking about someone other than his family.

But did that mean he loved her? Yeah, he still was afraid to answer that question, even though he knew he was going to have to.

Soon.

She may have said I love you in her sleep, but it would only be a matter of time before she said it out loud. He didn't want to be caught off guard or risk saying the wrong thing and ruining what they had because he was being...cautious.

14

It took four days, but baby Asher was finally home.

Courtney stood over his bassinet and just stared at him in awe. "He's perfect," she said in a hushed tone. "Absolutely perfect."

Beside her, Scarlett nodded. "I know, right? I made that!"

"You know you weren't alone in that," she teased. "I think Mason gets some of the credit here."

"Yeah, yeah, yeah...I know, but...I did most of it."

It was pointless to argue.

"So come and sit down and tell me what's going on with you. How's the job hunt going? Any leads?"

Sighing, she sat down on the sofa. "None close to here. I did get a couple of responses for positions I applied for weeks ago though."

"Really? Where are they located?"

"Raleigh."

Scarlett's eyes went wide. "Raleigh? I thought you never applied to any there? I thought you were waiting until you moved?"

"Yeah, well...I sent a few right before the wedding." She looked over with a sad smile. "Now I don't know what to do."

With a sigh of her own, Scarlett leaned back against the sofa cushions. "Wow. I can't believe nothing is available here. How is that even possible?" Then she cursed. "I knew Mason should have pushed harder to get the whole medical practices search done sooner."

"It's not Mason's fault, Scar. It's just the way things are. I've looked at other jobs, but...none of them are what I want." Then she let out a mirthless laugh. "And believe it or not, I can't seem to get hired doing anything. I even got turned down when I applied at the grocery store for a cashier position." She shook her head. "Dean even offered to give me a job at the garage doing the billing."

Scarlett laughed. "Typical Dean. He's always looking to fix everyone's problems no matter what it takes."

Something about that statement felt like a punch in the gut.

"What do you mean?"

Turning her head to look at her, Scarlett shrugged. "I'm just saying that's the exact kind of thing Dean does. They don't need anyone to do billing for them. He and my dad are both lazy and hate working on the computer when they'd rather be working on cars. It takes them each like...a few hours a week total to do it all. If it was someone who knew what they were doing, it would be done in two hours tops. And that's doing all the billing for the week. Trust me. I've done it for them a time or two."

"Still, ...he mentioned answering phones..."

"Yeah, that would add maybe another hour a day."

"Oh."

"Of course, if they go through with adding on to the

business, then I could see them needing to hire someone." She smiled. "I always knew Dean wanted a garage of his own, but he never wanted to rock the boat. I think he was afraid my dad would be offended or something. Like he'd take it personally that Dean wanted to be the boss rather than the boss's son. Crazy, right?"

All she could do was nod. Dean had told her all about the conversation he'd had with his father and brothers over lunch and the possibility of him having his own garage excited him a lot. She never knew it was something he always wanted. He talked that entire night about all the things he would put in his own place and how he would run it that she couldn't help but get excited with him. It wasn't going to be something that happened right away, but she couldn't wait to see it all unfold.

They sat in silence for several minutes before Scarlett sat up straight before twisting so she was fully facing Courtney.

"Okay, I need to tell you something."

Oh, God...

"I did something," Scarlett said quickly, her eyes not quite meeting Courtney's. "And I want you to know that I did it because I love you so...you need to remember that. And I'm all hormonal right now so you need to keep that in mind."

Forcing herself to sit up straighter, she mimicked Scarlett's pose. "What did you do?"

Letting out a long breath, Scarlett finally met her gaze. "I was very distracted before the wedding with all the planning. Honestly, I still wish we had waited until after Asher was born, but...that's beside the point."

Courtney nodded and willed Scarlett to get to the point.

"Anyway, I didn't realize how serious you were about

moving until it was too late to do anything."

"Scar, we've been over this..."

"When you showed up here when I was put on bed rest, I knew I had to do something to convince you not to move," she went on. "I'd never been so relieved for a car to break down in my entire life."

"O-kay..."

"But I knew it was only a matter of time before your car would be fixed and you'd be on your way." Then her shoulders sagged. "So...I told Dean not to fix your car."

"What?!" she cried.

Nodding, Scarlett went on. "I told him to make up stuff and tell you more was wrong with it than there actually was and to do whatever it took to keep you here in Magnolia. I knew if you had a little more time, you'd find a job and wouldn't have to move." She paused. "I'm so sorry. I...I know it was selfish of me, but I didn't know what else to do!"

"Wait, so...my car wasn't...all the things Dean said were wrong..."

"They weren't," Scarlett admitted. "The hitch did break and you needed a tune-up and an oil change, but there wasn't anything majorly wrong."

She let out a shaky breath. "So then the job offer..."

"Probably another way he was doing what I asked of him," she said quietly.

Slowly, Courtney stood and willed herself not to cry. "I...I don't even know what to say."

Scarlett came to her feet. "I swear I didn't mean it in a bad way, Court! And I really badgered Dean to do this! You know how much he hates to lie, but I forced him to! I didn't even give him an option! I'm so sorry," she said, reaching for Courtney's hands. "Please tell me you understand!"

But she couldn't.

Not right now.

Pulling her hands away, she took a step back. It would have been easy to fight with her in the ways they always had–lots of yelling and screaming and drama. But with Asher sleeping a few feet away, Courtney knew she didn't want to do that.

Plus, it was time she grew up.

"I...I can't do this with you right now," she murmured, picking up her purse. "I...I just can't."

"Court, please!" Scarlett cried. "Don't go! We need to talk about this!"

"No." Walking to the door, she shook her head. "I need some time to think."

"You know you didn't want to move to Raleigh! It was going to be a mistake!"

"It was my mistake to make!" she countered, spinning around. "Just because you've got this great life going for yourself, doesn't give you the right to play around with mine! Now I'll never know if anything that's happened is true or if you had something to do with it!"

"I swear I just wanted what was best for you," Scarlett said miserably. "That's all I've ever wanted."

"No, Scarlett. You wanted what was best for *you*." And before she could say anything else, she walked out the door. She was still driving Scarlett's car but...that ended now. Walking over to it, she tossed the keys on the front seat and walked down the driveway and down the block. At the corner, she stopped, pulled up her Uber app, and called for a ride.

Ten minutes later, she was walking into Dean's house and knew that was going to change today too. There were still hours before he was going to be home, but she knew she'd need all of it to pack up her things and figure out where she was going to go. Now that she knew there wasn't anything major wrong with her car, she knew she wanted it back today. After that, she had no idea where she was going to go.

She could just go on with her original plan and go to Raleigh. Clearly there were jobs there for her and she could be there tonight.

It didn't matter that she hadn't talked to Dean about it. Knowing what she did now about how he had lied to her and was strictly following Scarlett's orders to keep her here told her that everything she thought they had was a lie. Everyone knew Dean looked out for his family and how he had a particular soft spot for his baby sister. If she asked him for something, he did it.

Apparently, that included toying with her.

Not that she thought their sleeping together the night of the wedding had anything to do with Scarlett.

It was just rotten timing.

If it were up to him, he probably would have been more than okay with them having a one-night thing. Her car breaking down complicated it and then he was stuck with her because he had a conscience.

Damn him.

She used to think it was admirable. Now it just pissed her off.

Walking around the bedroom, she began packing her things. She didn't have a lot here in his house, but there was still enough that it was going to take some time to get it all together. As angry as she was, she moved around calmly collecting her things—taking clothes out of the dryer and neatly folding them and wiping down the bathroom vanity after she packed up all her toiletries.

Never let it be said she left the place worse off than the way she first found it.

No way was she giving anyone ammunition to use against her.

For the first time in her life, Courtney was going to make damn sure that she didn't overreact or come off as being dramatic.

At least, she would hold off on that until she was alone and far away from Magnolia Sound.

Once her suitcases were packed, she walked around and straightened up some more and made some hard decisions.

There was no way she could drive to Raleigh tonight even if she got her car back. She was too emotional and considering how hard it was to drive with the trailer the last time, she was going to be extra cautious this time.

"Time to see if Magnolia on the Beach has any rooms," she said, pulling out her phone. Once she confirmed her room reservation, she wished she could just go there now and be done with it.

A sound by the front door caught her attention and she looked up to see a very frazzled-looking Dean coming through the door.

"What are you doing home?" she asked, cursing the slight tremor in her voice.

"Scarlett called."

Of course she did.

With a small eye roll, she crossed her arms. "And we all know you jump when she tells you to, right?"

Tossing his keys onto the kitchen island, he frowned at her. "What?"

"Oh, please. Spare me. Scarlett told me how she asked you to lie to me about my car and you did!" Then she began to pace. "You stood here, day after day, and lied to me, Dean!"

"Yeah, okay, I know that sounds bad, but you have to know it's not the only reason I did it!" he countered.

"Right. You did it because that's just who you are—good ol' Dean Jones, helping out everyone who needs a hand, riding to the rescue," she said with disgust. "Well I've got news for you, I don't want to be rescued! I had a plan! I had a chance at getting my life together!"

"You had an escape plan because you weren't getting your way here!" he yelled and they both froze at his words and tone.

Courtney knew her eyes were wide and her heart was racing like mad. She couldn't believe he was saying this to her even as she knew she shouldn't be surprised—especially since the truth was now out.

With a nod, she began to pace again. "Yup. That's me. Losing my job and my home makes me a drama queen," she said, her voice dripping with sarcasm. "Not all of us have built-in careers and family businesses to turn to. Some of us actually have to search for a job. Not that you'd understand that."

"What the hell is that supposed to mean?" he demanded.

"It means you and Scarlett don't understand what I'm dealing with! You always wanted to be a mechanic and your father owns the only garage here in Magnolia! It's not like you had to look real hard for work! And the same with Scarlett! She had the garage as her backup when she was trying to get her social media business off the ground! So don't you dare judge me because I had to take some extreme measures to find a job!"

In typical frustrated Dean mode, he raked both hands

through his hair and sighed. "Okay, I think we both need to sit down and talk about this."

But Courtney shook her head. "No, I'm done talking about this. And on top of that, I don't think I could believe anything you have to say to me." She paused and let out her own long breath. "I'd like to go get my car please."

"Not until we're done here," he argued.

"Oh, we're done," she said sadly. "Believe me, we're done."

"Court, come on. If you'd just listen..."

"You've had weeks to talk to me about this, Dean. *Weeks!*" Tears began to sting her eyes and she refused to cry in front of him. Turning her back, she quickly wiped them away before facing him again. "You know, I was so happy to have this time to get to know you. I thought I was so lucky that my car broke down," she said, forcing herself to stay calm. "But now I wish it all never happened–the car breaking down, sleeping with you, or even kissing you after the rehearsal dinner. I wish it all never happened."

He was standing so still that he didn't even blink. "You don't mean that."

But she nodded. "I really do." When he didn't respond, she said, "Now, are you going to take me to get my car or do I need to call for a ride?"

She saw him swallow hard right before he nodded. Wordlessly, she went to get her luggage, but Dean beat her to it. He carried them out to his truck and loaded them in. The drive to the shop was spent in total silence and once they were there, she walked inside to pay for the repairs.

"Courtney," Domenic said when he saw her, "there's no charge for this. You're family."

That almost broke her, but she held firm. "I appreciate the offer, Mr. J, but I'd prefer to pay for it."

He eventually caved but she knew he charged her way less than he should have. He came around the desk and hugged her. "Don't be too hard on them," he said softly. "They both care about you."

"It doesn't really feel that way."

Pulling back, Domenic's expression was a little sad. "I did my family a great disservice."

That wasn't at all what she was expecting. "What do you mean?"

"I mean I let Dean take on a lot of responsibility–looking after his siblings and looking after me. He was too young to have to do so much, but...I had no idea what to do back then. He just had a knack for taking care of all of us and I never did a thing to stop him. At the time, I swore I needed the help, but then I got too lazy to change it."

"Mr. J, don't say that..."

"The last few weeks, I saw a difference in Dean–a lightness–that I swear I hadn't seen since he was a boy. Since before my wife died. We talked about the two of you the night Asher was born and you have to know, even before that, he was struggling with this whole car situation as well as his feelings." He paused. "I don't think he was ever expecting any of this. You. Just...give him a chance to explain."

She couldn't speak, couldn't utter a single word even if she tried. So she hugged him one more time and walked out the door.

The house was dark and he didn't care.

Courtney was gone and he didn't do a thing to stop her.

He knew it was all going to come back and bite him in

the ass; he knew it as soon as Scarlett proposed this ridiculous scheme. Why the hell did he listen to her? Sure, most of her life she had known exactly what to do or say to get him to do what she wanted, but why did he do it this time? Especially when he knew it was going to hurt Courtney if she found out? Why did he put his sister's needs first?

"Because I'm an idiot," he murmured.

Sitting on his sofa in the dark wasn't exactly the best way he could handle the situation, but he literally had no idea what to do. For the first time in a really long time, he felt lost.

Much like he had when his mother had died.

He remembered not having time to grieve because he'd been too concerned with his siblings and wanted to make sure they were all okay. He'd gotten through it then and he knew he'd get through it now, but...it was going to take some time.

The house was quiet and lifeless and he realized how much those few weeks with Courtney living here changed that. The silence never used to bother him, but it did now. All the nights he'd come home after work and relish the peace and time to himself, he now knew he was going to dread them.

"You have no one to blame but yourself."

If he were spiteful, he'd blame Scarlett too, but he knew she was suffering just like he was.

At least she had Mason and the baby to help her, though. He had no one.

Resting his head back, he wondered where Courtney was and how she was doing. Her trailer was still here and he wanted to offer to hook it up for her, but she had pulled out of the garage parking lot like the hounds of hell were after her.

That meant she was still here in Magnolia, but...where?

She wasn't talking to Scarlett, her parents were still away...granted, he knew she had a ton of friends here in town, but...

The urge to get in his truck and go look for her was strong and he knew he wouldn't be able to rest until he saw for himself that she was someplace safe and okay. Getting up, he grabbed his keys and decided he'd drive all night until he knew where she was.

He made it to the front door when someone knocked on it. Praying it was Courtney, he pulled it open and groaned.

Hunter.

"Dude, this is not a good time."

But his brother wasn't paying any attention and walked in. "I heard what happened with Court and wanted to make sure you're okay."

Still holding the door open, he glanced at his brother. "Did you talk to Scarlett?"

"No. Courtney."

"What?!" he cried. "Where is she? Is she all right?"

Hunter held out a hand to stop him. "She's pretty damn upset and seriously hating you and Scarlett right now."

"Where is she?" he repeated.

"I promised her I wouldn't tell."

Rage, pure and simple, coursed through him. He slowly advanced on his brother with every intention of beating the shit out of him if he didn't tell him where Courtney was. They were almost toe to toe, when Hunter grinned.

"I'm just here to get the trailer, so...let's not do this," he said firmly. "You screwed up and you know it. Court's a good friend, and right now, I'm one hundred percent on her side."

"How can you even say that? You know how I feel about

her!"

"I thought I did, but the fact that you let her go says otherwise!"

"This is ridiculous," Dean murmured. "Just tell me where she is so I can go make this right."

"Nuh-uh. Not going to happen. Unlike you and our sister, I'm no liar. I told her I would keep her secret and I will," Hunter stated.

"Dammit, Hunter!" he yelled, lunging forward.

But his brother was faster and–honestly–a little stronger. He shoved Dean away without batting an eye. "You need to calm the hell down! She's devastated that two of the people that mean the most to her lied to her! Give her at least tonight to calm down. If you care about her at all, you'll do that!"

"What if she leaves? What if you bring her the trailer and she takes off, huh? Then what will I do?"

Hunter's shoulders sagged slightly. "She's not going anywhere tonight, I swear. Just...give her a little time, okay?"

All the fight left him. Collapsing onto the couch with his head falling forward, he felt completely discouraged. "I waited too long," he said, his voice gruff and quiet. "I meant to come clean–meant to confess about it all–but..."

"But you didn't," his brother said, sitting down beside him. "You know, we may tease you a lot about being overly cautious, but this time, you really were. You were afraid to take the chance and tell her how you felt and look what happened."

Lifting his head, he looked at Hunter. "What if I tell her that I don't want her to go and she leaves anyway? What if I tell her I love her and it's too late?"

"What if none of that happens and it all works out,

huh? Dude, you are usually a very confident person. What is it about this situation that has you so freaked out?"

"Because it's not just me this time," Dean confessed. "And Courtney's not some random woman who doesn't mean anything. She's been a part of our lives since...forever. If things don't work out, it's going to be awkward forever. Her friendship with Scarlett would be ruined..."

"I'm thinking Scarlett's responsible for that one more than you. And you know how many times the two of them have had horrendous fights and then got over it? Do you not remember the screeching and crying and dramatic exits when they were in high school?" Hunter asked, laughing. "It was like a soap opera once a week in our living room! And they always got over it and are still friends. Well...not today, but we all know they're going to make up."

But Dean wasn't so sure.

"Look, all I'm saying is that you need to stop being so damn afraid here. If you really love her, then you're going to have to man up and say it and to hell with the consequences!"

"Tell me where she is."

Hunter stood and shook his head. "Not tonight. Tonight, I'm going to get the trailer."

"Then I'll just follow you and see where you take it," Dean countered.

"Then you'll be following me to my house because that's where I'm taking it."

"She's staying with you?" Jumping to his feet, all the rage was back.

Laughing, Hunter clapped him on the shoulder. "No, she's not staying with me. I'm just getting the trailer for her and keeping it at my house so she can get it when she's ready."

"Hunter..."

"We're not talking about this anymore. Do yourself a favor and get your head out of your ass. I promise to call you tomorrow and let you know what's going on if anything's changed, okay?"

"Why are you being such a prick?"

With a smile, Hunter turned to walk out the door. "Because I care about you both. But you deserve to suffer a little." With a wave, he left.

Dean walked out the door behind him and together they got the trailer hitched to the back of Hunter's SUV.

"It's going to be alright, Dean," Hunter said solemnly. "Try to remember that."

"I can't force her to stay," he said, hating to admit it out loud. "There's nothing here for her—no job, her family's gone..."

Rolling his eyes, Hunter said, "They'll be back in like eight weeks or something. It's not permanent. The job thing is a big factor, but not something that she can't overcome. Although..."

"Although what?"

"She did mention that she got a couple of job offers from dental offices in Raleigh."

"Shit."

"Yeah, I know. Maybe you mean more to her than a job?" Then he laughed. "Probably not right now, this moment, but...basically..."

"I hope so. I really do."

Hunter was quiet for a long moment. "What if...she doesn't feel like she has a choice and still wants to go?"

His heart squeezed hard at the thought of her leaving Magnolia and, therefore, leaving him. "I honestly don't know."

15

"WHAT ARE YOU DOING HERE?"

"Hunter told me where you were."

Groaning, Courtney stepped aside and watched as Scarlett, with Asher in a carrier, walked into the hotel room. "He said he wouldn't tell."

"No, he said he wouldn't tell Dean where you were. He made no such promise about me."

"Awesome. Lying by omission. Great family trait," she mumbled before going and sitting on the bed.

Scarlett carefully sat on the small sofa in the corner of the room and adjusted the carrier she was wearing with Asher snuggled against her chest. She rubbed his tiny back as she got settled. "You can't just leave town like this."

"Oh really? What are you going to do, go out and slash my tires?"

With a small smile, Scarlett replied, "Fine. I deserve that. But that's not what I meant."

"Then what did you mean?"

"If you want to be mad at me, fine. You and I both know

we'll get over it. But don't take this out on Dean, okay? It's not his fault."

"You don't have any idea what you're talking about."

Scarlett's smile grew and took on an almost mischievous quality. "Oh really?"

"Yeah, really."

"Care to explain?" she asked, hoping she sounded bored, even though she was beyond curious.

"It's no secret that Dean is the one we all turn to when we're in need. Hell, sometimes we don't even have to go to him; he just sees a need and does what he can to help out."

This so wasn't helping...

"He spends so much time taking care of everyone else, that he rarely does anything for himself," Scarlett went on. "But he never *ever* did anything that would hurt anyone."

Until now...

"The day I asked him to lie about your car, I knew he was going to tell me no. Like...before I even picked up the phone, I knew he was going to say no. You see, for all the times I brag about getting my way, especially with him, his sense of honor always prevails. So when I got him to easily agree, it made me wonder why."

In no mood to play this game or prolong this conversation, Courtney interrupted, "You want to know why he agreed?" she asked sarcastically. "I'll tell you why, it's because..."

"Because he's in love with you," Scarlett said confidently.

"No. Because he was sleeping with me. Big difference."

Neither said a word for several long moments.

"I hate that you kept it a secret from me," Scarlett finally said. "That you wouldn't tell me what was going on."

She rolled her eyes. "Do not put this all on me to try to excuse your bad behavior."

"That's not what I'm doing!" Asher jumped a little in her arms before she quietly repeated, "That's not what I'm doing."

"I've had a crush on your brother since I was like fifteen years old and you never once noticed. And really, it's none of your business."

Chuckling softly, Scarlett smiled again. "You honestly think I didn't notice? You're no James Bond, Court. You were always asking about him or staring at him and of course I knew! I've been waiting for the two of you to get your acts together and figure it out because I knew he was into you too! Granted, not as long as you were into him, but...still!"

"Wait...what are you...I mean...why didn't you say anything?"

With a shrug, Scarlett explained. "At first, I figured it was just you being you. Back when we were younger, you had a new crush every week. Then as we got older, I just figured you'd eventually move on. Then I noticed a change in my brother and thought 'Finally!' but he's a doofus who moves at a snail's pace."

It was hard not to agree.

"I saw you kiss him the night of the rehearsal dinner."

"What? Why didn't you...?"

"Say anything?" She shrugged again. "If you remember correctly, I had all my own drama I was dealing with–like fitting my beachball belly into my wedding gown." She rolled her eyes. "I still can't believe I did that."

"Oh, stop. You looked beautiful and you know it. Maybe in a year or two you and Mason can renew your vows and you can wear a normal-sized gown."

"Maybe. Not that it matters. That whole ceremony was really for everyone else." She paused. "I meant what I said though, Court. I wish you would have talked to me."

"We both thought you'd freak out–and not in a good way," she corrected. "At the time, it seemed easier not to say anything."

"Wow."

"Then we were going to tell you Saturday night when you and Mason came for dinner."

"You were going to be at Dean's?"

She nodded. "I was staying with Dean." Then she figured she might as well spill it all. "I never stayed at your place. Your old place. I went home with Dean the night of the wedding and then after my car broke down, I went home with him again and never left."

"Holy. Crap! Are you kidding me?"

"Nope."

"Then what are you doing here? Why aren't you back at Dean's? What is happening right now?"

Frowning, she looked at Scarlett like she'd lost her mind. "Um...because he lied to me. And now I don't trust him and..."

"We already established he lied about the car because I asked him to! You can't hold that against him! And in the grand scheme of things, it's a tiny issue!"

Shaking her head, she flung herself back on the bed. "Don't you see? It's not just about the car, Scarlett. He was killing time until you told him it was okay to let me know about the car or...or until I found a job!"

"Oh, my God! How can you even think that? You know Dean would never do that! He's not that devious!"

"That's the thing, Scar. I don't know that! I never thought Dean would be the kind of guy to lie about anything and this was pretty big! If he was serious about me, he shouldn't have needed a ruse to keep me here! He knew how I felt! I told him the night of your wedding! So if he really had feelings for me, he shouldn't have lied. All he needed to do was ask me to stay and I would have."

Groaning, Scarlett looked devastated. "I really screwed this up, didn't I?"

"Well...you certainly didn't help," she muttered.

"What can I do?"

But before Courtney could answer, Asher let out a tiny cry and she looked over to see him squirming against Scarlett.

It was the cutest thing she'd ever seen.

"Is he okay?"

Nodding, Scarlett carefully lifted him out of his carrier and kissed him. "He's probably hungry."

"Oh. Do you need to go?"

"Not as long as you don't mind me whipping out a boob right now and feeding him."

Laughing softly, she said, "At least you're whipping it out for a good reason."

"Mardi Gras was a good reason."

"Says you."

And just like that, she knew they were going to be okay.

For Courtney and Dean, however, the jury was still out.

"Dude, it is seven o'clock in the morning! What is wrong with you?"

Not even remotely remorseful, Dean took a sip of coffee from his travel mug. "I'm here merely as a courtesy. I need to get the trailer hitched to my truck. I would have done it without you, but I didn't have the keys to your SUV to move it."

Hunter yawned broadly and scratched his head. "You can't steal her trailer and prevent her from leaving. That's not going to go over well."

"That's not what I'm doing."

"Then what are you doing?"

Dean motioned to his own truck and watched his brother's expression go from mildly curious to wide-eyed shock.

"What the hell...?"

The back of Dean's truck was filled with luggage, and boxes, and assorted items from his house.

Late last night it hit him that it didn't matter if Courtney still wanted to leave because he would go with her. He had a solid career, which meant he could find a job almost anywhere. She was struggling and if her only option was to move, then he was moving with her. He was prepared to beg and grovel if necessary, but either way, she was going to know he was serious about her–that he loved her–and that meant he was going to be wherever it was that she needed to be.

Even if that meant leaving Magnolia Sound.

"Well?" he finally prompted his brother.

"You're serious about this?"

He nodded. "I've never been more serious in my entire life."

Chuckling, Hunter shook his head. "And that's really saying something since you're the most serious guy I know." He yawned again. "Hang out and I'll help you get the trailer switched over."

"Thanks, man."

"You know I made her a promise..."

"And you're not breaking it. Scarlett already called me and told me where Courtney is so...you're safe."

He laughed. "Not really. I'm the one who told her!"

"Then you've just firmly established the fact that you're the blabbermouth of the family and no one should ever tell you their secrets."

He shrugged. "I can live with that."

Fifteen minutes later, he was pulling out of the driveway and kicking himself for not realizing where Courtney was sooner. The night he picked her up in the tow truck she had mentioned going to Magnolia on the Beach. How could he have forgotten?

There was some mild traffic as he made his way through town and he was mindful of the trailer he was pulling as he drove. When he pulled up to the hotel, he drove around toward the back where Scarlett told him her room was–number 112. He spotted her car parked right in front of the door and carefully parked his truck next to it–even though it meant the trailer was sticking way out.

His heart was beating wildly and he acted before he could second-guess himself.

Then he beeped the horn.

And beeped it again.

And then a third until several people began opening doors and peeking out behind their curtains to see what kind of idiot was being so loud so early in the morning. But he didn't care about them or what they thought; there was only one person he wanted to see.

Only one person whose opinion mattered.

He climbed out of the truck and walked around to lean against the hood while he sipped his coffee and waited for his girl.

Courtney slowly opened her door and looked out, her

eyes going wide. She looked around as she stepped out of the room. "What in the world are you doing? Are you crazy?"

He drank in the sight of her–tousled hair, no makeup, a threadbare tank top, and flannel shorts, and she was the most beautiful woman in the world. Straightening, he nodded. "I am." Several people hurled curses at him while others slammed their doors, but he wasn't fazed.

She spotted the trailer and did her own cursing. "I'm going to kill Hunter when I see him!"

"Don't be mad at him. He didn't tell me where you were."

"And yet, here you are," she said dryly.

"Yeah, but...Scarlett called and told me. Then I had to go wrestle the trailer away from Hunter. But you should know he put up a good fight and is completely on your side."

"Well...I guess that helps." She turned to walk back into her room when she stopped. Her gaze on his truck narrowed. He knew exactly what she was seeing and could tell she was confused. "What...why is all that stuff in the truck?"

Suddenly calm, Dean placed his travel mug on the hood of the truck and walked over to her. It took every ounce of self-control not to reach out and touch her, but he refrained.

For now.

"If I had to choose between staying here in Magnolia without you or moving away so I could be with you, I'd choose moving. If you're going to Raleigh, then that's where I'm going too."

She didn't smile or even blink. "You're forgetting something."

"Really?"

She nodded. "No one asked you to move. Hell, no one invited you to move." Crossing her arms over her chest, she looked and sounded like her usual sassy self and he felt the first rays of hope.

"Is that right?"

Another nod.

"Hate to break it to you, but I'm going to be where you are and we're going to make this work."

"Why?" she cried. "Why are you even doing this? We all know you only let me stay with you because of your obsessive need to take care of everything and everybody! You felt sorry for me because I'm weak and a mess and..."

He couldn't hold back any longer. Reaching out, he grasped her shoulders and gave her a gentle shake. "That's where you're wrong," he hissed. "I didn't do it because I thought you were weak or couldn't take care of yourself. I did it because you're important to me. Because I love you!"

She gasped and looked up him in shock. "What?" she whispered.

"I am so in love with you, Courtney Baker," he said, carefully pulling her closer. "I was so afraid to say it sooner, but as everyone keeps pointing out to me, I'm overly cautious. But I'm not afraid anymore, and I'm sorry for not saying it sooner, for not letting you know how much you mean to me."

"Dean, I..."

He didn't let her finish because he knew he'd already made a mess of everything by not talking. There were things he needed to say–things he needed to specifically say to her–that couldn't wait.

"You are everything I have ever wanted," he said earnestly. "Most women don't stick around because I'm so involved with my family and looking after them, but you understood that. For the last several weeks, you never put any demands on me or tried to tell me not to help them out. You know me. You know everything about me but more than anything, you accept me." He paused, slowly wrapping his arms around her waist.

"Dean..."

"I thought I was doing okay," he went on. "I thought I was happy with where my life was at. Then you kissed me and I realized just how wrong I was. But more than that, you came home with me and eventually stayed with me and turned my house into a home. You gave me something to look forward to every day. You gave me a purpose." His voice cracked. "I would count down the minutes until I could get home and see your smiling face." He rested his forehead against hers and was thankful when she didn't pull away. "Last night was hell for me. I went home and realized I have nothing without you. So...please let me go with you. I promise to do better and that I'll never lie to you again."

"Dean..."

"But you really do need to take better care of your car—that's not something I'm ever going to stop saying," he explained. "You need to be safe and I want to spend every day of the rest of my life taking care of you to make sure you stay that way."

"*OH MY GOD!*" she cried. "Can I please say something?"

"Hey! Can you guys speak up?" Someone called out. "If you're going to wake people up, then you need to speak loud enough for us to hear why!"

"Um...maybe we should take this inside," she said, glaring in the direction of the voice.

"Okay," he agreed and smiled when she took him by the

hand and led him into the hotel room. Once the door was closed, she pulled her hand from his. "So..."

She walked several steps away from him before turning around and facing him. "I don't know how to believe you," she finally said, and he saw the sadness in her eyes, and heard it in her voice. "I feel like these last several weeks were based on a lie."

"No, they weren't," he replied softly as he walked toward her. "We started long before your car broke down, Court, and we both know it. The car was just the nudge we needed to admit it."

Staring at him, she let out a long breath. "You can't say that. If I hadn't kissed you that night, I wouldn't be here right now."

"Here in this spot exactly? Probably not. But you need to know I still would have picked you up the night your car got stuck and I still would have brought you home with me." He closed the distance between them. "And I would have done my damnedest to seduce you."

With a snort, she laughed. "No you wouldn't have. You would have fought it and I still would have kissed you first."

He knew she was only partly teasing. "Here's the thing, Court," he reached for her hands. "You are far braver than I ever was and probably ever will be. I'm both in awe of you and a little intimidated."

"Seriously?"

Nodding, he said, "Yeah. You go after what you want, even when it's hard. You're moving to a completely different city—one that's hours away from your friends and family—because it's what you need to do. You're totally this kickass woman and..." Pausing, he shook his head before meeting her gaze. "And I don't know what it is that I can bring to this relationship because I need you far more than you need me."

"What? How can you even say that?" Her expression finally softened toward him, and for the first time since he showed up, he felt optimistic. "You are the most thoughtful and caring and giving person I've ever met!"

"But you don't *need* me, Courtney," he said slowly. "If I walked away right now, you would go on and make this move and be okay. You'd find a job and totally be the best at it and meet a guy who would spend every single day wondering how he got so lucky."

"That's ridiculous."

"No. It's really not." He squeezed her hand. "But if you walked away right now, I would be utterly and completely lost. There would be no love or laughter in my life."

"Oh, stop. You know that's not true. You have an amazing family..."

"Who I've let be the center of my whole world for far too long. I want something–someone–for me! I want you, Courtney. Please. I'm so sorry for...for everything. For lying about the car, for not asking you sooner not to move away... but mostly, for not saying something sooner about how I felt. I should have told you a long time ago–before the wedding, before the rehearsal..."

He never got to finish because his arms were full of Courtney as she pressed up against him and kissed him. His arms banded tighter around her as he kissed her like his life depended on it.

And it did.

He maneuvered them–or maybe she was the one maneuvering them–until they fell onto the bed. They rolled around until he had her pinned beneath him. Breaking the kiss, he looked down at her. "I love you, Court. Now and forever. And if moving is what you want to do, I'm serious about going with you."

"You can think about that right now?" She pressed up against him in a most provocative way. "We can talk about that a little later, right?"

"We can do whatever it is that you want," he vowed.

"I want you to make love to me," she said, her voice all sultry and sexy.

"Damn, how did I ever get this lucky?"

"Is that something you really want to discuss right this minute?" Squirming beneath him, Courtney pulled the tank top she was wearing up and over her head.

Hell, he probably couldn't utter a single word if someone put a gun to his head.

Sitting up, he whipped his own shirt off. She smiled up at him and he loved how she managed to look both sweet and sexy at the same time.

"Dean?"

"Hmm?"

"I love you."

Greatest way to start the day. Ever.

"Do you have a hotel in Raleigh booked?"

"No."

"Is there anything we need to pick up before we go?"

"No.

"Do we need to get on the road soon?"

"Nope."

He sighed. "Um, Court, we kind of need a plan here. I thought we were heading out today."

She was way too comfortable to even think about

getting up and moving. With her head on his shoulder, her hand on his bare chest, and their legs tangled together, this was pretty much bliss. "I never said anything about leaving today. There's no plan."

"Oh."

Slowly, she lifted her head. "Oh? You sound disappointed."

"Well, I sort of planned on leaving town in a blaze of glory," he said casually. "I called my father and told him not to expect me in again. Ever. I packed up my house. I submitted all the receipts to Mason late last night and made him write me a check for all the work we did on the house... and I threatened to kick Kyle's ass just because he was annoying me. So...yeah. Blaze of glory. Lingering here in the hotel just feels like I'm hiding out and afraid my entire family is going to retaliate and try to talk us out of leaving."

She put her head back down. "Good. Let them do that." With a yawn, she closed her eyes.

"Wait, you want them to talk us out of leaving?"

"Yup."

"But...why?"

"Mmm...because this is home," she said sleepily. "And I'll find a job eventually, right? In the meantime, I can do billing for the garage or wait tables at the Mystic Magnolia..." Another yawn. "Or...I can flip houses. I did a really good job on Scarlett's."

He laughed softly. "Oh, you're going to flip houses? All by yourself?"

"Well...maybe not completely by myself. You can help."

Placing a kiss on top of her head, Dean chuckled. "Gee, thanks."

"But that reminds me, you said Mason cut you a check, right?"

"Uh...yeah."

"Where's my cut?"

Laughing out loud, he hugged her close. "Tell you what, how about we take the money and go away for the weekend? Anyplace you want."

"Hmm...anyplace?"

He nodded.

"What if all I want is to go home to your place?"

"Then we'll take the money and use it to pamper ourselves–massages, a nice dinner out, that sort of thing."

"Or..." she countered. "We can take it and invest in another house that we can totally renovate together for ourselves."

"I think you're overestimating how much Mason paid me..."

Kissing his chest, she snuggled in close. "It was just a suggestion."

Dean was quiet for so long that she figured he had fallen asleep. Opening one eye, she looked up and saw him staring at the ceiling.

"Hey, you okay?" she asked.

"Yeah, just thinking."

"About...?"

"Another house." Then he sighed. "If we're staying, I'd probably want to go ahead with the expansion on the garage–you know, the second location."

She nodded.

"That's going to take a lot of time. I'm not sure I'd be able to do them both."

Lifting herself up again, she smiled. "I wasn't trying to pressure you into anything. We were just joking around. Maybe sometime down the road we can do that, but...the garage has to come first."

"Are you sure?"

She nodded again. "Absolutely. I know that's your dream and I never want to be the person who robs you of that."

He kissed her soundly. "Damn. I really am the luckiest guy in the world."

"Oh stop. If you're the luckiest guy, then I am certainly the luckiest girl."

Groaning, he guided her head back to his shoulder. "We're not going to be that couple, are we? The ones who are all about telling everyone how in love they are?"

"If any two people deserve to do that, it's us!"

With another kiss on her head, he said, "Yeah. You're right."

Courtney was just about asleep when he said her name. "Yes?"

"What time is checkout?"

"I asked for the late checkout so...one o'clock? How come?"

"Because I'm having a hard time keeping my eyes open and would love to sleep for a bit before we go home."

Home.

Yeah. She really liked the sound of that.

EPILOGUE

"Okay, I'm not trying to say that you're not pulling your weight, but..."

"Oh, I'm totally not pulling my weight," Courtney said, glancing at her phone.

"Are you telling me you don't even feel bad about making me do all the work?" Dean asked. "Need I remind you how this was all your idea?"

She nodded. "I know."

"Court, come on. This is crazy."

Sighing dramatically, she slipped her phone into her back pocket. "Fine. What do you want me to do?"

"How about you go get the iPad from the truck so we can see if we're on the right track? I've been taking measurements and I can't keep track of it all in my head."

They were looking at a house on the Sound side of town that Dean got a lead on for them to possibly flip. At the time she had originally suggested it, she'd only been partially kidding. Now the thought of them doing it for real was kind of exciting.

Except...there was no way they would be able to afford

this house. It didn't need any extensive renovations, but it was a little outdated. A good refreshing was really what it needed, but even with that it had to be over their price range. The location was great; it was right on the water...if it was in their range, it would almost be too good to be true.

She walked out to the truck and grabbed the tablet before going back inside. Dean wasn't where she left him. Walking through the living room, she went to the kitchen and didn't see him. He wasn't in any of the three bedrooms or the garage. "Dean?"

"Out here!"

She stepped out the sliding glass doors onto the deck and still didn't see him. "Out here where?"

Then she saw him walking along the long dock down on the water. It was easily a hundred feet long and there was a small gazebo at the end with benches to sit on. Why was he heading out there? Was he checking on whether or not any of the wood needed to be replaced?

"Court!" he called out. "Come down here and check this out!"

Walking down the stairs to the grass, she couldn't help but laugh. They already had so much going on that she didn't know why he was even considering this project. The work for the second garage for Jones Automotive was starting next month. Dean and his father had opted to buy a piece of property on the south end of town and build something new rather than renovating an existing building. They were easily looking at around six to eight months for it to be finished. Once they were ready to sign the papers and get things started, he had explained to her how all of his money was going toward the business, so...again, why was he even thinking of this place?

At the end of the dock, she found him sitting on one of

the benches with his legs stretched out in front of him. He reached out and gently pulled her into his lap.

"This is some view, huh?"

She nodded. "It really is. This is sort of like the setup Mason and Scarlett have at the new place."

"Yeah, but they have a slip for the boat. This is just to enjoy the view."

Wrapping her arms around him, she rested her head against his. "This all looks to be in really good shape."

"The dock's fairly new. Maybe three years old."

They sat in companionable silence for several minutes before she asked, "Dean?"

"Hmm?"

"What are we doing here? This house doesn't need much and it's got to be way out of our budget."

"What if I told you it wasn't?"

"Then I'd say something was seriously wrong with it–like bad plumbing or water damage or mold or all the electrical is bad..."

"The plumbing and electrical passed inspection. There's no water damage or mold. Just a little house that needs some TLC."

Straightening, she looked at him and frowned. "What are you saying–that you've already done the inspections and you want to buy and flip this place?"

"Um, no." Carefully, he guided her to stand up and then did the same. With his arm around her, Dean pointed out to the view. "I know it's a cliche, but...this is kind of a million-dollar view."

She looked out at the Sound. "That it is."

"And I would think anyone who lived here would love it, right?"

"Well...yeah. It's gorgeous. Who wouldn't love it?"

He grew quiet, but his gaze stayed on the water. "Do you love it?"

"Dean, it doesn't matter if I love it or not. If we're just going to flip it..."

"What if we flipped it for us," he said and she heard the slight tremor in his voice–the uncertainty.

"Us? As in you and me owning a place that belonged to the two of us? Like from the very beginning?"

Looking at her, he nodded. "Yeah. Like from this day forward."

She let out her own shaky breath. "I like the sound of that a lot."

Now he turned to stand right in front of her. "Court, this is something I really want–a place that we get to put our own stamp on and a place where we really start our lives. I'm not saying it has to be this house; we can start looking online together until we find the perfect place for us."

The house checked all her boxes and she knew they'd be crazy to let it slip through their fingers. And if Dean already knew it was something they could afford, why wait?

"I really like this house and I can already envision some of the things I want to do with it! I saw some great ideas for a bathroom that I think we can try here! When can we start?"

"Well, there is one thing we need to take care of before we can put in an offer."

"Really? What?"

He dropped to one knee in front of her, her hand in his. "Courtney Baker, I am so glad you took a chance that night not so long ago. You kissed me and I haven't been the same since. I can't remember a time when you weren't in my life, and I want you there every day for the rest of my life." He paused and pulled a small ring box from his pocket. Opening it, he asked, "Will you marry me?"

"Oh my God," she whispered as her hands went over her mouth.

"This ring was my mother's. My dad's been holding on to it for me, for this moment. But if you want something different, that's fine too. I know it's not particularly flashy and a little more antique in design..."

When she saw the nervous look on Dean's face, she immediately lowered her hands. The ring was spectacular and she almost wanted to pinch herself to make sure she wasn't dreaming.

"Um...Court?" he prompted.

With a happy laugh, she nodded. "Yes! Yes, I will marry you!" He stood and kissed her soundly before stepping back to place the ring on her finger. Courtney held her hand up and simply stood in awe of it all. She faced the water as Dean moved behind her, wrapping his arms around her waist. "I think this was the most perfect day ever."

"You think so?"

She nodded as tears stung her eyes. "Do you know how many times I dreamed of this? How all the times Scarlett and I would play wedding dress-up, you were always who I wanted the groom to be? This is like a dream...and it still feels hard to believe sometimes."

Kissing her cheek, he said, "It shouldn't. This is always where we were meant to be. I mean, one day you were just a friend."

She smiled and looked over her shoulder at him. "And then one day, you were mine."

Dean smiled back. "And you were mine."

IN CASE YOU DIDN'T KNOW

A PREVIEW

Chapter One

"Success." Mason Bishop looked around the room with a satisfied grin. Sure, he was alone and talking to himself, but he was alone in a place of his own and it was beyond exciting. It was something he should have done a long time ago, but...here he was.

Collapsing down on his new sectional, he studied his surroundings with a sense of accomplishment. Had he known how satisfying it was going to feel, he might not have moved back in with his family after he finished college five years ago. Hindsight and all. Relaxing against the cushions he realized that as much as he hated the way things had gone down a week ago, it was exactly the impetus he needed to get him here.

Of course the fact that his cousin Sam kept poking at him because he still lived with his parents helped moved things along, but...

As if on cue, his phone rang and Sam's name came on the screen.

"Hey!"

"So?" Sam asked giddily. "Is it glorious? Please tell me it's glorious!"

Mason couldn't help but laugh. "I just put the last of the boxes in the trash so I haven't had the time for it to feel particularly glorious yet, but..."

"Okay, fine. Pretend, for crying out loud. You're in your own place and it's filled with your own stuff. Doesn't it feel great?"

It would be fun to keep needling each other, but to what end? "You know what? It does," he said with a big grin. "I slept here last night but there were boxes and crap everywhere. Now everything is put away and...yeah, I guess it is kind of glorious."

"There you go! Now don't you feel like a complete idiot for waiting for so long?"

"Weren't you living with your mom up until a couple of months ago?"

"Dude, that was totally different. I'd been living on my own up in Virginia for years. It was only when I was forced to move here that I *chose* to live with my mother. Apples and oranges."

"Maybe."

"No maybes about it," Sam countered. "And now Shelby and I are living together and it's awesome."

"You sure that's a good idea? Moving in together so soon? Her father's a pastor. The gossip mill must be going crazy with the news!"

"Thanks. Like I needed the reminder," Sam deadpanned.

"And?"

"And what?"

"C'mon, are you telling me there's been no backlash? No one spouting how you're living in sin and whatnot?"

Sam let out a low laugh. "Oh, they spout it all the time, but we're good with it. We both know this is it for us and if anyone really starts hassling us, we're more than okay with going to the courthouse, making it legal, and shutting everyone up."

Mason was pretty sure his jaw hit the floor. "Are you serious? Making it...? Who are you and what have you done with my cousin?!"

That just made Sam laugh harder. "When you know, you know. And with Shelby...I know."

And damn if he couldn't hear his cousin's smile.

It was enough to make a guy sick.

"Wow...just..." He let out a long breath. "I never thought I'd live to see the day."

"Yeah, well...me either. But like I said, she's it for me. But I appreciate the uh...concern." He laughed again. "That's what that was, right? You being concerned?"

"Um...yeah. Sure. We can call it that," Mason said with a snicker. "We're family and we just look out for each other, right?"

"Yes, we do. But enough about me. Weren't we talking about you and the decisions you're making for your own life?" He paused. "You know I was seriously just thinking of your own sanity, Mason. Every day I watched you die a little more while under your parents' thumbs."

"I know and now that it's done, I can't believe I didn't do it sooner–like as soon as I graduated college."

"Hell, I'm still surprised you opted to move back here at all."

Raking a hand through his hair, he looked up at the ceiling. "I tossed around the idea of moving somewhere else, but...believe it or not, I like it here. I see all the things I want to do and help change. And if it means I have to live under the watchful eye of my folks, I'll live."

"They'll get hobbies eventually, right?" Sam teased.

"God, I hope so."

"They will. And either way, this move is going to be great for you. Trust me."

He didn't need his cousin to tell him that. He already knew it.

He could feel it too.

Last night when he'd carried in the last box and closed the door behind him, Mason felt like he had taken his first free breath.

Sad, right?

"I do trust you and I know the time was right because everything fell into place. The house–even though it's only a rental–is the perfect size for me. In a couple of years, I might be ready to buy a place, but for now this works."

"If you'd make a damn decision on the bar Pops left you, you know you could have afforded something of your own. I mean, why are you holding on to this place? Let it go already!"

Yeah, everyone had been in his face about The Mystic Magnolia and Mason had to admit, the whole thing still stumped him. Everyone else got an inheritance that made sense except him. Granted, he never felt the closeness to Pops his sisters or his cousins did, but to be left a decrepit old bar just seemed like a slap in the face.

Although–if he were being honest–he'd admit there was one *tiny* reason he was still holding on to it...

"I'll deal with it when I'm ready," he stated, unwilling to let his mind wander any more than it already had. "The lawyer said there wasn't a rush. Everything is being handled–bills are being paid and all so...I'm still trying to wrap my brain around it all."

"You mean why Pops gave you the place only old locals go to?" Sam teased. "And I mean *old*! No one under the age of sixty-five goes there!"

"Okay, that's not *that* old..."

"C'mon, fess up. Pops took you there when you were younger, didn't he?" Sam prodded. "The place must hold some significance to you and that's why he felt like you should be the one to have it."

"Why would I go to a bar with my great-grandfather? That's just...it's weird, Sam."

"Some could say it was like bonding, but whatever."

"Look, Pops never took me to The Mystic Magnolia or any other bar so...I'm stumped."

"Did he give you a letter? I thought we all got letters."

Rubbing a hand over his face, Mason let out a long breath. "He said a lot of things in my letter but none explained why he thought I should get that place."

"Really? Huh...that's strange. What did he say?"

Ugh...this really wasn't something he wanted to talk about right now. He was feeling all good and proud of himself and was ready to order a pizza. The thought of being able to kick back and enjoy it here in his new place was awesome. But now his cousin was crapping all over his good mood.

"Look, you um...you wanna come over for some pizza?" he said, hoping to change the subject. "I was just getting ready to order one when you called."

Luckily, Sam could be easily distracted.

"Wish I could, but rain check, okay? Shelby and I have dinner plans with Jake and Mallory. You wanna join us?"

The laugh escaped before he could stop it. "Right. Why

wouldn't I want to be the fifth wheel at dinner? I think I'll pass."

Catching his meaning, Sam laughed. "Yeah. Okay, I get it. Are you going to the benefit concert tomorrow night?"

"Shit," he murmured. "Is that tomorrow?"

Sam chuckled. "Yup. I think your mom bought out the entire VIP section."

He groaned. "Of course she did." He paused. "Wait, the Magnolia Amphitheater has a VIP section? Seriously?"

"Sure. Most places do."

"Still, that place isn't all that big—like 2,500 seats max."

"And that has to do with VIP seats...why?"

He groaned again. "Never mind. It doesn't really matter. We'll all be there so...wait, who's playing?"

"A couple of bands, I think. I didn't pay much attention either, but they're all somewhat local."

"Go have dinner and tell everyone I said hey and I'll see you at the show tomorrow."

"Yeah, sure. Sounds like a plan. Have a good night."

"You too."

After he hung up, Mason stretched his arms out along the top of the sofa cushions and smiled. He could order some pizza and maybe invite some friends over, instead of his parents and the brutal conversation he'd normally had with them over dinner. It was always about what other people his age were doing or who had just gotten engaged or who would be a suitable spouse for him. Seriously, he loved his parents but their obsession with his life had gotten out of control.

The breaking point was ten days ago.

He had come home from work to find his mother drinking wine with a woman he'd never met before. Leslie...something. Mason had figured she was involved in one of his mother's many charity projects and said a brief hello, then went to go change so he could go for a run.

That's when it all went wrong.

"Mason, sweetie," his mother said in her best Southern drawl. "You can't go for a run. You have dinner reservations in thirty minutes with Leslie."

The rage he felt in that moment was like nothing he'd ever felt before. In the past, he dealt with being introduced to women his parents thought would be a good match for him and being asked to take out their friends' daughters, but this was the first time he had been so blatantly ambushed in his own home.

Forcing a smile onto his face, he looked at Leslie and said, "I'm so sorry you were misled, but...I already have plans this evening." When he turned to leave the room, his mother had jumped to her feet and started to berate him for being rude.

"Rude?" he snapped. "You made dinner reservations for me with a stranger without talking to me about it and *I'm* being rude? This is it! I'm not doing this anymore! You have interfered with my life for the last time!"

The argument went on for hours and even though his father came home and tried to calm things down, it was too late. The damage was done. Mason had walked to his room, packed a bag and walked out.

And hadn't talked to either parent since.

He spent a week staying at Magnolia on the Beach–a small local hotel–and frantically combed the real estate ads looking for a place to live. The house was a complete godsend and when it was available immediately, he knew it was meant to be his. Furnishing it was a breeze since his cousin Mallory, who owned the local decor place, helped him and then his sisters both took turns bringing some of his things from home over to him. They could be total pains in the ass at times, but he was thankful for them right now.

It was quiet and for a long minute he sat there and enjoyed it and then...not so much. He wasn't used to the silence at all. Suddenly the thought of sitting home eating pizza wasn't quite so appealing, but then again, neither was going out to a bar or going out to eat alone.

Maybe he should've been the fifth wheel.

"This is ridiculous," he murmured coming to his feet. He'd lived in this town his entire life. Surely he could go out and grab something to eat, maybe run into a friend or two and kill some time before coming back here alone.

Or maybe...not alone.

Hell, he could finally bring a woman home instead of either going to her place or going to a motel!

The idea had merit.

But then...it didn't.

Honestly, he was tired, sweaty, and hungry. There was no shame in admitting that a quiet night in his own home was really what he wanted. Still, now he didn't want pizza, he wanted something with a little more substance. Feeling like he had a bit of a plan, he walked with purpose into his new en-suite bathroom to shower so he could go out and grab something to eat before settling in for the night with some Netflix.

"I think my virginity is growing back."

"Engine grease under your fingernails isn't very attractive, Scar. Maybe that's why guys aren't banging down your door to ask you out. But that's just my opinion."

Scarlett Jones looked down at her hands and frowned.

Damn.

With a shrug, she walked back into her bathroom to rewash her hands. Yeah, she wasn't a girly girl. She grew up working in her father's garage alongside him and her three brothers and it turned out, she really had a gift for working on motorcycles. If the engine grease and the smell of gasoline on her didn't turn guys off, the fact that she was fiercely independent did.

Did it bother her? Yes.

Enough to make her quit? No.

Glancing up at her reflection, Scarlett couldn't help but wonder what was wrong with her. In just about every other aspect of her life, she was confident—sometimes overly so. She was smart and caring and always willing to help out anyone in need. Everyone was always saying how great she was.

And yet, she hadn't been in a relationship in a long time.

Like...a really long time.

Hence the fear of her virginity growing back.

Turning off the water, she shook out her hands as she continued to stare at herself in the mirror. While there wasn't anything particularly remarkable about her, she was bold enough to know she was attractive, long, wavy brown hair, dark brown eyes, and if she did say so herself, a pretty kick-ass body. So why couldn't she seem to attract a decent guy?

"You're not pissed at me, are you?"

Reaching for a hand towel, Scarlett pulled herself from her thoughts and looked over at her best friend Courtney. With a smile, she replied, "Nah. That would be a pretty stupid reason to be mad. I had grease under my nails and you were just pointing it out. No biggie."

Only...it did bother her.

Not that Courtney pointed it out, but that it was there in the first place and she hadn't noticed it.

And it probably wasn't the first time.

"Are you sure? Because you just sort of got up and walked away."

Scarlett tossed the towel aside before holding up her hands and wiggling her fingers. "To get rid of the grease!" With a small laugh, she walked past Courtney and back into her bedroom. "Okay, where are we going tonight? Do I need to change?"

Looking down at herself, she seriously hoped not. She was comfortable. For the most part, they stuck to the local pubs and going out in jeans and a nice top were fine. But lately, Courtney had been wanting to broaden their horizons and that meant dressing up more.

Courtney walked across the room and flopped down on the bed with a dramatic sigh.

That can't be good, Scarlett thought, but waited her friend out.

Busying herself with straightening up her room, she mentally prayed her friend would just say what was on her mind.

"I think I want to move," she finally said and Scarlett immediately gasped in shock.

"Wait...why? Where would you go?"

Sitting up, Courtney flipped her hair over her shoulder and sighed again. "Anywhere. I'm just never going to do anything or meet anyone if I stay here. I'm over small-town life."

They'd had this conversation multiple times and for the most part, Scarlett was used to it. Walking over, she sat down on the bed beside her. "Okay, what brought this on?

Last weekend we went out and had a great time and I seem to remember seeing you make out with Mike Ryan." Then she winked. "And I distinctly remember watching you wave goodbye to me as you left with him."

Courtney fell back on the bed. "Yeah, and it was good and the sex was good, but...it's like it's always the same guys! We've been hanging out with the same people we've known since elementary school!"

"That's not true. We're heading into the peak tourist season! You know it's going to be crazy around here for the next six weeks or so. Maybe you'll meet someone..."

"You don't get it, Scar. I don't want to be the girl the tourists hook up with for a quick weekend fling or the girl the locals pass the time with until they can hit on the tourists! I'm just...I'm ready for a change!"

"Okay, okay," she soothed, falling back next to Court-ney. "How about this...let's just go out tonight and grab something to eat and then we'll pick up some ice cream on the way home and have a mellow night. How does that sound?"

"Boring," Courtney said with a pout. "And the exact reason why I'm done with small-town life."

"Hey! I'm kind of taking offense to that! I know I'm not the most exciting person in the world, but..." Sitting up, Scarlett immediately bounced off the bed.

"You're right, you're right, you're right," Courtney said, standing up. "That was uncalled for." She gave Scarlett a long hug before pulling back. "I'm just in a funk and I'm bored and...don't listen to me. I'll get over it."

And the thing was, Scarlett knew she would, but it didn't mean she could just ignore the situation either.

"Look," she began cautiously, "I'm bored too. It's not

like a whole lot of exciting stuff happens around here or that I've got all kinds of interesting things going on..."

"Now that's not true. You could be doing so much more if you would just share your hobby with..."

"Lalalalala!" Scarlett cried out before stopping to glare at her friend. "I swore you to secrecy and you promised never to bring it up!"

Courtney looked around the room in confusion. "Who's going to hear me? It's just the two of us!"

There was a slight chance she was being paranoid, but there was no way she was going to tell anyone other than Courtney what she'd been doing in her spare time.

"Fine. Whatever," she murmured. "Can we go grab something to eat now? I'm starving."

And yeah, there was a little snap in her voice that she instantly regretted.

They walked out of the bedroom and Scarlett picked up her purse and keys, then followed Courtney out the door.

"So not the fun night I was hoping for," she said under her breath. At her car, she paused and apologized. "I'm sorry I snapped at you. That was wrong of me."

Courtney–ever the drama queen–merely shrugged.

Awesome.

"You want to go to Café Magnolia or The Sand Bar for burgers?"

"Ugh...I know their burgers are legendary, but why won't they change the name of the damn place? It's not very appetizing to go eat somewhere that has the word 'sand' in its title."

"So you want to go to the Café?"

"I didn't say that," Courtney was quick to amend. "I mean, we both know a girls' night requires burgers."

"And fries," Scarlett said with a grin as they climbed into her car.

The Sand Bar was like most of the businesses in Magnolia Sound–an institution. It had been around for at least twenty years and was in need of a renovation, but business was too good to close down and get it done. When the hurricane hit a little more than eight months ago, it seemed like the logical time to finally freshen the place up. Unfortunately, old Mr. Hawkins simply fixed the roof, replaced a couple of windows and declared The Sand Bar open again just a week after Hurricane Amelia blew through.

"I'm getting the bacon cheeseburger, fries, and possibly onion rings," Courtney declared as they drove along Main Street. Turning her head, she grinned at Scarlett. "And I think you should share an order of fried pickles with me."

Her stomach hurt just thinking about all the food, but she kept that to herself. Fried pickles definitely weren't her thing, but she'd eat a couple and move on. "Sure. Why not?"

The parking lot was crowded, but that wasn't anything new. The location was prime–on the beach side of the street–and it had indoor and outdoor seating, live entertainment, and a full bar. Honestly, Scarlett never cared much for coming here to drink, though. She was all about the food. Once they parked and started making their way toward the front entrance, she was more than ready to eat.

Courtney worked her way through the crowd and managed to find them a small booth in the corner.

"How do you do that?"

"Do what?"

"Always find us a place to sit?"

"It's my lone superpower," she said dryly as she flagged a waiter over. Once their orders were placed, Courtney began scanning the room. "I swear, even the tourists are the same."

Scarlett looked around and frowned. "How can you tell?"

"Because we've been doing this for what feels like forever. Maybe there will be some different faces at the concert tomorrow. You're still coming with me, right?"

Their server came back and placed their drinks down and Scarlett eagerly reached for hers. There was no way she could admit she wasn't looking forward to the concert, but she still needed a little sweet tea to bide her time.

"Nice delay tactic." Courtney knew her too well. With a weary sigh, she asked, "Tell me why you don't want to go."

"I don't know. The amphitheater is small and the crowds are going to be crazy! We're going to be up in the nosebleed section and packed in like sardines! And on top of that, it's going to be ninety degrees out! Call me crazy, but that is not my idea of a good time."

"Why are you like this?" Courtney whined. "It's like you just refuse to have fun!"

"That's ridiculous! I have fun all the time! I just don't find it enjoyable to stand around and sweat when I don't have to!"

"You work in your dad's garage and it's always hot in there! Every time I've ever seen you there, you're sweating!"

"And that's because I have to be there!" she cried with more than a little frustration. "When I'm there, I'm working. I work, because I need money! And sometimes that means working in a building with little to no air conditioning!"

"Scarlett..."

"I'm forced to sweat for work so why would I choose to

get sweaty on a night out when I'm supposed to be having fun?"

"Look, we both know you don't have to work at the garage. You choose to."

"I need the income..."

"Yeah, yeah, yeah...I get it. You use the second job to feed your hobby supplies," she said with a hint of sarcasm. "You work too much and you're always saving and you live frugally. It's admirable."

"But...?"

"But...you are way too uptight! No one is thinking about it being hot out, Scarlett! We're all like 'Yay! Concert!' Why can't you do the same?"

"When have I ever simply followed the herd, Court? That's not me."

"Okay, fine. It's not, but...can't you just do it this once? C'mon! It's going to be so much fun! For one night can't you forget about your jobs and be a little carefree? You might actually enjoy it."

So many comments were on the tip of her tongue–most of them snarky–but Scarlett opted to keep them to herself. It was easy for people like Courtney to be carefree and not obsess about finances. And while she didn't begrudge her friend having a family who always was and probably always would be financially stable, there was also no way for her to fully understand the anxiety that plagued her daily.

Growing up poor–and knowing that everyone you knew wasn't–wasn't something you got over. From the time Scarlett first started school, she knew she was different. Besides never having anything new for herself, she was dressed more like a boy than a girl. Looking back now she could almost laugh about it, but back then, it was beyond painful. Her father had done the best he could and she loved him for it. She just wished someone had stepped in and tried to explain to Dominic Jones that raising a daughter was very different from raising sons. Her brothers were all fine–in their own annoying ways–all three of them. But they were boys who were raised by a strong male role model.

They'd also had more time with their mother before she died from colon cancer when Scarlett was four. Kandace Jones had fought hard to win her battle with the deadly disease, but it was too much for her. There were days when her memories of her mother were so strong it was as if she were sitting right there with her, and other days it was like she couldn't remember a thing. Those days were devastating.

Still, her father had struggled to raise four kids on his own and apparently it was easier to treat them all equally–like boys–rather than figuring out that Scarlett wanted nothing more than to be treated like a girl.

Something she still struggled with.

Maybe that was another reason why she couldn't seem to find anyone she was interested in dating. It was hard to find the balance between being the girly-girl she longed to be and the tough-as-nails mechanic she presented to the world.

A damn dilemma indeed.

Although if anyone who didn't know much about her dared to look in her closet, they'd only see the girly stuff.

Way too much of it.

"Hey," Courtney said with a growing smile. "Just when you thought there were no new faces in the crowd..."

Scarlett turned her head and tried to see who her friend was talking about. "Who are you looking at?"

"I don't think I've seen him here before. I mean...I suppose it's possible, but I always heard he tended to hit bars and restaurants out of town–especially since we graduated."

Frowning, Scarlett continued to scan the crowd. "So it's someone we know?"

"Oh, good Lord. I think he got even better looking..."

Now her curiosity was seriously piqued. Still, not one face in the crowd looked familiar and with a huff of frustration, she faced Courtney again. "Who the hell are you talking about?"

"Mason Bishop," she replied before taking a sip of her beer. "He's a little too pretty for my taste, but still, you have to appreciate a fine-looking man." Putting her drink down, she looked at Scarlett. "What's with the face?"

Doing her best to put a relaxed smile on her face, she replied, "What do you mean?"

"You were practically scowling. Why?"

With a shrug, Scarlett reached for her own drink and wished it were alcohol. "I really wasn't."

"Yes, you were. Now spill it. What's up?"

If there was one thing Scarlett was certain of, it was that Courtney would continue to badger her until she answered her.

So she did.

"Guys like Mason? They're what's wrong with the world!"

Courtney's eyes went wide. "Um...what?"

Nodding, she looked over her shoulder and glared briefly when she spotted him. When she turned back to Courtney, she explained. "Everything comes easy to guys like him. Like it's not enough that he comes from one of the founding families here in town, but his folks are wealthy and successful, his sisters are both super nice and pretty, and he looks like a damn model!"

"Scarlett..."

"No, I'm serious! Do you remember what he was like in school?"

"Uh...yeah..."

"Mr. Popularity! Captain of the baseball team, student body president, homecoming king, prom king...ugh! It was enough to make me sick!"

"Okay, if I didn't know him, I'd agree with you. All those things combined are a bit much. But Mason was always a nice guy, so..." She shrugged. "It's just who he is, Scar. What's the big deal?"

Rolling her eyes, she was about to go off on a rant when their server returned with their food. With a muttered thanks, she opted to reach for her burger and take a huge bite instead.

And damn...as far as distractions went, this was the best one yet. It was almost enough for her to forget what they were talking about.

"You should probably get to know him before you get so judgy," Courtney said as she picked up her own burger. "I bet if you spent some time talking to him..."

"Oh, I know him, Court. Back in middle school we were lab partners for a short time. He was semi-decent and kind of nice, but once high school hit, it was like he didn't even know me. So...I stand by my earlier opinion, thank you very much."

"Look, I get you have issues with people you think lead a privileged life..."

"You have no idea."

Courtney gave her a hard stare before she continued. "However, sometimes you have to remember that looks can be deceiving and you have no idea what goes on behind closed doors."

Doing her best to appear bored, she reached for an onion ring. "And sometimes it's all exactly as it seemed. Sometimes shiny happy people are exactly that—shiny happy people with no substance."

"Well damn."

With a shrug, Scarlett took another bite of her burger and pushed all thoughts of Mason Bishop completely out of her mind.

Read IN CASE YOU DIDN'T KNOW now!!
https://www.chasing-romance.com/in-case-you-didnt-know

ABOUT THE AUTHOR

Samantha Chase is a *New York Times* and *USA Today* bestseller of contemporary romance that's hotter than sweet, sweeter than hot. She released her debut novel in 2011 and currently has more than sixty titles under her belt – including *THE CHRISTMAS COTTAGE* which was a Hallmark Christmas movie in 2017! When she's not working on a new story, she spends her time reading romances, playing way too many games of Solitaire on Facebook, wearing a tiara while playing with her sassy pug Maylene...oh, and spending time with her husband of 28 years and their two sons in Wake Forest, North Carolina.

Where to Find Me:
Website: www.chasing-romance.com
Facebook: www.facebook.com/SamanthaChaseFanClub
Instagram:
https://www.instagram.com/samanthachaseromance/
Twitter: https://twitter.com/SamanthaChase3
Sign up for my mailing list and get exclusive content and chances to win members-only prizes!
https://www.chasing-romance.com/newsletter

ALSO BY SAMANTHA CHASE

The Enchanted Bridal Series:

The Wedding Season

Friday Night Brides

The Bridal Squad

Glam Squad & Groomsmen

The Magnolia Sound Series

Sunkissed Days

Remind Me

A Girl Like You

In Case You Didn't Know

All the Befores

And Then One Day

The Montgomery Brothers Series:

Wait for Me

Trust in Me

Stay with Me

More of Me

Return to You

Meant for You

I'll Be There

Until There Was Us

Suddenly Mine

A Dash of Christmas

The Shaughnessy Brothers Series:

Made for Us

Love Walks In

Always My Girl

This is Our Song

Sky Full of Stars

Holiday Spice

Tangled Up in You

Band on the Run Series:

One More Kiss

One More Promise

One More Moment

The Christmas Cottage Series:

The Christmas Cottage

Ever After

Silver Bell Falls Series:

Christmas in Silver Bell Falls

Christmas On Pointe

A Very Married Christmas

A Christmas Rescue

Christmas Inn Love

Life, Love & Babies Series:

The Baby Arrangement

Baby, Be Mine

Baby, I'm Yours

Preston's Mill Series:

Roommating

Speed Dating

Complicating

The Protectors Series:

Protecting His Best Friend's Sister

Protecting the Enemy

Protecting the Girl Next Door

Protecting the Movie Star

7 Brides for 7 Soldiers

Ford

7 Brides for 7 Blackthornes

Logan

Standalone Novels

Jordan's Return

Catering to the CEO

In the Eye of the Storm

A Touch of Heaven

Moonlight in Winter Park

Waiting for Midnight

Mistletoe Between Friends

Snowflake Inn

Wildest Dreams (currently unavailable)

Going My Way (currently unavailable)

Going to Be Yours (currently unavailable)

Seeking Forever (currently unavailable)

Made in the USA
San Bernardino, CA
20 May 2020